I woke up the next morning with an awful throbbing headache, a sense that I was in a dream, and a couple of seriously questionable flashbacks. I lay in the dark room for about five minutes, my hands clasped over my eyes and forehead, trying to make the spinning and thudding stop. When I finally sat up, I almost threw up, then almost screamed. On the opposite side of the bed, luckily as far as possible from me, was Aiden.

I left the room quietly and went upstairs to the kitchen. Everyone was still asleep.

I went to the fridge and got some water. Then I sat on a stool at the counter...and tried to piece together the night before.

* * *

Praise for Paige Harbison

"*New Girl* reads like *Rebecca,* as done by the CW.
I don't know about you, but that spells awesome to me."
—Leila Roy, *Bookshelves of Doom*

"Paige Harbison takes on mean girls with her debut novel about a queen bee stuck in limbo after a horrific accident. Following in the footsteps of her mom, Beth—author of *Shoe Addicts Anonymous,* which is being made into a movie starring Halle Berry— the twenty-one-year-old has already inked a deal to give her book the Hollywood treatment.
For fans of *Gossip Girl.*"
—Tommy Wesely, *Teen Vogue*

"Compellingly written from Bridget's point of view, *Here Lies Bridget* is an ideal read for victims of this abysmal behavior [bullying], offering keen and witty insight into the emotional motivations of privileged narcissists.... What's so engaging about *Here Lies Bridget* is its honest insight into Bridget's self-perception....
[A] solid and intriguing read."
—Susan Carpenter, *Los Angeles Times*

"The novel unfolds with a certain sweetness and a lack of cynicism, which I found refreshing. This may be because author Paige is only twenty years old, so her connection with a young audience is natural and easy. I appreciate the book's message and if I had kids, I'd feel comfortable allowing girls as young as twelve to read it."
—*New York Times* bestselling author Jen Lancaster
on *Here Lies Bridget*

Books by Paige Harbison
available from Harlequin TEEN

HERE LIES BRIDGET
NEW GIRL
ANYTHING TO HAVE YOU

ANYTHING
TO HAVE
YOU

PAIGE HARBISON

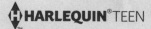
HARLEQUIN®TEEN

Recycling programs
for this product may
not exist in your area.

ISBN-13: 978-0-373-21088-6

ANYTHING TO HAVE YOU

Printed in U.S.A.

HARLEQUIN® TEEN
www.HarlequinTEEN.com

To Emily, my best friend, and to all the others in the world
who have had to really learn what friendship means and what it doesn't.

"It is easier to forgive an enemy than to forgive a friend."

—William Blake

Part I

NATALIE

CHAPTER ONE

End of January, Senior Year

I HEARD HER before I saw her. Music blasted from inside her car despite the fact that she was in a quiet neighborhood. I climbed in, and she turned down the volume.

"So *fucking* cold outside," Brooke said as I buckled my seat belt.

"It's winter, it's supposed to be cold outside."

She rolled her eyes and turned around in my driveway. "I'm moving to, like, California or something. I can't stand this. Okay, so," she said. "Justin continues to not notice me, despite my employment of slutty tank tops."

"Who cares about Justin? He's a junior, for one thing, and he's related to Reed, which means he's likely insane."

"And I really thought this bra would do the trick, too." She ignored me and pushed up her push-up. "My tits look totally awesome—there is no explanation for how he has not dropped to his knees in obsession yet. I mean, look at me, I am, like, an adorable fucking snow bunny."

She raised her eyebrows at me, and I surveyed her pink cheeks, pitch-black mascara, ribbon-blond hair and absurd fluffy white coat.

Only this girl could pull that off.

I sighed as she looked back at the road.

"Well," I said, "he is also friends with Aiden. Maybe he's got some kind of…integrity?"

"Hah! That moron? Come on." She shook her head, no doubt in the world. "He's not picking up on it or something."

I doubted that.

"All right, so he's not aware that you're trying to get him to want to bang you—"

"I want him to *want* to bang me. I would never actually do that with him. Ew."

"Okay…so you want him to *want* to bang you. Maybe you shouldn't be doing that."

"I mean, I know that? But this isn't about cheating on Aiden. Or breaking up with him or anything. I need to know Justin wants me, and that he would have me if he could."

"You know that's insanely selfish, right?"

"It is not."

"Oh no, it is."

"It's an attention thing! Aiden and I have been together for what, like…a year?"

"More than that, but go on."

"So, I mean, it has gotten a little…stale. And I don't know… I totally don't want to *not* be with him. But sometimes a girl's got to get some attention on the side. I mean, come on. This is the last semester of high school that we will ever have. Shouldn't I be living it up, being young and all that?"

"I still don't understand why you want to stay with him if you need that."

"Do you really not?"

"No, I don't! You're not even eighteen yet, and you're in a relationship you clearly don't want to be in. I'm just saying—"

"You wouldn't understand."

"I am pret-ty stupid."

"I'm sorry but you wouldn't!" she said. "You've never really even had a boyfriend, Nat!"

"Yeah, that's because when I know it isn't right, I don't stick around because he's hot or because I *wish* I had those feelings."

"Can we not argue about this?"

"We're not arguing, we're…discussing." Things were tense for a split second before we both started laughing. "I'm just saying, I don't think you should feel trapped into something that's not right. You know your options are endless, and no one can blame you for wanting to—"

"You're the one that we should be talking about."

"Me? Why?"

"Because! You're a freakin' hottie with a body and yet you spend all your time at home nowadays."

"A hottie with a body? What decade are you from? And hey, I'm not at home right now!"

"You know what I mean, Natalie. I don't get why you do that. I'll never understand it. You get asked out by guys more often than makes sense for how little you talk to people, and yet you choose to spend time all alone."

"I choose me, Brooke!" I quoted the public service announcement on unhealthy relationships we had recently been forced to watch. Apparently none of the rest of the video had affected Brooke much.

"As I was saying, if you could not interrupt—everyone's all about you, and you ignore them and don't do anything. People still ask where you are at parties. How many events do you get invited to that you don't deign to go to, or that you instantly decline on Facebook?"

She pulled onto a street a few blocks from "our" Chinese restaurant and parallel parked.

I watched the tires in the side view mirror. "What is your point exactly?"

"My point—oh, shit—" she rolled up on the curb and then fixed it "—is that everyone knows you're awesome. What girl in her right mind doesn't bother using her popularity?" She turned off the engine and stared at me.

"I'm not into the partying stuff so much, and that's all anyone does anymore. I'm sorry! I know you like it, but…hanging around drinking disgusting beer that tastes like sewer water and taking shots of raspberry-flavored nail polish remover while someone's mom is out of town is not fun to me. Neither is sitting in someone's basement watching a bunch of guys in knitted hats smoke weed, or getting hit on by scumbags who aren't even sure what I *just* said my name was."

"First off, everyone knows your name. But…you know what, you're right in a *way.* I'll admit it can be like that on occasion. But it can also be really fun. And when it is, it's worth it. I have some fairly epic stories. And, yes, Nat, you are happy. But you won't have anything crazy to look back on if you carry on like this. When I'm old and haggard, I'll have so many ridiculous stories. I'm afraid of your biggest regret being that you didn't live it up."

We got out of the car and—no surprise to me—she was distracted from her bad-influence-best-friend monologue by a cute guy playing a guitar under a heater.

"Ooh!"

He looked a couple years older than us and was Urban Outfitted from loose knitted hat to moccasins. His case was open and filled with the pocket change of passersby. Brooke snaked her way to the front of the small crowd shivering around him.

"And you were so cold a minute ago!" I yelled after her. I groaned and then followed her.

The singer's eyes locked on hers, and he smiled as he sang the next few lines directly to her. She smiled coyly back, looking from his puppy-dog eyes to his khakis and back again. Good ol' Brooke. She turned and gave me an excited shrug. She pulled a twenty from her purse and tossed it into his battered guitar case before walking demurely back to me. What I would give to have a twenty-dollar bill I didn't mind tossing to the wind.

"He's really hot, isn't he?"

I looked at him. He was cute. But it was cuter that she thought he was superhot. Something about him wasn't mainstream attractive.

"Come on, Miss Casanova," I said, looping my arm through hers. Brooke was, as my dad put it, "boy crazy."

"Thank you, you're gorgeous!" he shouted after us—well, after Brooke—as we made our way down the street face-first into a gust of chilly, wintry wind.

"Do you think I was meant to meet him? Like fate and all that?"

"Him? My God, Brooke." I laughed. "No, no, no. Let's go get our food."

"Fine. But he was really cute. And so good!"

"Yes, he was practically Paul McCartney."

She sighed, her attention and gaze already moving on to another subject. "I want to be twenty-one." She gestured at the people sitting in a nearby bar. "Look at them all—drinking and hanging out, not a care in the world. No school."

My ADD best friend. She wanted one thing badly, then wanted another even worse two seconds later.

"Uh-huh. Because as everyone knows, drinking is the universal sign for not having any troubles."

"Whoa," she said, halting completely. "Is that…*Reed* in there?"

We both stepped closer and peered through the window. "God." I shook my head. "I can't think of someone to better demonstrate my point."

James Reed was our local bad boy. There was something about him that made seemingly sane girls lose their minds. He was good-looking and extremely charming when he wanted to be. But he was also an obnoxious and contemptuous, self-obsessed douche bag. Here are the top things said about James Reed:

1. "I thought he really liked me!"
2. "One minute everything was fine, and then I never heard from him again!"
3. "*Fuck* him! No seriously, *fuck* Reed."
4. "What a jerk. I wonder if he likes me."

Here are the top things said *to* James Reed:

1. "I hate you, do not *ever* talk to me again."
2. "You're an *asshole*."
3. "Fine, *one more time,* but that's *it*."

It could be argued that I was biased, since I *might* have been one of those seemingly sane girls that fell for a charming line and a boyish dimple. I'm a smart girl, but I wasn't smart enough *fast enough* to escape his grasp unscathed.

"Look at him, leaning on the bar, surrounded by dumb girls," said Brooke. "Of course he's doing that. Of course he is."

She bit her lip, shaking her head but still staring at him.

I sometimes feared that she was one bad choice away from

becoming another girl burned by him. I didn't object on a jealous level, just because I had hooked up with him. Once I was away from him, I never again was able to see why I had been fooled by his whole shtick. I cared because he would burn Brooke, and she would be humiliated. And then I would probably have to kill him.

"How did he even…like, does he have a fake ID or…"

"Probably," I said. "Whatever, it's his felony."

"I bet we could get in. I look like I could be twenty-one, don't I?" She adjusted her clothes. "We should try."

"I am in leggings and a sweatshirt, and I'm wearing my glasses. For one thing."

"Exactly! You're being…ironic. And you're wearing thick-rimmed tortoiseshells! You will blend right in with all the hipsters! You'll snag some guy who would probably be cute if he didn't have a handlebar mustache, and I'll kick Reed in the balls for you. It'll be fun!"

"I'm wearing these so I can see, not so I can look trendy. And no need to kick him in the balls. I'm pretty sure some-one else will do that for us tonight. Come on, let's go order our food."

She let me lead her away, her focus stuck back on me.

"I think I've got something here, though. That's who you need—a slightly older guy who can understand your love of the Mamas and the Papas and who will watch your Hitchcock movies with you. That—" she pointed back at the hipster bar "—is where those guys are! Them, and a couple of skeezeballs like Reed, who somehow finagled their way in."

"I don't need a guy to do those things with!"

She threw her head back and groaned. "Okay, you're right. You don't need a guy who can necessarily do *that*. But you need a boyfriend, Nat. Or a boy toy at least. You are seven-teen and hot, and you haven't done, like, *anything*."

"Shh!" I looked around.

"Exactly! It's embarrassing. You should be embarrassed."

"I'm not a virgin, Brooke," I whispered.

"Basically you are. Because it was James 'the Dickwad' Reed, and I'm pretty sure anyone who hooks up with him is entitled to be in denial about doing so."

"Truth. But still. I'm not looking for someone to hook up with. And even if I was, I am not going to meet him at a Bethesda bar. Plus it's creepy. If a guy is old enough to drink legally and wants to hook up with me, he's weird already. I'm not into pedophiles."

"Oh, really, you're not into—Natalie, come on. This is a three- to four-year difference I'm talking about here!"

"Eh. Still."

"Look, I know you're into being all independent and everything, with your reading and listening to records while you knit scarves or whatever you do instead of having a social life—"

"I don't knit. I just *can* knit."

"In an argument where you're trying to say that you don't need to be more social, do you really think the sentence 'I just *can* knit' is going to win?"

"I am social! I'm out right now!"

"Nat…you know I don't count. It was only about a month ago that I invited you to a party and you said you couldn't come because you were busy, and I came over to force you, and I found you in an apron, cooking…whatever it was called."

"Coq au vin. It was delicious, thank you very much. And as you pointed out, winter is cold. Coq au vin is hot."

"You're basically a middle-aged woman. Worse than that, you're like a middle-aged woman suffering from empty-nest syndrome. You are too young, Natalie, to be spending your nights working your way through Julia Child's cookbook."

I shrugged. "What do you want me to say?"

"I want you to say that you will make an effort for the next few months. Not only is it senior year, but it's our last opportunity to do this stuff together. I don't know where either one of us is going to be next year for sure—I'll probably be in stupid Pennsylvania—but I know we won't be together. And I really miss my partner in crime."

I had nothing to say back. Brooke was rarely affectionate or sweet, and these were not the moments to argue with her.

"Especially prom," she added, grabbing my wrist and shaking it. "Prom, prom, prom. You haven't been to homecoming or prom since sophomore year, and I admit that it was lame that year."

"Brooke, are you asking me to prom?" I smiled wryly at her. "The answer is yes, a million times yes!"

Instead of laughing, she looked sad. "Look, it's not only about you having the high school experience. It's also that mine isn't complete without you there. Please come out more."

In a way, I knew she was right. I should go to events like prom and all that…but I never fit in at any of those must-do high school events. I used to go to big parties, and for me the experience was uncomfortable. All the girls waltzing around in too much makeup and crop-tops they couldn't pull off because of the beer gut they already had, and the guys flexing their arm muscles and puffing out their chests. People either acted drunker than they were, or they'd had way too much and were trying to seem sober. Any conversation you had would likely be forgotten by the morning, and any hookup you had you'd *hope* to forget by then. There had been a brief moment where I didn't hate it, but I'd walked away from my Reed mistake and suddenly had seen it all with new eyes.

The top five things you hear at a party:

1. "I am *so* fucked up."
2. "Who brought *her?*"
3. "I think I'm gonna vomit."
4. "I am way too high right now. No, seriously, I think I'm having a heart attack."
   a) Fun subcomment: "Can I get in trouble if I'm high and go to the emergency room?"
5. "*Ugh,* I'm gonna be so hung*over.*"

And then a lot of happy squealing matched only by weepy couple-fights.

But I did miss hanging out with Brooke. We used to have fun at some of those parties together.

"Fine."

"You mean it?" Her face lit up.

"Yes, but you're not *She's All That*–ing me and taking off my glasses, straightening my hair and putting me in your clothes."

"Of course not."

"And you're not going to then stand back, cross your arms and nod while the guy of my dreams double-takes at how gorgeous I've become."

"I know," she said, patting my back and leading me into the restaurant.

"Because in the end, it will turn out he liked me best before I got the makeover, anyway, so it's really a waste of time."

She shook her head, smiling. "You're lucky you're so attractive already, because you are a freaking weirdo."

CHAPTER TWO

IT WAS AN awful, bright kind of cold out today, only made worse by the sea of red and pink that I had been swimming in. I know it tends to be mostly bitter people who say they don't care about Valentine's Day, but I…really don't. It's dumb. I'll take burgers and fireworks over heart-shaped candies and roses any day.

I sat on a table outside of school at the end of the day, wearing no color that came close to pink, and checked the time on my phone. Fifteen minutes since the bell rang. I'd known I would be waiting, so I already had headphones in and was listening to my fifties doo-wop playlist. I sighed and sipped from the aluminum water bottle I had filled up.

I felt a tap on my shoulder and nearly spat the water out.

I turned to see Aiden Macmillan, Brooke's long-term, for-serious, if-they-get-married-they'll-be-the-definition-of-high-school-sweethearts boyfriend. The one with whom she considered herself to be in a "stale" relationship.

I took out my earbuds and scooted over. "Aiden, hi, sorry."

"It's all good. What are you listening to?"

"Um, the Fleetwoods right now."

"Ah, your doo-wop playlist."

"That's the one."

"That kinda day, I guess."

"Yes, the doo-*wop* in the temperature put me in the mood." I nudged him with my elbow.

"Oh, man," he said. "That was bad even for you."

"Shut up!"

"Just kidding. No Valentine's roses today?"

"My heart is breaking over it. Please."

"Right, right, I know you hate it…but I kinda got you a little valentine."

At first I couldn't tell if he was kidding. "What?"

"Yeah, really, I did." He handed me an envelope. It said, *Happy Pal-entine's Day.*

"Hah! And *I've* got corny jokes."

I opened it, and out fell a package of what looked like some kind of seasoning.

"My mom swears by it." He shrugged. "I dunno, it's probably dumb. I know you like to cook and thought you would like it. I was going to give you a package of it randomly, but decided to give it to you on a holiday you hate instead."

"That's so nice of you. And…and weird."

"I know, I kinda see that now."

He messed up his hair and looked out into the parking lot, where people and cars were all weaving around one another to leave. "So to change the subject…did you see it's supposed to blizzard this weekend?"

"No…is it really?"

"Yeah, it's supposed to be a couple of feet."

"Wow. Time to get out the snowshoes, I guess."

"And the toboggan."

"Toboggan! Oh, my God, seriously, though, I love sledding. Why is that a thing reserved for kids?"

"Me, too. And in fact, it's pretty dangerous, as far as sports and leisure activities are concerned. So really it shouldn't be for kids at all."

"You probably didn't do a lot of sledding in Texas as a child, anyway."

"Nope, only when I visited my aunt up here for Christmas and we got lucky enough for it to not just be gray and cold."

"So almost never, then. That's probably my least favorite thing about our winters. Not only do they drag on for weeks longer than you want them to, but most days it's just ugly out."

"I completely agree. If I'm going to live somewhere with four seasons, I want four *real* seasons."

"Exactly," I said. "My cousins live up in Michigan, and as awful as Michigan can be—"

Brooke appeared behind Aiden, and I stopped talking.

Always dressed impeccably, she had also not lowered herself to wear anything in theme today. She was in black velvet leggings, a navy blazer and a sheer black tank top. The only thing arguably holiday-related was the Tiffany's filagree heart necklace she was wearing on a long chain. She clicked toward us in her heeled ankle-boots, rolling her eyes dramatically.

"Ugh! I am so sorry, you guys, Mr. Andrews was nagging me for, like, ten minutes about how, for *this* essay, I need to 'arrange my thoughts' and 'write an outline.' Ugh. Okay, let's get out of this soul-sucking hellhole."

We climbed into Aiden's Jeep. We rode with him whenever Brooke woke up early enough.

Brooke buckled her seat belt and turned to me. "Oh, did he give you that seasoning stuff?"

"Yeah, just now." Okay, so she had known about it. That was less weird, then.

"I don't know what it is, but every time his mom cooks, the food is amazing and it's because of that stuff. So now you can cook me food whenever I want it and I don't have to wait for his mom to let me come over." She gave me a cheesy grin. "Oh, okay, so here's our new mission, Aiden. We have to find Natalie a boyfriend."

I leaned back against the headrest. "Brooke..."

"Oh, shush, I know better than you. I'm thinking she needs a hipster-type guy."

"I told you, I don't want some weird poser who wears non-prescription Ray-Bans. It's really not my thing."

"That shouldn't be anybody's thing," said Aiden.

"Agreed."

"No, guys," Brooke said, "not the annoying kind of hipster who's just catching on to the mainstream hipster thing, more someone who is a little off-kilter, but not to an annoying extent."

"I already think he sounds lame."

"Nat, be real, I'm not saying he needs to be *exactly* anything. I mean someone who is into the same things as you. You're not going to date, like, a football player." She gestured at Aiden. "I don't see that being something you're into. Or maybe you need someone who is your total opposite. I don't know! It's going to be fun to shop you around. Which is why—" she pulled out her phone and opened up Facebook "—we are going to this tomorrow night."

I took the phone and looked at it. "Stupid Cupid Rager?"

"Yes. It's at Alexa's place, have you been there? Well, it's huge and has a pool table and a movie theater, and is the best. We're hoping to get snowed in there. It's even better in summer because of the pool in the back, but whatever. It'll be fun, anyway. She has a hot tub!"

"Snowed in?" I groaned. "That seems like it could be kind of a nightmare."

"Yeah," Aiden agreed. "There are more than a few people I would rather not be locked in a house with."

"God, Mom and Dad, chill out. It's going to be *fun* god-dammit."

Aiden's eyes shifted to mine in the rearview. I stifled my grin.

"Point is," Brooke went on, "there'll be a ton of people there and it's going to be awesome. Lots of guys. And Alexa used to go to Northwest, so I think we might not already know and be sick of them all. Bonus!"

"Does Natalie even want a boyfriend?"

"Aiden. Every girl secretly wants a boyfriend, no matter what they cop to. It's how the world works."

"Brooke, I'm not searching that desperately. I'm actually not even searching. You are. For me. Without being asked."

"I know you're not, you're doing the opposite! You're hiding! And what happens if you squander your youth and beauty by not even trying?" She glanced back at me again. "You're always going to be pretty but you know what I'm trying to say."

"I don't see the point in wasting time or youth on some drunk LAX bro, either."

"Then you haven't met some of the LAX bros I know. What?" Aiden was giving her a look. She rolled her eyes and turned back to me. "He's being jealous. So will you go?"

"I don't know…"

"Come on! You promised!"

She gave me her best puppy-dog eyes. They didn't work on me ordinarily, but I had promised. And I didn't have any plans.

"Fine! Fine, if it's that important to you, I'll go."

She squealed.

"Go to the party, Natalie."

"But I don't *wanna*." I was bent over the back of the couch, a listless sack of un-fun. My father was in the kitchen making us egg salad sandwiches and trying to convince me to be a teenager.

"Brooke is right—there are certain things you have to do at your age. Even if it's not fun, you'll be with your best friend. And Aiden, you two are friends."

"Yeah, I know. But Brooke tends to gets wasted and wander off, and then I'm left alone."

"Tell her in the beginning of the night, say, 'Brooke, I would really appreciate if you could make an effort—'"

"Dad, Dad, Dad," I cut him off, pushing myself off the couch and holding up a hand. "Do you really see that being a real conversation? No, she's going to do what she wants, and it would be incredibly loserish of me to have a *conversation* about sticking by my side."

"Fair enough." He cut my sandwich diagonally, and then cut his down the middle. "Then hang out with Aiden."

He turned around and gave me a look.

"Shut up!" I said, covering my face with the neck of my hoodie.

"Aiden and Natalie, sittin' in a tree…"

"Dad! He's Brooke's boyfriend, I don't know why you're so intent on me having a crush on him."

"I'm not getting in your business. All I know is, my daughter is a big fan of his, and I like him." He shrugged and brought over the sandwiches. "The guy watches football with me while you and Brooke shriek upstairs, doing your makeup and comparing split ends or whatever it is you do. Can't help but like him."

"Yep, you nailed it, Dad. 'No, Brooke, my split ends are better than your split ends!'"

"I say go, be *careful*—" he handed me my plate "—don't get housed or make mistakes, but have fun. Let Brooke force you to have a good time. Gotta admit, I see where she's coming from. You do hang out with your dad too much. You're, like, so uncool."

I laughed and unpaused the episode of *The Office* we were watching. And resigned myself to attending the Stupid Cupid Rager. When even your dad tells you you're a pitiful homebody, you really ought to get out of the house.

WE PARKED ON the street and made our way up to the house. It was already starting to snow. Brooke, Aiden and I left footprints in the white dust as we walked.

Inside, I saw exactly what I expected to see. A room full of wasted people shouting, guffawing, flirting and mostly trying to look hot.

"Yup," I said to Brooke and Aiden. "Pretty much exactly how I remembered it."

Aiden laughed, but Brooke punched me on the arm. "Give it a chance!"

Alexa, the good host, came over to greet us. "You guys! You got *Natalie* to come?" She extended her arms for a hug, her mouth agape.

"Alexa, hi!" I hugged her back and gave her a little pat on the shoulder. "Good to see you, thanks for having me."

"Oh, anytime, girl. Well, any time my mom goes out of town." She giggled. "Does this mean you're going to finally hang out with us again?"

Brooke gave me a look that a mother might give a daughter who needs to say *thank you*.

"Yeah, definitely. Senior year and all that." I smiled enthusiastically to try to make up for how lame I sounded. Brooke looked pleased, then turned from us and scurried away to talk to other people.

"Oh, I know, I'm so excited! But so sad, too. I'm going to miss everyone so much." She shook her head. "May is getting closer and closer every day."

There was a small drop in my stomach. I, too, was dreading the end of the year, but not for the same reasons a girl like Alexa was. While hers was more of a melancholy dread, mine was outright terror at the fact that I had no clear "next step."

"Crazy!" She downed the rest of whatever was in her red cup and swayed a little. "Ohmigod, so you have to come take a shot with me right now."

"Shots? Eee…I don't know…"

I remembered all too well the feeling of throwing up after too much liquor. I had been part of the group when we were freshmen and sophomores. We had mostly gone to the movies or gotten dropped off at the mall to go shopping—I was usually tagging along, never having much money—or we had sleepovers. It wasn't until the end of sophomore year when Brooke had gotten hold of a few bottles of wine that things started to change. Then it was a hop, skip and a jump to the big parties they were still into.

That unfortunate night with Reed, I had done shots.

"Just one!" Alexa insisted.

"Um—" I didn't know how to get out of it. I lacked the ability to put my foot down, like I knew I should. I had an incessant need to please people, but almost none of the wherewithal to do so.

"Natalieeeee!" said Brooke, coming up to us. She had taken off her coat and was wearing a tight red tank top with a black bra. Her necklace dangled scandalously between her boobs.

She grabbed me by the shoulders. "Natalie is letting me be

her party godmother this year. Which means she's actually going to have some fun and stop sitting at home all the time."

"Sick! We're going to have such a blast! The rest of this year is going to be insane. I mean, how could it not be? We already got accepted to schools for next year, so who gives a fuck?"

There was a whoop from the people around us. Brooke ambled away again.

My cheeks went slightly hot, and I wanted to make sure no one tried to ask me about my plans.

"You're going to Arizona, right?" I asked Alexa, recalling what Brooke had told me. One of my few skills was remembering details about people. This would be great if I actually knew any of them well anymore and could come off more like a good friend and less like a stalker.

"Yes! I'm ready to bake in the sun. I can't stand this cold weather. My aunt lives out there and absolutely loves it. I've heard people either love it or hate it there. I hope I love it, ya know?"

"Oh, I'm sure you will. And hey, if you don't, you can always soak up a good base tan and a few credits and go somewhere else, right?"

She smiled at me, looking like that somehow actually made her feel better. "Exactly. Exactly! You're totally right, Natalie. That's how I need to look at it."

I basked in the glow of her approval and became suddenly desperate for more. "Okay, let's do a shot."

She squealed and pulled me over to the counter, where Brooke had gone to squeal with a girl named Bethany, who I had always disliked. For almost no reason—she just bugged me.

"Brookie! Natalie said she'd do a shot!"

Brooke looked surprised, but she smiled. "That's my girl!"

It was kind of funny to see Brooke in her element. I was

used to slightly dopey Brooke, who was a little off the wall and could always crack me up or unselfconsciously pull an ugly face. But here she was, her hair swooshed to one shoulder, confidently chatting with the people around her while she poured vodka into a shaker with ice and whatever else. She really was good at the whole "being the queen" thing.

She had that smile that looked real every time. She sounded interested, surprised, shocked, or however it was you wanted her to sound when you told her something. She made the people around her feel interesting, funny or attractive, and all the while it was clear that she was the most interesting, funny and attractive person in the room.

I came off as the opposite. I didn't want to take a shot, so I immediately felt like the prude. Which sucked. Because honestly, I simply didn't want to.

When I talked to people, I felt like I could never think of the right response or anything clever to say. I was fine with people I really knew. Smart, and even funny sometimes. But with strangers or acquaintances, I was a mess.

"Ready?" asked Brooke, handing me my first two ounces of regret. "It's not that bad, I promise."

"To senior freaking year!" screamed Alexa. Everyone cheered.

I took the shot and was unable to play it cool, reaching for something, anything, else to shoot back afterward, but there was nothing. I became the unwilling center of attention as everyone around me, clearly unfazed by the sting, laughed or looked at me like I was their little sister or something. Someone even went, "Aww!"

"Oh, God, was it really that bad for you?" Brooke hugged me. "I'm so *sorry,* Nat. Whoo!" She widened her eyes. "All right, that'll probably do you for a while. I wanna play darts, come play with me!"

She grabbed me by the hand and dragged me through the party, and up onto the stage that is her life.

CHAPTER THREE

THE SUN HAD ALREADY set completely, the promised snow had come and accumulated into inches and most everyone was well on their way to blacking out. You know, your typical "eight at night."

I had given in to the atmosphere and had a couple drinks. Which for me was enough. I was starting to remember that being drunk and a girl at a party wasn't half-bad. For one thing, it was much easier to talk to people. I was joking and chatting without overthinking everything, or worrying about what everyone thought of me. I was pretty much only ever this comfortable with Brooke, Aiden and my dad. At one point I took an objective look at the scene I was living out and realized I was sitting with five guys, all of whom, I knew, would be happy to get in my pants.

It was never going to happen with any of them, but it still felt good.

At this particular moment, Brooke wasn't in the room, and I was still holding up okay on my own. We had made our way to the basement, and she was outside with a group of people. How she was managing it I didn't know, since it was about two degrees out there. Inside, though, was sweltering. I excused myself and went to the bathroom to splash my face with cool water. I looked good, I decided upon seeing my reflection and the makeup I had allowed Brooke to apply. I looked like a normal teenage girl. Right now—maybe it was the vodka, maybe the high of attention—I felt like one of them. Something I didn't usually feel.

I hadn't locked the door, and Alexa burst through crying.

"Oh, sorry," she said, and started to back out.

"No, no, Alexa, come in." I opened the door and motioned for her to join me.

She sniffed and came back. "Thanks."

I put the lid down on the toilet and shut the door. "What's going on?"

Alexa took a shuddering breath, the kind you have only after crying deeply. "It's so *stupid*. The guy I've been kind of talking to was supposed to come over, but now he's *not,* and I hate being so upset about it, but I can't help it!"

"And this was…Reed's friend Sam, right? The guy who had the New Year's party?" Again, obsessive detail-remembering.

She nodded. "Uh-huh. I had met him before, and I thought it mattered when he invited me and Brooke—" she looked at me "—and you…you were supposed to come, too."

I started to give an excuse for not going, but saw that she didn't care right now, so I shut my mouth again and listened.

"Right, well, anyway, I thought it mattered, but then Brooke talked to Reed, and it turned out *he* invited us, not Sam, even though it was Sam's party. And I was flirting some with Sam that night, and he seemed into me, and then I left when Brooke wanted to leave, thinking that it was good to play a little hard to get, you know? And we have texted some, and he said he might come tonight, but now he isn't, and I feel like shit! I even went and got a Brazilian done and everything, because I thought I might…you know."

So much for hard to get.

"Look, Alexa, he's just some dumb guy. Guys are always talking about you and how pretty you are. I know that doesn't make you feel better right now since you don't want them, you want this guy Sam. But you'll move past it, I promise. And I bet it won't take that long. You're going to be fine, and someone else will come along and actually get the fact that you're awesome. I mean, who is this Sam guy to think he can treat you like any old nothing-girl?"

I talked to her like I would have talked to Brooke. And apparently it worked. Her expression relaxed, and she said, "Yeah! Really. I am *not* some dumb bitch."

"No, definitely not. And just think, when he looks back on this, after you don't talk to him anymore, he'll remember that you left on New Year's, anyway. So you totally didn't even seem into him."

"Exactly!" She smiled. "Okay. How bad is my makeup?" She stood and looked in the mirror. "Oh, God, I've totally ruined it!"

"No, you're fine, come here."

She turned and looked up to the ceiling, allowing me to touch up the eye makeup with a Q-tip I had found in the medicine cabinet. Again, this was an activity usually reserved for Brooke's breakdowns.

"That's so much better," she said, looking at her reflection, and then to me. "You want to go get mani-pedis sometime this week? I've got about three hundred dollars in credit for Red Door Spa from birthday gift cards."

She shook her head like this was actually a problem.

"Sure, that would be fun."

"Okay, do you still have the same number?"

"Yep, same old one."

She exhaled and looked cheerfully at me. "All right, let's kill these drinks."

She held up hers, and I copied. Clearly we were both going to finish our drinks right now. I knew it was stupid. I had already had a lot. But this was the bonding kind of drinking that was hard to say no to without coming off like a complete bore.

"All right, here's to not taking shit from asshole guys!" she said.

"Cheers to that."

We chugged, and then she put her cup up in the air. "Whoo! Oh, Natalie, I'm so glad you're hanging out again. This is going to be awesome. We've all missed you."

She pulled open the door, and we rejoined the party.

"Oops, sorry, Eric." Alexa pushed past Eric Hornby, who was rounding the corner toward us. He was one of the most sought-after guys, the Brad Pitt of our school. It didn't hurt that he looked like an Abercrombie & Fitch model, and he was as rich as you could get. The guy who everyone had a crush on. It was a given.

"Sorry," I said, too, giving him a brief smile and making to move past him.

"Your drink is empty. I have some in the fridge down here if you want one. It's better than the crap they've got upstairs." He gave one of his half smiles that made all girls' legs turn to jelly. I was no particular exception.

"Oh, sure, what've you got?" I would rather hold a full drink than keep being offered more.

I followed him into the next room, which was unfurnished and held storage boxes and the laundry area. He opened a refrigerator, a normal white one that looked like mine at home, unlike the expensive one upstairs. That one had a screen and Wi-Fi. God knows what for.

"I've got some Goose Island beer. What kind of beer do you like, do you know?"

I made a face. "Basically…no beer."

He nodded. "Okay, so probably not an IPA, then."

"I don't even know what IPA means."

"India Pale Ale. It's really hoppy." He leaned down into the fridge.

"That still means nothing to me."

He pulled out a green bottle, which he opened and handed to me. "My uncle owns a brewery and made me learn about all this stuff. It's pretty interesting, actually. I'm thinking about working for him after I get out of school."

"That's cool. What is this?" I read the label. Stella Artois. A woman my dad used to date drank this.

"It's a Stella. Nothing special, but you'll probably like it more than other ones I've got in here. Pretty mild."

I took a sip and nodded. "I do like it. It's better than Miller Lite, or the awful shots Brooke and Alexa keep doing."

He grimaced. "Yeah, not much of a shot guy myself."

"Yuck." I leaned against the fridge.

"Hey…do you remember when we were in English class together in seventh grade, and we read *The Outsiders?*"

"I remember that you didn't read the book, and you called me at five o'clock in the morning the day of our test so I could meet you before school and brief you on the plot. Is that what you mean?"

He laughed, looking shy. "Yeah. That's what I mean."

"Yes, I remember." I sipped from the green bottle, needing to do something.

"I have a confession." He gave a nervous laugh before looking down at the ground. "I had read the whole book. Twice, actually. It's one of my favorites."

I stared at him. "What?"

"I had a crush on you, and I wanted to see you."

I laughed. "No way."

"Yep…I was afraid you thought I was stupid or something, since all I did was play sports, and you were so smart and everything." He shrugged. "Twelve-year-old-boy logic."

I laughed, my heart giving the skip that was unavoidable with a Brad Pitt type. "Well…I guess that explains how you got an A on the test. I knew I didn't brief you *that* well."

"You remember that?"

"Yep…"

His gaze caught mine again, and I laughed once and then looked around, feeling kind of awkward.

"So shall we…" I gestured at the door that would lead us back to the party.

"Of course, yeah, sorry."

I felt bad dismissing him, so I continued talking to him as we went out into the hall. "So. How's lacrosse?"

"Good, looks like we might be pretty strong this year."

He might as well have said something more about IPA beers.

"Cool. Good for you guys."

I looked up and saw Brooke, who had just sauntered inside and onto the stairs. She wasn't alone.

Oh, no.

The telltale signs of a drunken Brooke:

1. She has her sexy, suggestive eyes on full blast.
2. She's with someone who isn't Aiden.
3. She's swaying ever so slightly.

"Hey, Brooke!" I shouted to her. She waved at me without looking and kept talking to Justin, who was wearing an exceptionally douchey flat-brim hat and no shirt. That part, I don't blame him for. He'd worked hard for that six-pack. Or maybe he hadn't. I didn't know.

I called her name again, but this time she didn't acknowledge me. Which brings me to:

4. She is belligerently only interested in what she wants to do, and even I cannot easily pull her out of it.

"So have you gotten any acceptance letters back yet? I'm sure you got into a bunch of places with your GPA."

"Uh—"

Brooke was grinning at Justin and biting her lip. He took a step closer to her. If I said anything more she would yell at me and keep talking to him somewhere else.

"I have to go upstairs," I said to Eric. "I'll see you in a few."

I went up the steps and whispered sharply as I walked by her. *Stop, Brooke.*

She pretended not to hear me. I went into the kitchen, where a group was letting out a shout. They were playing some game, and clearly Aiden had just gotten eliminated. He pounded his beer, to the cheering of those around him, and then slammed it flat on the counter. He straightened up, smiling, and was intercepted by Bethany. She pointed behind her, toward where I had just come from. He took off his hat, tossed it on the table and strode toward the stairs. I could only hope Brooke hadn't pushed the limits beyond what I had seen by the time he got to her.

"Brooke, what the fuck?" Aiden's voice carried from where we were, down into the stairwell, and the crowd around us froze.

Everyone in the kitchen was alert now. The music still thudded loudly, the house still vibrated with the normal party sounds, but all of us surveying the scene were silent.

A moment later, Brooke stomped up the stairs, holding her hands up in a *what?* motion, and they started fighting. Justin seemed to have jumped ship the second Aiden approached.

Smart move.

"You are so *fucking* controlling!" And there's the last drunk–Brooke sign:

5. She has messed up and is now being a bitch about it.

The scene played out like a soap opera on mute, and I knew the characters well enough to write in the dialogue myself. Brooke crossed her arms and said something to him, probably about how it wasn't a big deal and she was just messing around. Aiden showed every physical sign of exasperation as he told her, I was sure, that it was not okay. She railed something back at him and pushed him on the shoulders despite the fact that he is a good six or seven inches taller than her, and he reared back his head, clearly angry. She looked challengingly up at him, but he looked away. She said one more thing, and Aiden raised his hands and then walked down the stairs. Even from his back, I could see that he was pissed.

Brooke's confident posture melted a little as she put one hand on her hip and one over her mouth. I went over to her.

"You okay?"

"No! He's being such an asshole." Her last word was muffled by the coming of tears.

I hesitated. It never goes well when I tell her that Aiden is not actually wrong and that she is, in fact, being a bitch. Her embarrassment gives way to anger every time. I told myself to wait until tomorrow, when she would be sober and an iota more accepting of criticism.

The other girls from the kitchen, including Bethany, came

over to comfort her. Ha, really, Bethany? As if she hadn't been the one to rat Brooke out! I knew I never liked her.

We went into a nearby guest bedroom, where Brooke sat sniffling at the end of the bed, surrounded by supporters, and started complaining.

"Like, I get that I was kind of close to Justin, but it's not like I was going to do anything! Aiden should know me well enough to know that. You know? I was just messing around!"

I didn't even know how she was getting through this with a straight face. She and I both knew damn well that she was flirting with Justin so that he would want her. Which is the only reason anyone flirts, so…was she really claiming that she was just kidding?

"It's so rude," said one of the girls. "Like, you're your own person, you don't have to do what he wants you to do. You know what I mean? He's being so bossy."

"Exactly," chimed in another. "He is seriously domineering."

I almost laughed. That was such an inaccurate descriptor for Aiden.

The first girl continued. "It might even be emotionally abusive."

Oh, for God's sake.

"Maybe," said Brooke. "I mean, like, I get it, but he's so jealous *all the time.*"

No wonder she messed up almost nightly. She had a chorus of dumb girls telling her she was in the right.

I was witness to this pity party, hosted by and for Brooke, for another half an hour. She complained, bitching about Aiden, defending Aiden, pretending to be overly sorry for her actions, then suddenly playing the victim again. The girls handled the emotional waves like pro surfers, supporting her sycophantically with every ebb and flow.

She shook her head violently and then obviously regretted

it. "Bethany, can you find me some headache stuff? I have to go out there, anyway—I just remembered I'm on the beer pong list."

Bethany scurried off, and the team of ladies-in-waiting dispersed, each giving Brooke a hug as if she had been through a train wreck and made it out alive or something.

Brooke reported for duty at the beer pong table. She became very busy with everyone else at the party then, and I knew she was trying to save face and look like she didn't care about the drama that had just happened. I had nothing to contribute to that cause, so I went downstairs to look for my phone. I found it on a bookshelf where I had been talking to people earlier. I texted my dad to tell him everything was fine and that we were staying there for the night. He answered after only a few seconds, telling me to have fun and be careful.

"Nattie, come here, girl."

I clicked off the screen and looked up to see Aiden beckoning me over to him.

He was sitting with a bunch of people, including Eric. It was a much different scene than the weepy girl-fest that had occurred upstairs. Everyone down here was in perfectly high spirits.

Aiden, like most of the guys, now had his shirt off. Why Brooke felt the need to get attention from anyone in the world besides Aiden, I could not imagine. How does a relationship get stale when you're dating *that?*

As I walked over to him, he smiled and pulled me onto his lap.

I fell with a small squeal, and then pushed off and slid into the space on the couch next to him.

He put his arm around me. It felt friendly, but his bare skin on what was exposed of mine made me prickle. He was warm, and it felt strange—and yet also very natural—that I should

be this close to him, encompassed by his body. "This girl...
she is the fucking best, dude, seriously."

I tried to pretend this was how he normally acted with me.

"She's hot, too," said a guy I had seen around but didn't
know. He must be new to the group.

"Dude, right?" Aiden winked at me. "But she never comes
out at all, so no one gets to know her. See, most of these other
people—" he gestured around us "—got to hang out with you
back when you were a little social butterfly. But ever since I
moved here, you haven't been."

The timing of that was slightly suspect. I wondered if he
noticed that.

"Try not to take it too personally, Aiden. I only *kind* of hate
hanging out with you."

"Hoh! Nattie's got jokes, huh?" He bent his head toward
my ear, and I tried not to shiver. What was happening? "We're
about to play a game, you want in?"

"Yeah, sure."

"What's the game?"

"Fuck the dealer?"

"Who's the dealer?"

"This time it's me."

We locked eyes for a second "Oh—okay."

"Yep, you got lucky."

We looked away from each other, and he went on to explain the rules of the card game to me, patiently repeating
anything I forgot or didn't understand.

We played for a good hour, and when the game started to
die out—it's one of those games that can go on forever, due
to multiple rounds—he and I were the only ones left sitting.
Despite the fact that the third cushion was now open, we were
still right next to each other.

The alcohol was starting to make me feel like I had one eye

covered or something. I was only soaking in half of what was going on, and not getting the depth of any of it.

"Are you glad you came?" asked Aiden.

I nodded and took a sip of the rum and Coke he had made me, and which I had not admitted to not wanting. "I am. I didn't know...or, I didn't think it would be fun."

He put a hand over his heart. "Damn. What a cruel thing to say."

"Not you!" I giggled—oh, God, had I? Had I just *giggled?* "Just, like...I don't know, I didn't think it would be. I don't know!"

"Well, now you know, right?"

"I do. I think...I think I'm also a little drunk."

"You think so, huh?"

I shoved him lightly on the shoulder. "Don't judge me, jerk, you're drunk, too!"

"I'm not drunk." He smiled at the look I gave him. "Okay, I am a little drunk."

"Mmm-hmm, that's what I thought. Plus you made me finish this drink, and that's what tipped me over from tipsy down into the drunk zone."

"Oh, so it's *my* fault, I see how it is."

"Yeah, so if my head's in the toilet tomorrow, you know who I'm going to blame, don't you?" I patted him on the chest, my fingers lingering for a moment.

"You just wanted an opportunity to touch these ripped pecs...." He flexed and smiled at me cockily.

"Ohhh, right," I said. "That's definitely it."

"Hey." He held up his hands in surrender. "I'm not saying I wouldn't take the same opportunity."

It wasn't clear if this was a flirtatious comment or a jokingly vain one. But still, my own chest filled with a sharp but pleasant chill. Our gazes met, and for a moment I felt sexy.

Like Brooke always seemed to. I felt like I was affecting Aiden in the way that—well, I guess, in the way that he was, very suddenly, affecting me.

"Is that right?"

He furrowed his brow and sucked in air. "Oh, man. No question."

"Yeah, yeah, yeah. Don't give me that."

"Why wouldn't you believe me? You're a hot girl, and I'm a guy." I guess that settled it. It was a flirtatious comment. "Come on. Isn't that a rule of nature or somethin'?"

The real reason that he shouldn't feel that way about me was because he was Brooke's boyfriend. But for some reason I didn't want to bring her up.

"Yes, I'm a girl, but I'm just boring old Natalie, and you're Aiden."

"I don't think…that your connotation of your name and *my* connotio—connotation—" he worked through his slur with a smile "—are the same."

The words made my heart pound, and I could come up with nothing to say.

"Huh." I became very aware of the hand he still had on my knee. It hadn't seemed weird before. I was facing him with my legs pulled up. But he tightened his fingers a little, and warmth surged through my whole body. Our smiles faded, and we didn't unlock our eyes.

Suddenly I shook my head. Oh, my God, what was I thinking? What was I doing? This was why people shouldn't drink. It affected judgment. That was why I was feeling this way. I would never sit this close to Aiden usually.

"Have you ever been in a hot tub when it's cold out?" he asked.

I started. "I've barely been in a hot tub at all. One time at a Holiday Inn when I was in Florida. And it was hot out and overall a ghastly experience."

"No way. And you're the Northerner. Well, get ready."

"We can't—"

"It's happening, Shepherds, no fighting it." He stood and held out a hand to me.

"Oh—"

"Nope! The decision has been made."

Temptation and curiosity got the better of me. Okay, temptation, curiosity, Aiden and several drinks got the better of me.

He led me to the sliding glass door and opened it for me. There were other people around at least.

"Give me, like, two seconds and I'll meet you out there," I said.

I should have known, as I went upstairs to see where Brooke was, that what I was doing was wrong. I should have recognized that, by checking on Brooke, I was checking out whether or not I would get caught. And I should have understood that the thrill I felt when I found her passed out on the couch next to Alexa was not the thrill a best friend should feel.

I remember looking at her and starting to feel guilty and stupid for the moment of flirtation downstairs. That didn't mean that my heart wasn't still pounding or that my skin didn't feel like it was on fire from the excitement.

I saw Eric in the kitchen, where he was refilling a drink. Shirt off. All by himself.

I hadn't really noticed before, but *damn*. He really had the body of a Grecian god.

As luck would have it, that was when my mind went fuzzy. I remembered him saying something, laughing, and then it all goes black.

CHAPTER FOUR

I WOKE UP the next morning with an awful throbbing headache, a sense that I was in a dream and a couple of seriously questionable flashbacks. I lay in the dark room for about five minutes, my hands clasped over my eyes and forehead, trying to make the spinning and thudding stop. When I finally sat up, I almost threw up, then almost screamed. On the opposite side of the bed, luckily as far as possible from me, was Aiden.

My heart plunged and I became hot and cold all at once. The only light was the gray glow from the other side of the blinds in the tiny basement window. I got out of bed and realized I was wearing a sweatshirt I knew to be Aiden's, my pair of hot-pink cheeky underwear and nothing else. Socks, though, weirdly. I guess even when completely hammered, I don't like to sleep with icy toes.

I pulled on my jeans. I winced as I pulled them up all the way.

Whoa.

I was sore, in the region that Brooke had started demurely

referring to as "Brazil" after reading *Bergdorf Blondes* by Plum Sykes when she was fourteen. I had only felt this particular Brazilian soreness once in my life.

Last time I had gone to a party.

Last time I had done shots.

Last time I had had sex.

Holy. Cow.

I looked at the bed, where Aiden was sleeping on his stomach, shirtless.

No. There was absolutely no possible way. Right? No way. No, no, no.

How could I not remember? I had never blacked out before. Even the night with Reed, I had known what I was doing. It was stupid, but I had known. Was blacking out really that literal? Did you really *completely* forget things that happened? Even enormous, life-changing, multiple-friendship-ruining events?

Could alcohol really change your personality so much? I would never do that to Brooke.

I tore off the sweatshirt, turned my bare back to Aiden and pulled a tank top from my bag. I left the room quietly and went upstairs to the kitchen. Everyone was still asleep. But Brooke wasn't on the couch with Alexa anymore. *Shit*.

What if she had come downstairs, seen us in the same room together, or worse, seen something more NC-17 and left? I hadn't checked my phone to see if there was some kind of furious "our friendship is over" text.

I went to the fridge and got some water, and then riffled through the cabinets until I found headache medicine. I then sat on a stool at the counter and tried to piece together the night before.

Brooke and Aiden and had gotten into a fight. The girls were all being stupidly supportive of her. I'd gone downstairs.

Played a drinking game. Then...I remembered Aiden and me on the couch. He'd asked me if I had been in a hot tub in the snow. I'd run into Eric in the kitchen.

There was a gap then, and I remembered being in my bra and underwear—really, me?—freezing cold in the snow, and then getting into the tub. Aiden was there, Eric was there and a couple other people I didn't really know that well, including Reed, which had annoyed me. But then...unless I'm going crazy...I recall him actually being pretty fun. I remembered laughing a lot. Playing Never Have I Ever—a game that makes me basically Glinda the Good Witch. Reed had dared Bethany and her friend Megan to make out, and they had. Hah! Eventually, I remembered, Reed had left, and it had been down to Bethany, Megan, Eric, Aiden and me.

Then the other girls had left, and it was just Eric, Aiden and me. What had we talked about? I remembered feeling flattered by something someone said. I remembered cracking up loudly at something else.

I had an infuriatingly vague memory of talking to Eric alone outside as I pulled a towel closer to my trembling, wet body. He had kissed me.

How Aiden and I had ended up in a room together, I had no recollection.

"Good *God,* I feel like utter hell."

Brooke came out of the hallway and into the kitchen in sweatpants and only a bra.

"Brooke! Whose pants are those?"

"Morning, sunshine. I don't know. I fell asleep over there—" she pointed to the couch "—and at some point relocated. I think these pants might be Alexa's little brother's." She chuckled and massaged her temples.

She clearly had not gone downstairs and seen anything she could misinterpret.

"Nice," I said.

"I totally blacked out after Aiden's and my fight."

Thank. God.

"Uh, so did I."

"No way!" she trilled, and then covered her mouth to stifle her volume. "So proud of you, Nattie."

"It's not like it's super positive, though...."

She shrugged. "I mean, whatever. It happens." She suddenly looked devious. "Sooo, I went downstairs after waking up from a little catnap, after you all were in the tub and I saw you outside...."

At first my heart clenched, but then I realized it couldn't have anything to do with Aiden, or she wouldn't be treating the news like it was an exciting bit of gossip.

She moved closer and dropped her voice. "You were making out with *Eric Hornby.*" She mouthed, *Oh my fucking God.*

A more distinct flash came back. His hand on my jaw, and his lips on mine. He was warm still, from the tub, and the air was icy cold.

"You saw that? Yeah, I really...hardly remember it."

"Well," she said, "you two looked pret-ty into it, if you ask me. Which you didn't, for some reason. Jesus, if you don't remember it, aren't you even curious how you two looked together? You looked perfect, by the way, positively adorable. You have exactly that right height difference. I would have thought you would think he was too perfect looking, but honestly, I think he's right on the cusp of being too pretty."

The truth was I did find him a little too pretty. Sparkling green eyes with sandy brown lashes, a nose carved from marble and lips that were just big enough without becoming weird and gross. His cheekbones could win *People* magazine's Sexiest contest all on their own. But I tended to be more into the

Ryan Gosling type than the James Marsden type. Still hot. But less like a Disney Prince.

So…I had been making out with Eric. And had seemed into it.

Of course I hadn't hooked up with *Aiden*. It wasn't exactly a relief, since I didn't want to have slept with Eric Hornby, either, but I should have known that even my drunk, blacked-out brain wouldn't allow me to betray my best friend. Or sleep with Aiden, who was also a good friend.

My stomach flipped. Had I had enough sense to use a condom? I wasn't on birth control or anything. It had always felt like a waste, since I had no boyfriend and no real prospects. Did I even really know how to use a condom? What if we had but had put it on wrong or…inside out or something?

"Where did you sleep even?" she asked, sticking her hand in a box of Apple Jacks.

Plummet. "Downstairs. I don't even know who else was down there, it was dark. I came up here to find ibuprofen."

She laughed. "'Atta girl. Where's Aiden? He didn't leave, did he?"

I remembered his hand on my knee, and the way he had flirted. I cringed. What had been up with me last night? Why had I ended up in his room? Why was I slutting it up left and right? Next thing, someone was going to say they'd seen me giving Reed a BJ in the bathroom or something.

Ew.

I wanted to curl up in a ball. "I don't know. Probably not?"

"Well, I'm dying to get out of here and get some Chipotle. You look downstairs, I'll look in these rooms. I swear to God if I find him in bed with another girl, he is going to wake up to a solid punch in the balls and no girlfriend."

"I'll…go look."

"Thanks, love. I need some Pedialyte or something…."

I went downstairs to where I knew Aiden was, and opened the door to find him awake and sitting on the edge of the bed putting on his shoes.

I flipped on the light and shut the door. "Hey."

"Hey."

"How the hell did *this* happen?" I gestured at the bed.

He shook his head and gave me an *I have no idea* look.

"I guess…I guess it's good no one came in," I said.

"Yeah, it is." He bit the inside of his cheek, as I knew he usually did when he was nervous. "Are you…good?"

"Me? Yeah, no, I'm fine."

I wanted to ask if he knew what had happened with Eric, but it seemed weird to talk about it with him for some reason.

"I don't want it to be awkward or anything," he said.

"No, me, neither. I just…I mean, if Brooke found out…"

"She would kill us both."

"I mean, she probably wouldn't freak *too* too much. We just slept together. Or, you know, next to each other. It's not like we hooked up."

I searched his face for a sign that maybe I was wrong about it being Eric, and that maybe it was actually Aiden.

But his face went blank, and he just nodded. "Right, no big deal." He went back to putting his shoes on.

"Nattie," shouted Brooke, clearly not concerned about waking the sleeping people, who were bound to be nursing brutal hangovers the second they were roused.

I reopened the door, thinking it was sketchy to have it shut.

"Yeah, coming!" I tried to whisper-shout.

"Aiden down there?"

I still felt guilty, but I reminded myself I had no reason to. Except that it still didn't look good that I had slept in the same room as him. And that if anyone had seen us talking on the couch, they could make us both look bad.

"Yeah, he's down here," I replied.

"Is he with a girl?"

I swallowed. "Just me."

"Thank God. Well, tell him to hurry his ass up, I'm starving." I heard her depart from the top of the stairs.

I looked back to Aiden. "Hurry your ass up, Brooke is starving."

"So I hear."

"Hey, um…" I looked into the basement living room. I dropped my voice and moved in a little toward him. "Do you think maybe we should say you slept out there on that little couch?"

He looked where I was pointing. Justin lay passed out on one of the couches, but a love seat was empty.

"Looks like I got a terrible night's sleep." His tone had changed. Suddenly he sounded like hardened Aiden. The one I was used to hearing after he and Brooke fought. All curt responses and no joking. Had I made him mad? Was it my fault somehow? Had I creepily and stalkerishly climbed into bed with him?

"Do you…have my sweatshirt?" he asked, standing.

He remembered enough to know that I had worn it. Yeah…I would have to ask him for some clarification on the night's happenings at a better time.

"Oh, yeah, it's over here."

I tossed it to him, quickly gathered my stuff and went upstairs to Brooke.

"Is he coming?"

"Yeah, he's getting dressed."

"Dressed? What, was he…naked?"

"No, no." I laughed nervously. "Putting his shoes on and whatever."

Reed came out of the hallway, wearing only dark, low-hanging jeans. It looked like he wasn't even wearing boxers or anything. He rubbed his face and went over to the fridge. He pulled out a beer and popped it open.

I observed his body, which was covered in tattoos. They wrapped around his ribs, disappeared down his pants and laced his collarbone. He was so gross. I would never understand why I'd thought sleeping with him—or even touching him—was a good idea.

"Seriously? A beer right now?" Brooke asked with a sneer.

"Would you prefer to take a shot with me instead?"

She clicked her tongue and then grinned, trying, and succeeding, at being Dangerous, Sexy Brooke. "Maybe."

He gestured at the counter. "Pour it up."

Brooke gave a tilt of the head that said, *Act like I won't do it.* She then walked over to the counter, poured two shots of whiskey and handed him one.

"No chaser?" he asked.

"Do I look like a pussy to you? Oh, wait, everything does."

"Oh-*ho!*"

"Bottoms up, dickwad."

In unison, they clanged the glasses together, tapped them on the counter and took them. Admittedly, they took them like champs. They set down the glasses, each glaring at the other, waiting for one to waver. Then he laughed and crossed his arms at her.

"Oh, my God, Reed. You are so beyond disgusting," she said.

It was obvious to me, and probably to anyone else, that she didn't actually find him disgusting, and that she was in fact pleased at his evident approval of her. What was happening to my best friend? Parties do weird things to people.

He leaned against the counter and looked at her with a smirk. "My disgustingness seems to work for me."

She glared at him. "I have *no* idea how you ever get girls."

"No? Maybe you should ask your bestie over there."

I was startled at suddenly being involved in the conversation. I wanted to say something nasty back but I lacked the guts to actually do that. Luckily, I had Brooke as my mouthpiece.

"Hey, Reed, why don't you go fuck yourself?"

He shrugged. "Got too many girls offering to do it for me."

Megan and Bethany emerged at that moment, both wearing very few clothes and very funny expressions. They said hi and then started giggling by the pantry.

Brooke looked at Reed and cocked her head to the side and mouthed, *No fucking way…*

He held up three fingers and nodded.

She made a face that communicated all the *ew* now circulating through the room.

So, last weekend, I was watching Netflix and doing yoga by myself and falling asleep at ten at night. This weekend, I was blacking out, waking up in bed with my best friend's boyfriend with hazy memories of making out with the school's most eligible potential prom king, and a threesome had happened in the same house.

Lovely.

Thank God we hadn't ended up snowed in. I didn't know that I could have dealt with an entire weekend stuck with all these people plus the mystery of what had happened the night before.

The ride home was awkward as could be. Aiden and Brooke were clearly still in a fight. Brooke sat with crossed legs, staring out the window, saying nothing. Aiden drove without speaking except to say, "Later," when he dropped me off.

So much for my first night back in the game.

ONCE HOME, I spent the entire day in and out of panic attacks about what had happened with Eric. I thought about messaging him a couple of times, to clarify what had happened, perhaps find out what had prompted me to even want to do such a thing, and maybe—hopefully—confirm that we had used protection. But even though we apparently had gotten to know each other pretty well, I felt weird trying to talk to him. We had hardly ever spoken in our lives, and we had never said anything of importance. And maybe it was stupid, but I kind of felt like he should try to talk to me first. He hadn't seemed that drunk. Why had he let me go through with it? He was surely aware that I was hammered, right? Shouldn't he have done the noble thing and not hooked up with me?

Instead of doing the smart thing and trying to figure out what exactly my body had been up to while my brain was in Blackout Land, I curled up in a ball and cried over soap operas all day. I would have stayed like that probably forever if my dad hadn't called me downstairs for our weekly tradition of Sunday Diner Dinners.

I managed to haul myself from bed all the way to a red vinyl booth. I felt this weird guilt sitting across from my dad, knowing that I had had sex the night before. I didn't know why, exactly. Part of me wanted to talk about it, especially since I hadn't said it out loud at all yet, not even to Brooke. But as close as I was to my dad, this was just too weird.

I set down my patty melt, feeling a little queasy, even though it was as delicious as ever, and surveyed my father. I knew he would be disappointed in me if I told him what had happened at the party. It was the saddest thing in the world to disappoint him.

Maybe it was his blue eyes, which had a shape to them that made him always look soft and kind, and even a little sad. He had aged in the past couple of years, gray starting to fleck his sideburns and stubble, and the lines around his eyes and mouth starting to deepen. He had creases in his cheeks, signs of a lifetime of smiling and laughing. My dad was one of those men who really looked like an older version of the young, attractive guy he had once been. He didn't look like any regular older guy. He still looked like himself.

As if he knew something was up, and he probably did, he asked, "How did last night go?"

"What?" My face flushed red. "Oh, it was fun. It was fine."

"Did you have anything to drink?"

"Umm…"

He laughed and shook his head.

"Are you mad?"

"No, I'm not mad. You didn't drive, and you know better than to get in the car with someone who's been drinking. I'm not worried about you. You're a smart girl." He gestured at me with his fork. "Don't make a habit of it, or I will get concerned."

Smart girl. Was I? I didn't feel like it right now. My dad's lack of concern about the situation was based on the fact that I had always made smart choices. He knew I had removed myself from my social group when they started getting into that stuff, and that I wasn't the type of daughter that needed to be worried about. It made my heart hurt a little to imagine his reaction if he knew the truth. If he knew that I had drunk too much liquor, had sex with someone I hardly knew and woken up in bed with a different guy. Not just any guy, either, but my best friend's boyfriend.

Actually, he was a big fan of Aiden's, so that probably wouldn't be the worst part of it.

Marcy, our favorite waitress, came over with our refills. "Here you go, guys. How's that patty melt?"

"It is possibly the greatest thing I have ever consumed in the history of my life."

"Marcy, you'll never guess what little Natalie did last night."

"Ooh, what?" She tightened her shoulders excitedly, and sat down on the bench next to my dad.

"She went to a party."

Marcy gave a small squeal, knowing exactly how much of a shock this was. "Well, little miss Natalie. Are we going to have to check you into rehab? Don't tell me you're going down the path of Lindsay Lohan."

I rolled my eyes good-naturedly. "Yeah, yeah, yeah…"

"Did you want any coffee or anything tonight?" Marcy asked my dad. The way she looked at him was so cute that it got me to smile and stop obsessing about last night for a second. It was so obvious she was crushing on him.

"Yeah, sure. And—"

"And one big slice of coconut cream pie. I know, John." She gave him a wink and turned to go back to the kitchen.

"Would you ask her out already?"

"Cool your arrows there, Cupid, Valentine's Day is over." I was letting out an exasperated sigh when my phone rang. Aiden.

My stomach did about nine somersaults. It wasn't hugely out of the ordinary for him to give me a call. Usually he was looking for Brooke, or asking a question about school. But I had a feeling this was about yesterday.

"I'll…be right back." I scurried outside and answered. "Hello?"

"Hey, Nattie."

"Hey. Uh, what's up?"

"Are you at the diner with your dad?"

I gave a small laugh at the predictability of my routine and Aiden's awareness of it. "Yeah, why?"

He hesitated. "Do you mind if I stop by for a sec?"

"Um, no, that's fine."

That *was* out of the ordinary.

"Okay, I'll be there in, like, five minutes."

CHAPTER FIVE

I WENT BACK in, appreciating the warm gusts of heated air that beat down on our table. I cleared my throat and tried not to make eye contact with either my dad or Marcy. Which was difficult, since they were both staring at me.

"Was that a *boy*, Miss Natalie?"

"No...I mean, yeah, but it's Brooke's boyfriend." I avoided my dad's gaze.

"Ooh, that tall one? She showed me a picture of him a long time ago when she first met him. He is *cute*. They're still together? That's so sweet."

"Yeah, they're pretty cute. Um. Daddy, he's going to stop by here for a minute if that's okay."

He studied me, probably trying to figure out what was really going on—he didn't stand a chance, since even I didn't know—and Marcy elbowed him.

"That's fine, sweetie, I'll keep your dad company."

I spent the remaining few minutes trying to calm my unnecessarily wrought nerves and to not watch every set of headlights. I failed, though, and finally one of the sets of headlights was his. He pulled into the lot and parked right outside. I looked down at my Sprite, but found myself watching him step out of his Jeep, lock it and make his way inside.

He looked particularly good, wearing a pair of dark jeans he'd had forever, a gray T-shirt and a black zip-up that was not zipped up. I really wished it was, since I realized my gaze had dropped to his abdomen. I had a flash of what it would be like to race my hand up under the cotton and feel his warm skin.

Whoa. That thought was super not okay. *Get ahold of yourself, Shepherds.*

He walked over to our table, and I could smell his body wash. I had always liked it, but it seemed like an odd thing to notice, much less to compliment.

"Hey, all," he said. "Mr. Shepherds, how you been? He held out his hand and gave my dad a firm handshake.

"Hey, guy, good, good, how are you?"

I blushed a little at my dad's enthusiastic greeting.

"And you're…Marcy, is it?" Aiden shook her hand, too, and I noticed that his grip was considerably softer.

"Yes, it is," she said, blushing a little.

"Natalie says you're their favorite waitress, and she'll accept diner fare from no one else, so I figured it must be you."

"Oh." Marcy waved a hand at me, blushing even more than I was.

"Do you all mind if I steal Natalie away for a few?"

"Of course!" responded Marcy, not my dad. "Here, why don't you two settle up here at the counter, and I'll grab you a nice piece of coconut cream pie. Natalie and John get it every time they come in, and I know you'll love it."

"Sounds awesome," he said.

I couldn't help but like a guy who didn't hate dessert. It seemed like so many guys did.

We sat down on the red vinyl stools, silent as we waited for Marcy to return from the kitchen. My stomach churned and I bit my tongue as I tried to both think of something to say and stop myself from talking. She came back after only about a minute, coming over with one small plate with a perfect slice of pie on it, and two forks.

"Enjoy." She smiled, and went back over to my dad. She sat in my spot and started in on my half of his pie, and—I sus-pected—on distracting him from my conversation with Aiden.

"You have the first bite," I said, pointing to the sharp top of the triangle. "It's the best part until you get to the back crust."

"You sure? I don't want to steal your favorite bite."

"Oh, please, I have it at least once a week."

He laughed and took the bite. His eyebrows went up and he nodded. "That's extremely delicious pie."

A smile tensed my cheeks as that hint of an accent showed through on the word *pie*. I wanted to tease him for it, like I might ordinarily do, but something stopped me.

"Isn't it? It's my favorite."

"Yeah. Wow." He took another bite.

I liked that he liked it. I didn't know why.

"So…what's up?" I asked.

"I wanted to make sure everything was cool about last night."

"Oh, you mean—" I dropped my voice "—sleeping in the same bed? I didn't tell Brooke. She didn't ask, either, I don't think it matters. I say, let's not bring it up."

He looked at me for a long moment, looking a little frozen, and then took another bite. "Yeah."

I became conscious suddenly of my increasingly strong heartbeat. "Or do you mean…"

He waited for me to go on.

"I know we were flirting…when we were playing cards

and all," I said. After sitting around feeling guilty and dehydrated all day, I had begun to fear that maybe I had been the initiator more than I realized, and that perhaps it had all been in my drunken brain that he had been flirting with me, too. "I'm really sorry about that. I totally didn't mean to be like that. I mean, Brooke is my best friend."

"Right. I guess we'll forget about the whole thing. I'm sorry, too."

"You have no reason to be sorry, I was being a flirt. I don't know. I must have picked up the habit from Brooke and not even noticed." I laughed, feeling nervous and knowing I was talking a lot.

"She's certainly flirtatious."

"Hey...I know she acts how she acts, but that's just because she's *like* that. It's nothing to do with you or how she feels about you."

That felt better. That made up for how I had acted a little bit: doing some damage control for her.

"Right," he said again. He seemed to go into deep thought, and I felt suddenly like I had made him angry again.

I took a deep breath, glanced at my dad's table to be sure they weren't looking at us and then asked, "Aiden...we didn't hook up...did we?"

Oh my God, oh my God, oh my God. I couldn't believe I had asked that. But no, it was good that I'd asked, I needed to know. Needed to be sure. Because while the evidence pointed to Eric...I had woken up with Aiden, and if I was forced to choose sober who I would rather kiss, I knew who that would be. Even admitting that to myself was difficult, but there it was.

He hesitated, probably thinking I was an idiot, and then said, "No. We didn't."

"Right. Of course not. It's really embarrassing how little I remember. It's pretty messed up."

"Not a good feeling, I'm sure."

His tone was still clipped and impatient-sounding.

"So, um, I guess let's go back to normal. Is that okay?" I asked.

"Yeah. Sure." He gave me a tight smile that didn't quite meet his eyes. "Well, I better head out. You should, too, the roads are getting kinda tricky out there."

"We will. I guess I'll see you in the morning—you're picking us up?"

"School's canceled tomorrow, I just heard it on the radio."

"Nu-uh, really?"

"Really really." He still looked annoyed. I longed to bring him out of whatever it was.

"Well…Tuesday, then, I guess."

"Tuesday it is." He pulled out a ten-dollar bill and put it under the plate I had just taken the last bite off of.

"Oh, you don't have to—"

"Natalie, it's fine."

He stood, and we both walked over to my table. Dammit. I had probably just made him feel super weird.

"Nice to see you guys, have a good night. Drive safely. I was just telling Nattie—Natalie—that the roads are getting kind of slick."

"Yes, we're going to head out pretty soon here. Nice seeing you again, Aiden, keep your eye out for other drivers."

He gave another tight-lipped smile and a nod before waving and walking out. I watched as he made his way to the car and got in. He took a second before starting the car, running a hand through his hair and staring at the wheel. After a second, he started it up and pulled out of the spot quickly and effortlessly.

I watched him go, not sure at all how to feel. Something was different. Something was up with him. If we had hooked up, and I didn't remember, I couldn't really see him not telling me. If he was mad at me for hooking up with Eric, that would be weird, too. Maybe he thought it was my fault I had stayed in the bed with him. Maybe he was right. Maybe he felt weird about having to lie to Brooke about it.

I thought for a second about simply telling her, but quickly decided that, no, that was a stupid idea. She really would kill us both.

BROOKE TEXTED ME not long after and told me she wanted to come pick me up to sleep over. My dad agreed to let me, but only if he drove me, because of the weather.

"You're not hungover at all?" I asked her, walking in and tossing my bag on the steps.

"Oh, Nattie." She laughed. "It would take a lot more to get me hungover."

"But you were pretty drunk," I said.

"Yeah, but I usually only get hungover if I don't eat or something. Anyway, hi!" Brooke plopped herself on the couch in the living room. "Did you have more fun than you thought you would last night?"

"I did, actually…yeah. You and Aiden okay after the whole Justin thing?"

She waved a hand. "He told me to forget it and that we all make mistakes or whatever. It was surprisingly relaxed of him."

I didn't know exactly what I was feeling. Relief, I suppose, that no one had said something like, *Oh, yeah, Natalie and Aiden were being completely weird together.*

It was upsetting and strange, not being able to tell her something. Aiden was probably feeling the same way, since

I doubted he had ever lied to her or withheld anything from her, either.

"Well, that's good, I'm glad he wasn't too pissed at you."

"Definitely. But I am going to do what you were talking about, and be a better girlfriend. You're so right. I need to stop trying to get attention from other guys. Aiden is everything I ever wanted. He's smart, protective, hot as all get out and, I mean…he's all about me. And you know what I love?"

"What?"

She smiled and bit her lip. "Sometimes when he's pissed or drunk or tired or whatever? A tiny bit of that Texas accent comes out. And *God,* it's hot. Because it's not like a redneck accent. It's like…like a Southern gentleman accent."

I bit my lip, remembering how, only an hour ago, I had heard that very accent.

Brooke looked proud of herself. "I really need to stop acting like he's not enough."

"Yeah. Probably a good idea."

"I've been freaking out, because no matter where I go next year, I won't be near him. Or you. Unless I go to Towson." She mimed a gun at her temple. "He'll be at College Park being all successful and busy with his vet program, and I'll be a million miles away. It'll never work unless I stay here."

"Right…but I'll only be here because I'm an idiot who hasn't figured herself out yet. And my dad only gave me one semester to figure it out, and then he's reportedly going to start applying to places for me."

Brooke groaned. "Maybe I'll stay here, get knocked up and live off Aiden and his vet money, have beautiful children and spend my afternoons at, like, Bikram yoga or something."

I took the throw pillow from next to me and tossed it at her face. "You are a lost cause."

"I know it!" She squeezed the pillow and bent over it with

a groan. "Okay, but point is! I'm not breaking up with Aiden, because even if we are doomed for a breakup, I'd like to enjoy the rest of the year with him. I love him, ya know?"

"Are you *in* love with him?"

She opened her mouth to speak, but evidently couldn't bring herself to say that, yes, she was in love with Aiden. She started smiling, and I shook my head and said, "That's what I'm saying."

"Ugh, Nattie...I mean, if we were older, yes, it would be selfish. But what, am I holding him back from meeting someone new or something? No, there's, like, three months left in high school. I'm pretty sure he knows who he's going to know until next fall."

I became suddenly conscious of my facial expression.

"And what would the point be in being single now," she went on, "right when you find a boy?"

"I did not find a boy!"

"Yes, you did, and he's superhot, named Eric Hornby, and I'm so excited!" She spewed the words quickly and bounced up and down. "Which is why—" she stood up and went into her purse "—we're going to have a spa night."

"Spa... *What did I say?* I said no movie-style makeover!"

"It's not a makeover! At all. It's a spa night. We're going to refresh ourselves. I'm not saying you need to do anything to *look* better, but every girl *feels* better with freshly buffed skin, shiny nails and perfect eyebrows."

We both knew that she was a magician when it came to all things appearance-related. She nodded at me, knowing I was going to let her do her magic.

I sighed, resigned.

"Yay! We're going to beautify ourselves. I repeat...it's a spa night, not a makeover." She squealed and ran over to hug me.

"This is going to be the best time ever. Ohmigod. We can double date. How fucking cute is that? Ooh, game night!"

"You are getting way, way ahead of yourself," I said as she went over to her speakers and put on the new Black Keys album.

The music wasn't on for a full verse before Brooke's mom came into the kitchen looking irritable but perfectly put together, as she always did. It must be where Brooke got it.

"Brooke, turn that down, honestly. I'm scrambling to get my things together, I really can't listen to you blast music right now."

Brooke rolled her eyes at me, but said, "All right, sorry."

"Now, I'm gone until Wednesday, I need you to really get on this college thing. If you don't make up your mind—"

"Mom, I am, I told you. I went to the guidance office, but I have to go back at the end of the week when I have an appointment with my counselor."

She shook her head and pulled her Kindle and its charger from the wall by the desk. "It's so incredibly last second. You should have been on top of this a lot sooner."

"I know that, you already yelled at me about this a hundred times, what's the point in continuing to talk about it? I'm doing what I can now, so just stop."

Her mom raised her eyebrows in a signature move that had always intimidated me. "You want to adjust your attitude?"

"I can't do anything about it right now, regardless, so I don't see why we have to go on and on about it."

"Because if I don't bring it up, you will choose to forget about it, and then you'll end up loafing around here next year."

"That is not true! I—"

"Look, Brooke, I don't have time to argue about this right now. I have to make sure this flight is still taking off because of the weather."

"You brought it up! Jesus."

"Watch it, Brooke."

Brooke took a deep breath that filled her chest, and then sat on the couch next to me. She stared at the wall with her arms crossed, saying nothing but gnawing on her thumbnail until her mom left, talking loudly on her cell phone about a layover she wanted to avoid.

Once she was gone, Brooke popped up, said nothing about the verbal squabble and went back to being her normal self. Like always. I had come to know and expect this.

"I'll be right back," she said, and disappeared upstairs and out of sight as I turned up the music. She returned with the Tiffany Blue crate full of bottles, lotions and tools that usually sat on the bottom of her bathroom shelf.

The first thing she did was slather some horrid oil in my hair and wrap it up in a little terry-cloth turban. The second thing she did was pop a bottle of champagne.

"I had Aiden get one of his friends to bring us some bubbly. I think it's necessary."

I laughed and took the glass she handed me.

"Now," she said. "You might want to down that first glass."

"Oh, no, why…?" The thought of drinking again made my stomach turn, but as always, I had trouble saying no to her. She was the only person who consistently had this effect on me.

"Because this mask is going to burn a little."

It did. The next seven processes we did were equally uncomfortable. There was so much burning, tingling, plucking, pulling…and so therefore quite a few refilled glasses. I chucked two of them in the sink when she wasn't looking.

"All right, now on to the last portion."

"I'm dying to know why we're wearing your freshman-year bikinis, Brooke."

"Because!" She pulled a screw-top tub of nasty greenish-brown stuff from the blue crate. "Come on over."

"What is *that?*"

"It's, like…seaweed and oatmeal and honey and chamomile and about forty other things. Come here, I have to slather you!"

I took a few timid steps, and she took a handful and laid it on my bare stomach.

"Oh, my God, that is gross."

"It really is." She spread it around, grimacing. "But it's worth it! Because—and I'm really sorry this is how it is—boys like girls who are put together." She gave a *what can I say?* shrug. "What do you want to be? Do you want to be a Pretty Girl with a capital *P* and a capital *G?* Or just a regular ol' pretty girl?"

"I mean, I guess…the first one?"

"Well, there are a couple of things you have to be before you can be a Pretty Girl. I'm not saying you should slab on the makeup until you end up with a three-layer cake on your face, but you have to take extra-special care of yourself. You don't end up with skin that is the softest he has ever felt by using a regular soap bar and nothing else. Or hair that is so shiny that he wants to reach out and touch it, and find out if it really is as smooth as it looks.

"You don't end up with lips he longs to kiss again and again when you don't slough them off with a sugar scrub every once in a while. When he imagines you, he should think of every sensation of you before he remembers how you look. How you sound when you laugh at a joke he makes, how your soft, sun-kissed shoulder feels in his calloused hand, how your lips taste like sugar and how when you get *just* close enough to him, he can catch a slight breeze of you and he'll always remember that you smell like flowers and sunshine." She finished covering me in the mud, looking nonchalant, as if she hadn't just recited words that could have carried a whole ad campaign.

I gawked at her. I had never heard her be so profound, had never had so much insight into how she became the glistening goddess she was. "Wow, Brooke."

It did make perfect sense, though, that Brooke's entire outlook was based on appearance. Her foundation of life and love started with the belief that you needed to look and, thusly or at the very least, feel beautiful.

"It is only then," she went on to say, "that he should remember that you've got a bangin' bod and ass that don't quit."

"*And* back to the Brooke I know and love."

She laughed and handed me the tub to slather her up. "I'm just saying. In movies, when they picture the girl who got away or who changed them completely, it's never just a nice-looking girl being average and having normal problems. The girls are always laughing in the sunlight, moving a strand of perfect Aniston hair back from their eyelashes or lying in bed, with brushed, flossed and whitened teeth, no grocery store mascara in the corners of their eyes or hair filled with nasty product residue. You go for natural, but you make it the natural you choose. And of course, to top it all off, you need sparkling confidence and daring wit. Honestly, all of these things get you to the point that makes you the most confident, and that's what causes the 'smiling in the sunshine' effect more than anything else. And you've already got wit, so you're totally on your way."

I thought about what she'd said as she stood, arms out for me to rub in the grossness, and took a sip from her glass.

She really was an oddly wise and glamorous girl.

When I finished, we washed our hands and champagne glass stems, then put the final potion on our faces. She grabbed four slices of cucumber, and we took some towels and lay them down in front of the enormous hearth in her living room. She had at some point lit a fire.

We lay down, side by side, and covered our eyes with the cucumbers.

"I'm sorry if I'm pushing you too hard about finding a guy," she said after a few minutes. "I want someone to see you, and for you to feel the way that only a guy can make you feel. Maybe that's Eric, maybe it's not. But I want you to find someone."

"Isn't that against everything we're supposed to think now? As girls? Aren't we supposed to feel complete without the approval of a man and all that?"

I felt her wave away the comment. "Whatever. Be empowered. Be your own woman. But no matter how independent you are, no matter how much you love yourself, there's something only romance can make you feel."

"I guess I know what you mean."

"It's true, sorry 'bout it. People think I'm a slut sometimes, but I'm not. I'm not a sex addict. I don't crave attention so much that I'll sacrifice my dignity for it. I love *love*. Romantic love is different every single time, with every person. It's like having these lovely, sparkly little secrets with different boys. I love feeling those sparks fly. And I'll do anything to get them. But to lots of people, that means I'm a slut. And whatever. Maybe I am. Maybe that's what it is to be a slut."

I wanted to respond to this insight with something better, but all I could utter was, "You're not a slut, Brooke."

"Whatever," she said again. "I act how I act because that feeling is so addictive. The feeling that *you* are the girl in somebody's montage. Even when a romance is short-lived and lame, and disappointing, there's that moment…that moment where you feel like…a girl. Not a queen, not a goddess, not a supermodel. A girl, in the way that boys are supposed to think about us. Like the golden sunlit, breeze-in-the-hair girl that we all want to be."

I breathed deeply. I wanted to be that. She was right. That was what she had meant all along. Not that I needed a boyfriend because of social status or because of a date. But because I wanted and deserved a few glistening memories and moments with someone who saw me that way.

"Know what I mean, jelly bean?"

"Yeah, I do, actually."

I thought of Aiden. I pictured him walking into the diner last night. Shaking my dad's hand. The look on his face when he really liked the pie. I pictured his glances in the rearview at me in the backseat. I pictured his hand on my back, leading me through a doorway before him, but after Brooke. I imagined his hair, and wondered if it was soft.

Dammit. Dammit dammit dammit. Why was I having an Aiden montage?

"Okay, let's go rinse. I once left this stuff on too long and looked like I'd gotten a bad spray tan," said Brooke before leading me up the stairs.

I rinsed first and then sat on the sink in a towel while she did.

"So, Natalie," she said from behind the curtain.

"What?"

"Is there anything you aren't telling me about the party?"

All of my insides froze. "What?"

"I mean, you hooked up with Eric, right? I know you made out with him. But did something else happen? I remember that someone said they couldn't find you. I was still avoiding downstairs because I was pissed at Aiden, so I didn't go investigate. But I'm wondering what happened. You're kind of acting weird. Not like superweird, but you seem different to me."

"Do I?"

She ducked around the side of the curtain. "I'm your best friend, Nat, I think I know when you're acting weird."

Maybe she knew better than I even did.

"All right, whatever, have your secrets. But I think you like Eric. Do you like him? You should totally go to prom with him! You guys should hang out more. Oh, my God— you, me, him and Aiden are going to make, like, the most gorgeous prom group ever! If you're with him, you'll definitely get a nom, too." She nodded at me, agreeing with her own comment.

"A nom?"

"Prom queen nomination, duh."

It should have been obvious what she meant, but the idea was so foreign to me. Me, nominated for prom court? My life had already changed completely, but was that really possible? No way, right? And if it was, did I want it?

"That would be crazy," I said.

"It's really not. *You* are, but it's not. You're like this phantom It girl that everyone adores. But dating Eric will totally shoot you into the stratosphere of popularity."

"I don't really care about that stuff."

"No, I know. But what you can't fool me about—" she turned off the shower and grabbed her towel "—is the fact that you want to be in love just like I do. You can act blasé about everything else in the world, but I know you care about love. And I know you would do almost anything to meet the guy of your dreams."

"And this gross mud crap is that 'almost anything,' huh?"

She gave a hoot of laughter and said, "Pretty much!"

She did know me. And she was right. It was probably the only thing I did care about, even though it was something I barely pursued. But I wouldn't mind meeting a guy who made me happy. Someone to do things with. Someone to always have my back. Someone with whom I could exchange a look at a bad party, and he'd make an excuse for us and we would leave. We would go back to my house and watch movies on my couch. Getting snowed in would be fun, because we wouldn't be at a party.

The idea gave me a heart-twisting thrill. Followed by sadness and guilt as I recognized that I knew who I wanted that person to be.

And he had a slight accent that slipped out when he talked about pie.

CHAPTER SIX

I HADN'T EXPECTED Alexa to actually follow up with me about getting our nails done, but she did. She found me after school on Thursday and asked if I was "ready for a pedi." She laughed at her own rhyme. Before the party, I might not have said yes, but I did now. One of the things Brooke had told me about making friends with girls was that you would get one window in which to be friends with them. If you declined an invitation, or if you were un-fun at whatever it was, you were unlikely to get another invite.

I texted Brooke immediately, since she was taking her time to come outside, as usual. She told me to Go! Go! Have fun! Try not to forget any good gossip!

As we sat and chatted at the spa, I became grateful that Alexa was the kind of girl who was mostly interested in talking about herself. She was likable, so it didn't come off as annoying, and I didn't want to talk too much about myself, anyway.

But eventually the conversation did turn to me.

"So," she said, "I heard you hooked up with *Eric* last weekend!"

Judging by her openmouthed smile and the devilish gleam in her eye, this was not a problem to her.

"Oh, yeah. Is he telling people that?"

"God, no, honey, he's the perfect gentleman. People saw you guys making out and flirting and all and sort of put two and two together. And…okay, to be frank, someone saw a condom wrapper in the bathroom, and that was kind of the guess…. I hope you're not mad, but you know, people love to talk."

I hadn't thought the gossip I would take home to Brooke would be about *me*. At least it was…good news? Thank God I hadn't been *that* stupid.

My little spa date with Alexa wasn't the only social change for me.

After going to one party—well, and one slightly '90s-teen-movie-ish makeover/spa night—it was like I had moved up from the role of an extra at my school to a recurring guest star. I hadn't noticed how little eye contact I had been granted previously until suddenly everyone was locking eyes with me in the halls, either waving with a smile, giving a passing glance or looking at me like they were also wondering what the big deal about me was.

It was as if someone had called, "Action!" in my life, and I hadn't been expecting it, and now I was scrambling around trying to find and memorize the lines I was supposed to say.

This feeling really hit home when I ran into Eric in between classes the next week in school. I hadn't seen him much. All of my classes were pretty much in the same corner of the school, so I didn't do a lot of wandering around, and since I didn't usually eat lunch in the cafeteria, I didn't have much opportunity.

As soon as he saw me coming down the hall, he readjusted his backpack and gave me one of his red-carpet smiles. I smiled back, feeling slightly nauseated. I knew butterflies. And that was not what was happening in my stomach.

I was suddenly feeling the full extent of the weirdness about what had happened between us. This guy, this basic stranger—never mind that I had "known" him for years—had seen me naked. Had kissed me and touched me, and…God…had been *inside* me. I had fumbled drunkenly around in the dark with this person I hardly knew. On the one hand, I was still surprised that a guy as nice (and nonwasted) as Eric had actually followed through and allowed me to make such a mistake. It wasn't all on him, of course; it was my fault for being out of my own wits. But it still shocked me. He was renowned for his goodness.

I noticed that as he smiled at me, the people around us became mildly engaged in the scene. No one was whispering about us, as far as I could tell, but people seemed to be wondering. *Who is Eric smiling at? Why is he smiling at her? I heard they hooked up at Alexa's last party!*

"Hey, you," he said as he quickened to walk in step with me. That expression had always seemed sweet to me. Fond and comfortable, and something about it made it seem like the "you" in question was a relevant sort of person. It was a stupid and small thing, but I'd always kind of hoped for a guy to say it to me. And here one was.

"Hey," I said. What was I supposed to say now? "Um, so what's been going on?"

More glances from passersby.

"Not too much," he said. "Do you want to grab some lunch with me today? I've kept my eyes peeled for you, but I haven't seen you in the lunchroom or anywhere."

I imagined handsome, obsessed-over Eric standing in the

middle of a crowded cafeteria, scanning the faces of girls who would die to be with him, looking for me.

"Oh, I've had a lot of work to do. I was in the library."

He gave a look of understanding. "I've been doing a lot of homework, too. All this crap about second semester senior year being a breeze is bullshit."

I didn't actually agree with him. My course load had dropped off considerably. But considering that I had lied about studying in the library and not admitted to what I'd actually been doing, I felt like I had to nod and say, "Totally."

I had actually spent the past lunchtimes in an empty classroom watching *His Girl Friday* on my dad's iPad—which he had let me borrow and purchase my movie on with the promise that I would finally join him in watching *Moneyball* this weekend. Though I didn't in any way need to be bribed, I had accepted the trade, also promising to make the fried buffalo chicken cheese balls that I knew he loved.

"So…do you want to?"

"Want to what?" I asked, completely forgetting what he had asked.

"Grab some lunch with me today?"

"Oh, um…" I imagined Brooke's face if I told her I had said no because I wanted to start my next movie. "Sure."

"Awesome. I'll meet you out by the parking lot."

"Cool."

My next two classes seemed to go by quicker than ever, even though all I wanted was to slow down time and not find myself outside with Eric, wondering what we were supposed to talk about for the next forty-five minutes. The only topic I could think to bring up, was, *So…did we have sex? And did we in fact use and sloppily dispose of a condom?*

The fact that I didn't know the answer to those questions—

well, I pretty much knew the answer to the first one—was becoming more and more mortifying, particularly since I have a knack for believing that I imagine things. Like every time someone flirts with me, I start to think I made it up. It was seeming more embarrassingly unlikely that I had kissed Eric outside and somehow ended up having sex with him, and more likely that I had maybe been wasted, kissed him, fallen over something and injured my Brazilian territories, then scrambled stupidly and uninvited into bed with Aiden. If I were admitting any of this to Brooke, this is where she would give me a look like I was borderline committable and ask why, then, was he asking me to get lunch. To which I would respond, *Probably to talk to me about how awkward I was, and to make sure I don't accost him in the future.*

Brooke, I knew, would then tell me I was an idiot. But since I wasn't telling her any of this, I had to roll my own eyes and force myself out the door to meet him. Which was where I found myself now. He wasn't outside when I got there, and it took a huge effort to keep my feet planted on the chilly concrete and not to run inside and pretend that I had never come out. As I was weighing my options, he walked up.

"You all set?" he asked.

"Yep."

His car was, of course, parked right in front of the doors. This was just one of the lucky things that came with being one of life's A-listers, it seemed. The one and only time I had borrowed my dad's car and driven to school by myself, I had ended up having to park behind the tennis courts on the grass. I had then spent the rest of the day imagining how embarrassing it was going to be if my car got towed from my own high school. It hadn't happened, but it had seemed like a possibility.

Eric's car was a sleek black thing with dark brown leather seats and a nice audio system. Knowing nothing about cars, I wouldn't have appreciated it even if he had told me what kind it was—which he might have, I can't remember now—but I knew that it was a very nice car that probably cost an amount so large I would barely be able to fathom it.

I almost complimented it, but stopped myself when the words about to come out of my mouth were, *Your car is really pretty.*

"How does Panera sound for lunch?"

"Oh…"

It was the part of the invitation that had made me hesitate. Where most of the people I knew could afford a day or two (or more) going out to lunch, I couldn't. I didn't have an allowance, because my dad didn't have the money to give it to me. I worked summers at a restaurant nearby, but during the school year I couldn't. It was too much driving to ask of my dad or of Brooke, and I couldn't afford a car.

As if he'd read my mind—or maybe he knew I was broke—Eric added, "If that doesn't sound good, pick anywhere. It's on me, and I like just about everything. Except Indian food. Don't pick curry." He smiled.

"Panera sounds perfect—I was just thinking…if we had enough time to get there and back before next period."

"Don't worry about it, we do it all the time."

I didn't ask who "we" was. Just assumed it was people I envied. People with money, options and probably a plan for the coming fall.

He started talking about the lacrosse team. The fact that the game didn't interest me, and he didn't know it, was my fault, since I had feigned caring about it before. I couldn't listen, though. Not only did I hardly understand what he was describing, but I was distracted by my own thoughts and his hands on the steering wheel.

Had they been on my body last weekend? Something about

it seemed improbable, but that might have been my insecurities. I looked at his mouth as he spoke. It was a really nice mouth. My vague memory of kissing him wasn't bad. I had kissed only a few boys in my time, but I knew there was nothing about his kissing that wouldn't make a girl want to do it again.

Suddenly a flash came into my head of kissing in the bedroom, not just on the patio by the hot tub. A hand on my back, lifting me slightly off the mattress and into his kiss. *That* had been a good kiss. *That* had been the kind that made my knees go weak. Which wasn't a problem, I supposed, since I'd already been horizontal on a mattress.

I cringed a little. I had hooked up in a dark room, drunk, at a party. Again. Why had I been so stupid? *Twice?*

We got to Panera and parked. It was blindingly cold outside today, despite the sunshine, and as soon as we opened the door—actually, he opened it for me—a cozy gust of warm, heated air made me glad I had come.

I was a girl of simple joys.

He waited for me to order first, and then followed with his own order. I didn't know how to react when he pulled out his card and really did pay.

"Oh, you don't have to—"

"Hey. I asked you to lunch. And besides, I think the least I can do is buy you a meal."

Was that the going rate for blackout sex? And Aiden's ten-dollar throwdown at my diner...was that the price of a regrettable flirtation in a basement?

We settled at a table next to a fireplace, and I couldn't help but imagine how much I would love to be sitting here with someone I was severely crushing on.

Which made me even more aware of the fact that I was not severely crushing on Eric.

Which sucked, because as I looked at his gorgeous face, I could see that he seemed into me.

"So, I hope that was okay the other night...."

Was he asking me if he was good? How was I going to keep him from realizing that I had no recollection whatsoever?

"Oh, yeah, I mean..."

"I didn't mean to be too forward. I never do that, you know. I don't just hook up with girls to hook up with them."

I knew this to be true. Part of his appeal to all the girls at school was his unavailability. He'd had two girlfriends in high school, one for about eight months last year, and one freshman year, but besides that he was ungettable. He was flirtatious and obviously liked girls, but didn't date just to have a girlfriend. The first girl he'd dated had cheated on him and had gone on to weep endlessly for the next year or so. The girl he'd dated during our junior year was named Mandy, and she'd seemed really smart and interesting. She was a senior at the time, though, and had gone off to college in Indiana or somewhere to be smart and interesting there.

"I don't do that, either. And I know you don't. You don't need to apologize or worry about it." I shrugged. "It happened, it's fine."

They called our number, and he got up to get our food. I had ordered a bowl of soup, fearing the wrath of lettuce from a salad ending up wrapped around my teeth.

"So, anyway," he said, after we did the whole "yeah, your soup looks good, oh, yeah, so does your sandwich" thing, "I wanted to make sure that wasn't too weird for you, or that I totally turned you off or anything."

"No, no, of course not, it's fine," I said. "I guess...I guess in my ideal scenario, I wouldn't have been that wasted...."

"You don't usually party, and I know that," he scrambled to say. "I felt so weird about that. But I didn't want to seem...

however. I don't know. I was drinking, too, and I like you. I
didn't do too good a job holding back. I know I haven't gotten to know you very well yet—"

Or, really, at all, I thought.

"—but, we've been around each other forever, and you're
obviously beautiful and incredibly intelligent. I would really
like the chance to get to know you."

I'd heard that he was going to school for advertising—
everyone had started calling him Don Draper when he'd announced his major to friends—and I could see now that he
would be good at closing deals. I felt like I was a company,
and he had told me that he really liked my work and hoped
we could move forward with a project.

"That would be nice," I said. I didn't know what else to
say. Maybe we could like each other, and I wasn't giving him
a chance. He liked me. For whatever reason. Maybe the only
reason I didn't think I was into him was that I had never even
considered the possibility that he was…well, a possibility. And
I *had* slept with him. Didn't I owe him, and myself, the opportunity to get to know each other?

After that he asked me questions about myself—all the
right questions, doing exactly what you're supposed to do
when you're getting to know someone. I answered honestly,
if dully, and tried to ask questions back when they occurred
to me. I didn't like having all the pressure on me to come up
with interesting answers.

When we arrived back at school, we walked in just as everyone else was walking out of the cafeteria. The stares we
got were now incredibly obvious.

I wanted to say something to acknowledge the attention
but didn't know what. Thankfully, Brooke came out of the
cafeteria a few seconds later. When she was around, the burden to make conversation went to her. And she was fine with

that, so it worked. Aiden emerged a second later. I felt an immediate urge to leap away from Eric.

Brooke took Aiden's hand and they came over to us.

My eyes landed on their interlocked fingers, and I started to say hi in about ten different ways before clearing my throat and shifting my gaze to the tile flooring.

"Hey, guys," said Brooke. She looked at my coat and then smiled. "Where have you two been?"

"We grabbed some lunch at Panera," Eric answered for us.

Brooke and Aiden both raised their eyebrows, Brooke in glee, Aiden merely in surprise.

"Yeah, they have good soup," I explained stupidly.

Aiden chuckled, and I shot him a look.

"They sure do," said Brooke, as if the words had meant something more than that I really liked their soup. "Maybe we should all go sometime, the four of us. That'd be fun, wouldn't it, babe?"

Aiden shrugged. "Yeah, they have good sandwiches as well as good soup."

I knew he was teasing me, in the way he often did. It was this weird under-the-table joking we did that Brooke never really picked up on. Unlike usual, however, his new thing of seeming slightly irritated with me was laced into his tone.

"Well, Nattie and I have to head to English, so we'll see you boys later."

Brooke let go of Aiden's hand and grabbed mine, pulling me away.

"Bye, thanks for lunch," I said as Brooke led me into the crowd of people. I glanced at Aiden once before turning back.

"So oh-my-God tell me *everything,* are you guys totally in love?"

"I think...I think I had sex with him."

The words came out of my mouth, and I think I was expecting them even less than she was.

She stopped dead in the hall, not minding that people had to maneuver to stop from running into her. "What in the *fuck?*" She laughed, looking baffled. "Just now? What do you mean you *think* you...*what?*"

I groaned and pulled her out of the throng and into the theater hallway, which was less populated, but louder.

"What are you talking about?" she asked again.

"At the party. I was making out with him—as you know—and I kind of remember that, and then...I have some blacked-out flashes of hooking up with him in a dark room after that."

"Did you, like...could you tell the next morning?"

"Yeah, I mean, I was kind of sore and..." I shrugged. "I guess I'm sure it happened."

"Holy whore, are you kidding?" She laughed. "This is incredible. You, like, totally fucked our school's white whale. You fucked Moby *Dick!*"

She was thrilled by her own play on words, but I bit my lip and covered my eyes. "Oh, my God..."

"This is crazy."

"Okay, but you really can't tell anyone."

"I won't! But how did you not tell me? I even asked you the other day!"

"I know. But it's kind of weird since I'm not totally sure it happened? And I...I don't want anyone to know."

"That's fine. Okay, sure."

"No, I don't mean you can't tell anyone, but then you tell Aiden because he's your boyfriend and you tell each other everything. I mean *no one.*"

"Nattie, I get it. And I don't tell Aiden everything."

"I mean, because...what if I didn't, and I'm just wrong? There's definitely a chance that I'm wrong and nothing happened, and that I am completely losing my mind. Can you imagine anything more incredibly mortifying than thinking I had sex with someone when I didn't, and him finding out that I thought that?"

"Yeah, that would be embarrassing. Hi*lar*ious, but yeah, embarrassing."

"Brooke!"

"I pinky swear, all right? God!"

I hoped I could believe her.

CHAPTER SEVEN

FRIDAYS FOR SENIORS were different from Fridays for everyone else. The mornings were filled with either two long periods of Advanced Placement classes (for college credit), college preparation classes (usually filled with students whose parents had forced them into it), office assistant duties (in the main office, guidance or helping out a teacher in a specific subject) or with the morning off (an option usually chosen by students who didn't care at all about academics and adored sleeping in).

I was an assistant in the main office, which meant I answered phones and did boring filing. The job brought nothing very exciting to my day, but the secretaries in the office loved me, so it was an okay environment in which to spend a couple hours. I'd chosen it because it gave me Student Service Learning hours, and I needed them to graduate. My GPA was fine, it was the extracurricular stuff that I had fallen behind on.

Seniors spent the second half of their Fridays either at internships or doing a senior capstone project. Some students had a specific subject area for their project. Drama kids worked on directing and acting in one another's miniplays. Band students practiced for end-of-the-year performances. Artsy kids planned for a big show at the end of the semester at a gallery in Bethesda. People like me, who had no specific skills, did the generic capstone project, which worked on "team building and critical thinking." At least according to the paragraph in the description.

On Fridays, my dad would usually take me to school, but every once in a while Aiden would pick me up. This was on account of the fact that Brooke had taken the sleeping-in option, much to her parents' fury. Lately, I had declined Aiden's occasional night-before texts to pick me up. I felt awkward with him for whatever reason. So this morning, my dad dropped me off, giving me the hug and kiss on the forehead that he'd been giving me since my first day of kindergarten. I had always hated the kids in TV shows and movies who acted like it was such an enormous drag when their parents showed them affection. I thought it was adorable.

It had been about a month since the Stupid Cupid party, and in that time, I had hardly seen Aiden. Brooke had been driving me to and from school in her car. I wasn't sure why we hadn't gone with Aiden for so long. She said it was because he had stuff to do after school, but part of me wondered if they were on the brink of a breakup. When I wondered this, I got an irritatingly hopeful feeling in my chest.

Today he came into our capstone class and glanced up into the stadium-style seats and found me. At first it struck me as flattering or unusual that he should seek me out but then I realized he probably always did this, since we usually sat next to each other. This was just the first time I had also been watching for him. I usually stared at my phone or a school-book so that I could avoid exactly that: looking like I was looking for him.

The only open seat was behind me. I turned around as he sat down. "Hey," I said. "I feel like I haven't seen you in forever."

"I know. How are you?" His tone was a little chilly. For the first time, it occurred to me that if he and Brooke broke up, maybe he wouldn't talk to me anymore. I fussed anxiously with my hair.

"I'm good. Thank God it's Friday, right?"

Before he had a chance to respond, our teacher came in and called attention to the front of the room.

Halfway through class, we got the news that we were officially to start on our senior projects. After weeks of PowerPoint-heavy lectures on time management and organization, we were finally going to do something.

We all knew about Ms. Jean's final senior projects, because they tended to be relatively epic and awesome and things that encapsulated the past four years for us all. Her capstone class was the one to be in if you weren't in one of the specialized classes. Last year one team put together a tear-jerking video using collected footage that they'd gotten a bunch of people to donate, and they had given everyone a copy. I'd had my idea in mind since sophomore year, and I had been waiting and hoping no one would take it.

"As you know, the major focus of this class is the senior project. And once we are finished, so are you, with your entire high school career." She allowed people to clap and whoop. "The point of the project is not only to bring people together who might not already be friends and give you something to physically or mentally take away from high school—in addition, of course, to all the knowledge—" pause for laughter "—but also to put the power in your hands. I'm sure you know I am very loose with this assignment. I tell you no more than the fact that it is a senior project, who you're partnered with and whether what you suggest is asinine or insanely inappropriate. But even that I am flexible on."

More laughter from the class.

"Now, I take great pride in what my classes put out with this project. And I chose all of you specifically to be in my class when you filled out the application. This is not a project to screw around on, and it has become something that colleges look for from our school's graduates. It is not something to take lightly, and it is not something that you will ruin for future students.

"You are in this classroom, and doing work for the class on your own time, for a big portion of your senior year. I won't pretend that you don't have major things going on in the rest of your life, but I will say that you must find a way to do this and do it well. Not just for the grade. Not just for college. But for you. Because one of the most important questions you are going to have to ask yourselves, and in the end find a strong answer for, is this—what matters to you, and what matters to everyone else?"

No one was laughing now. People had begun to scribble down notes. I opened my red notebook—a five-subject one, for this class alone—and wrote down the questions.

Was everything going to strike a chord in me lately? Answering the question "What matters to you?" felt exhausting. I hardly knew.

"Maybe it's the same thing," she went on. "Maybe it's going to change throughout the semester. Maybe your answer now will be one you're embarrassed by at the end of college. But whatever it is, it has to be real. Find a way to do something that matters to you. And don't hand in a pencil and say that it encompasses everything you ever can or will do because it is the symbol of potential and possibility and also the ability to change. Clever that might be, but believe me, the boy who did that a few years ago got a failing grade."

She looked out at all of us again, and then took the glasses from the beaded chain around her neck and put them on her nose. She held out a hand and her TA brought over a yellow envelope. Ms. Jean leaned on her desk and gave a wicked smile.

"I can feel the tension in the room." Laughter. "Yes, this is the list of partners." She held it up. "The person—or people— that you will be spending your final semester working with, side by side. I chose your teams based on your applications. Some of you I've paired with compatible students. For some of you—those of you whom I believe need the challenge— I have paired with incompatible people. Because that's life." She smiled. "Have fun figuring out if your team is supposed to be compatible or not."

More laughter, but it was nervous now. Particularly mine.

We listened, all of us on the edge of our seats. When she got down the list to Aiden's name, I found myself almost knowing what was coming.

"...Natalie Shepherds."

I couldn't even turn to look at him at first. I waited for her to finish the list and tell us to get with our partners. He climbed over the row of seats and came to me.

When I finally looked at him, there was something intense in his expression. Maybe it was annoyance. I flushed red—as if I had anything to do with the pairing—and then whatever I'd seen was gone, and he looked normal.

Finally, I said, "Well, of course, right?"

He ran a hand through his hair. "Hey, at least neither of us is working with that girl." He gestured at Kylie Tamer, who was a nonstop chatterbox.

"She might talk a lot, but she's going to school for engineering next year." I wished again that my brain wasn't filled with so many details about other people's lives.

"Yeah, I was just kidding...I'm actually sorry about you getting me as a partner."

"Why?"

"Because I am...man, I am not creative. I'm all left brain."

"Well, I don't have a lot of that. So we'll be a good match!" I immediately regretted my choice of words. "Um. Yeah, so it doesn't matter, I have our project. I mean, if it sounds cool to you."

"Please," he said, leaning back in his chair to listen.

"Well. I thought of it forever ago and always intended to do it if I got into the class." I cleared my throat. "I think it would be really cool to make sort of a...a real-life Facebook or Tumblr-type thing. In the center of the school in the square. To plaster the wall with pictures of everyone throughout the semester. Like, let's say we get anyone who wants to...to donate three pictures of themselves. Because that's a lot of wall to cover. And then we put them up as sort of a base. Then toward the end of the year we can keep adding to it. Posters, ticket stubs, prom corsages, that sort of thing. The type of things people keep. And then at the end of the year we'll take high-res shots of the wall and give the pictures out to everyone."

His eyebrows were raised.

"What? Do you think it's lame?"

Immediately it sounded lame in my head.

"Are you kidding? I think that's an incredible idea."

"Really?"

"Absolutely, Natalie, that's crazy cool. I can see it now, too, people taking pictures in front of the wall or whatever."

"Exactly! Yes, that's exactly what I envisioned. Like, exactly what I envisioned."

I was thrilled at his acceptance of the idea, and by the fact that we were having a moment of acting normal again.

"Maybe rather than just asking people to donate pictures, we could rent out areas. So if a group of girls want to have their section all together, they can buy a square for five bucks or ten bucks or something. And then, in the end, we could do something where everyone could stand in front of it. We could get Mike, that camera kid, to take the pictures, and sell the prints. We could use the money to go toward a party. Like a graduation party for everyone."

"That's awesome. Wow. See, your left brain did help."

We went up to the front.

Ms. Jean, who was somehow both sharper and more pleasant-looking up close, raised her eyebrows at us. "Already?"

"Yeah," I said. "Um. Well, I kind of came up with the seed of the idea a couple of years ago, inspired by seeing what everyone else did, and I told Aiden just now, and he added a few things that I think will really total it all out."

"Go ahead."

I told her most of it, and Aiden pitched in the rest. When we finished, we waited anxiously. Her face was completely impassive. She thought for a full minute before responding.

"I think that idea has some incredible potential."

I let out a breath I hadn't realized I was holding.

"The key will be," she said, "to keep it from looking junky. I think you'll go wrong by having it too cluttered, and I think you'll go wrong by having it be too organized." She nodded at us, with a small smile. "I think you two will make a good team."

"Thank you, Ms. Jean," said Aiden before heading back to our seats.

"We've got our first accepted project of the year!" she said to the class at large. "But please, this is not a race! You have all week to solidify your ideas, so make sure you think them out properly!"

WE WALKED TO lunch together, both of us thrilled that our pitch had been accepted.

"I would be so completely lost right now if I we hadn't gotten paired up in that class."

I felt my cheeks go hot, but laughed. "I am somewhat of a hero."

"You are! Don't laugh."

"Well, yeah. I guess you would have been screwed."

"Totally screwed. So, um, we'll have to get together to work on this some."

At first I almost argued that, no, a double period was probably more than enough time to do it. But something stopped me.

"Yeah. We'll have to find some time."

"Right. I have my internship at the vet, too, so I kinda have to work around that."

"Oh, yeah, of course. No big deal at all. Whenever we can hook up—I—whenever we can get together, let's do it. Let's… whenever you have some time, we'll work on the project."

I glanced up to see that he wasn't looking at me but was laughing silently.

"Shut up!"

"What? I didn't say anything."

"My dad always calls it hooking up when you're both trying to make your schedules work and get together—oh, just be quiet."

But I couldn't help but smile back.

"Guys! There you are." Brooke came up to us. I felt a little deflated by her sudden appearance. For once, and only for a gleaming few seconds, it was as if Aiden and I had our own relationship, independent of her existence.

"Nattie, enough hiding in the library watching movies, you're eating with us today."

I allowed her to pull me into the lunchroom, and it became clear quickly why she was so eager to have me join them. Eric was sitting at the table, one of the three open seats next to him. He smiled when he saw me, and again I felt the audience around us.

I wanted to walk right back out. But instead, I smiled and greeted everyone as if I was not wishing I was elsewhere. I was such a brat. They were all being so nice to me, and all I could ever do was feel nervous and want to leave.

"You guys got partnered up today for Ms. Jean's class, right?" asked Brooke. "Who did you guys get partnered with?" She pulled the top off her Starbucks salad.

"We actually got paired together," I answered, possibly trying too hard to sound like I didn't care.

Brooke hesitated as she poured her salad dressing. "Oh, yeah? That's pretty lucky, then, huh?"

"Yeah, Nat already had an idea all mapped out and everything. I got totally lucky."

"Oh, yeah, the wall thing?" she asked. Of course I had told her about it a million years ago. "That's cool. So, Eric, when are you taking my friend on a real date?"

Whoa. Her tone had shifted to one I recognized. She was mad. Why was she being pissy-Brooke? Obviously I could guess it had something to do with Aiden. Possibly about Aiden and me being paired together?

The same reason it secretly thrilled me must be the same reason it seemed to be secretly upsetting her. I couldn't focus right then on what that must mean, because I was too busy being in shock at what she had said to Eric.

"Brooke," I said, with no idea what to follow it up with.

"What?" She smiled, but it wasn't a real smile. "You guys hooked up, I think the least he can do is earn it with a date."

I could see that Eric was uncomfortable, too. There was nothing I hated more than being put in a position of being rejected when I hadn't even made an offer or asked for the rejection.

If we hadn't been around other people, I would have smacked her in the arm and told her to stop being weird. But as little time as I felt like spending around them, I wanted these people to like me. I could think of absolutely nothing to say and was even starting to feel a little sick. I gave a short laugh.

"I was going to ask her if she wanted to do something, actually." He shifted his gaze to me. "You don't have to answer right now. But if you want to go out, we definitely can. I would really like that."

Aiden was staring incredulously at Brooke. She raised her eyebrows in a way that asked, *What?* while also confirming that she knew exactly what she had done.

I took a sip of my water, now feeling seriously sick. Out of nowhere, I had to actually steady my breathing in order not to wretch.

"You okay?" asked Aiden.

"Yes, I'm fine. Just…" The words were a struggle to get out. I took a deep breath. "I'm just feeling a little sick."

"There's been something going around," said Brooke. "If you go to the nurse I bet she'll let you go home. I totally would if I were you."

"Sick like nauseated?" asked Aiden.

"Yeah." Another wave. "I think I will go to the nurse."

"Oh, no, feel better, babe," said Alexa, who had sat down as the pukey feeling hit me.

"Want me to walk you?" asked Eric.

"No, don't worry about it," I said, trying to collect my lunch stuff.

"I'll get this, you go ahead," said Aiden. "Feel better."

"Thanks. I'll…see you."

I ducked out of the cafeteria and into the nearest bathroom, where I hurled up my entire breakfast.

CHAPTER EIGHT

I WAS IN the library a few days later, reading a book and trying not to get caught eating hummus and pita chips, when Eric walked up to me.

"Hey," he said, keeping his voice down.

"Hi." I shifted from the unattractively comfortable position I had been sitting in.

I had avoided him like the plague since Brooke had cornered him into asking me out. I didn't know what it meant exactly that I'd thrown up after talking about going on a date with Eric, but I did know that if I was to go on a date with him, I wouldn't want it to be because Brooke told him to ask me.

It was stupid that I was taking such huge steps to avoid him. I recognized that. He was a good guy—handsome, smart, funny, blah, blah, blah. All those things that girls say they want. But I just didn't have feelings for him. And as infuriating as it was, that mattered. People can't choose who to love, but if I could, it would have been great to choose him.

"Can I sit for a second?" He gestured at the chair next to me.

"Sure, of course."

He took his bag off and sat. "I like to be straightforward. So. That's what I have to do."

"Okay..."

"I like you. Brooke told me you like me, but I don't know that she's telling me the truth. I also don't know why she'd lie." He seemed genuinely confused by the notion. "So if you don't like me, that's okay. I understand. But if you do, I would really like to take you out. Movie. Grab a bite to eat. Minigolf—" he laughed "—whatever you want."

He really was such a nice guy. It was ridiculous that I kept hiding from him. What was I holding out for? Aiden? My best friend's boyfriend? That was stupid. Not only was Aiden too good a guy to ever do something like that—and I liked to think I wouldn't, either—but especially lately he had been so weird around me. To the point that I could no longer look back on the night of Alexa's party without a shudder. He probably knew I liked him—maybe before I even knew—and me crawling into bed with him must have come off so pathetic and stalkerish.

"Natalie?"

I shook Aiden from my mind. "Yes. I would love to go out. I'm sorry if I've seemed reluctant. I don't really go out with guys that often, and I'm bad at it."

He smiled, looking relieved. "You're fine. I'll see you around or text you and we'll do something soon, okay?"

I nodded, as if I wasn't going to continue avoiding him and pretend to be bad about answering texts. "Sounds perfect."

THE MORNING OF Brooke's birthday, March 20, she was in one of her grumpy morning moods. These tended to strike her most consistently on days where she had heard that school might be canceled, and then it wasn't. It had started snowing the night before at around seven, and the news had said that it was going to accumulate and likely make driving unsafe by nine the next morning. She'd been thrilled and had immediately jumped into action. She'd invited Alexa and me over, but my dad had told me no, since he didn't think the snow was going to stick. Brooke and I had both learned long ago that my dad meant no when he said it, and so she had given up pretty immediately on me making it. She was disappointed, but understood. She would come over this weekend, anyway, for our Brooke's Birthday Tradition, which was that we would watch either *Romeo & Juliet* or *Moulin Rouge!* and I would make her nachos from scratch.

I climbed into the car and sang her the first line of "Happy Birthday." She groaned, and I noticed that both she and Alexa were looking a little pale and raccoon-eyed and had the music uncharacteristically low. I learned that they'd stayed up drinking white zinfandel and watching old episodes of *The O.C.* until 4:00 a.m. Brooke's mom was out of town again, and her dad slept like the dead, so he hadn't even noticed that Alexa had come over.

"We're stopping at McDonald's," announced Brooke, pulling off. "I need some coffee."

"Why don't we go to Starbucks if you want coffee?" I asked.

"There's no drive-through Starbucks around here, and I can't possibly get out of the car until we have to."

Alexa nodded silently, her face almost completely hidden in her big fur hood.

I never ate McDonald's. I knew a lot of people were obsessed with the breakfast, but I had never particularly gotten the hype.

"Hi, yeah, can I have...can I have, God, like, four hash

browns and a large coffee? And what do you want?" She nudged Alexa.

"Large Diet Coke."

"That's it?"

She nodded again from her fur cave.

I looked at the menu, saw a picture of a breakfast sandwich and became suddenly ravenous.

"Okay, that's it," said Brooke.

"No, no, wait! Get me a sausage, egg and cheese biscuit."

"Really?"

"Yes, yes. Tell her. Oh! And orange juice."

She looked at me quizzically and then added it to the order.

"Oh, and do they have McFlurries at this time of day? God, I would kill for ice cream."

"What the hell is wrong with you, have you been anorexic for the past week and I haven't noticed or something?"

"It just sounds awesome right now."

"You're so weird sometimes. Yeah, ma'am? Can I also add a small Oreo McFlurry?"

"Anything else?"

"Anything else?" She directed this toward me, looking amused at my sudden appetite.

"No."

"No, that's it, thanks."

"Your total is $11.73. Next window please."

"And you're not even the hungover one," she said.

Alexa held up a weak, gloved hand. "Shh, you guys are talking, like, so loud."

IT WAS THE best sandwich I had ever consumed, and I ate the ice cream so fast I got brain freeze three times. I decided this was worth it, however, despite the confused looks I kept getting from Brooke.

"I am in shock that it's freaking snowing again," she complained as we walked toward our lockers. "And that we're in school today. Stupid snow couldn't have just accumulated? Couldn't have just been a little more dangerous out today?"

"It's not supposed to get really bad until, like, two, and then we're almost out, anyway."

Brooke groaned noisily and unselfconsciously, despite the fact that we were walking through the busy morning hallway.

"But we probably won't have school tomorrow!" I said, trying to cheer her up.

"Don't get my hopes up."

I stood with Brooke as she fiddled with her lock.

"I can never remember the stupid combination. It's what… to the left, then all the way around…and the numbers are… what? Thirty-two, eight, nine?"

"Oh, my God, Brooke. How do you not know by now?"

"I usually have my stuff in my bag. I want to see if Aiden put something in here for me today." She stepped back and allowed me to open it for her. "He better have. I've been a damn saint lately."

This distracted me, and I missed the third number.

"See, it's not that easy, you condescending bitch." Brooke was standing behind me with her arms crossed as I distractedly struggled with the lock.

I finally got it. "There you go. Whoa, Brooke!" I shut it almost all the way and turned back to her. "What the hell?"

"What?" She opened the door and saw what I saw. "What the fuck…"

I joined her at the locker, making sure we blocked the sight from any passing teachers. "Why is there a bottle of liquor in your locker?" I whispered.

Brooke laughed, looking seriously confused. "I have no idea. Whaaaat…wait."

She tilted her head as she picked up the bottle and found a scrap of paper. She held it up.

Happy birthday, let's see how much you can handle.

"Holy crap, do you have a secret admirer?"

She was furrowing her eyebrows at the note. "I guess. That's really weird. Maybe Aiden…?"

"Aiden would never risk getting you in trouble like that," I said.

"No, no, you're probably right."

"Then…any idea who it is?"

"Lotta people like drinking and a lotta people like me, Nattie." She gave a laugh that didn't quite sound like her own, and then went silent.

"Well. At least you know it's a guy. No girl has handwriting that bad."

The bell rang.

"Truth. Uh. Well, I should go to class."

I don't think I had ever heard her utter that sentence.

"Coming to lunch today, sport?"

The question was followed by a smack on my ass with a notebook.

I turned around, knowing exactly who it was. I exclaimed, but in that girlish way where you're smiling and are clearly not upset by whatever you're pretending to be annoyed about. "Aiden!"

I tilted my head at him. Why had he done that? And…did that mean we weren't acting awkward today?

He grinned at me. "Sorry, I'm excited. Guess what?"

"What?"

"I finally finished sketching out the measurements and stuff for our project."

"Really?"

We fell in step together on the way to the cafeteria. I hadn't intended to, but now it seemed I was going to lunch with everyone.

"Yup. Last night. Sorry we haven't been able to get together to work on it lately. My internship is running me ragged."

"Oh, no big deal, we don't really need to work together on it until later on, anyway." At once, I wished I hadn't said it.

But luckily, he insisted. "Well, we'll need to pretty soon, I think. Right?"

"Yeah…we probably should."

He held my gaze for a second and then laughed. "We better hook up soon, then."

For a second, I didn't realize that he was referencing my embarrassing phrasing from when we first got paired together. My heart skipped, stupidly, and then I remembered. "Right. Right."

We laughed and sat at the table.

He pulled his phone out of his pocket. "Brooke won't be coming to lunch today. She has to talk to one of her teachers about a grade."

"Typical Brooke. If you can't test your way to an A, talk your way into it."

He laughed again, just as Alexa and the others sat down.

"How you feelin', Alexa?" I asked.

"Like total shit."

She sat and lay her head down on folded arms on the table.

"Here, I'll be right back," I said. "You should eat something. I'll grab it for you."

I went to the lunch line and grabbed a cheeseburger with French fries, and a bottle of cranberry juice. I took it back to her and pulled ibuprofen from my purse. I always carried it with me, since I or someone around was always bound to need it at some point.

"You can have the headache medicine only after you've eaten half of the burger. Otherwise, you'll get sicker. And drink the cranberry juice, it'll help you get hydrated and get the rest of the toxins out of your system."

"You are, like, the best ever. Seriously, you're like a mom right now. Not my mom, of course, my mom is a total bitch. But you know what I mean." She took a bite of the burger. "Oh, my God, I haven't eaten shit food in so long. It's so good. Aw…look, here comes your boo."

She looked behind me. I turned.

Eric was coming toward us, and he pulled out a small bouquet of pink roses and gave them to me.

"What is this for?"

"It's a belated Valentine's Day bouquet. That was the day we started talking…and I felt like you deserved Valentine flowers, even if they're a month late."

"Ohh!" Alexa cooed.

"Ohh…" I didn't coo.

"That is so romantic," said Bethany.

The surprise of it all made me turn pinker than the roses. Everyone around us was watching. And I mean everyone. There was even a slight hush in the cafeteria as he leaned down to kiss me on the cheek.

"Thank you so much," I said, making sure to smile broadly.

According to the faces of every nearby girl, Eric had just done something wonderful. He was a dream of a boy. And all I could think was, *What a stupid gesture.*

I know that sounds totally screwed up, but I couldn't help it. It felt forced. Like imitating romantic gestures in movies or something. Also, I didn't care for the holiday, so having it come up again at the end of March seemed irritating.

I hated myself for these ungrateful thoughts. But I guess it doesn't matter how perfect someone is if they're not perfect for you.

How annoying.

Eric sat in the chair next to me, and everyone started chatting. I glanced at Aiden, who was back to looking expressionless. Gone was the jovial, joking Aiden of mere moments ago. My stomach tightened. Was Aiden mad that Eric had brought me flowers?

As I watched him swig from his bottle of water and avoid my gaze and the conversation, I got the feeling that, yes, he was mad. He cared.

And that made my heart skip far more than a bouquet of flowers from the most desirable guy in the school district.

CHAPTER NINE

THE RIDE HOME from school was tense, and I couldn't quite put my finger on why. Aiden had seemed pissy since lunch, and Brooke was quiet and seemed mad, too. Neither of them spoke most of the way. A couple minutes from my house, Aiden finally said something.

"So, are you going out with Eric tonight, Nat?" He looked at me in the rearview.

Brooke turned to face him, but he just looked back at the road. What was going on?

"Uh, no. I'm not. Probably going on a date with *Bonnie and Clyde*. I've never seen it."

"Oh, really? It's different than you'd expect. You'll like it, though, I think."

"Good. Yeah, I like movies."

Golly, the sentences I allowed out of my mouth.

I like movies? Come on, Shepherds, get it together.

"Me, too. Old movies are the best, though. Which is probably why that's all new movies are, anyway, just remakes."

"Right? I've said the same thing, like, a thousand times, haven't I, Brooke?"

"Yeah, you guys are, like, so on the same page."

Whoa. What was her deal?

"You okay?" Aiden asked her in a much quieter voice, putting a hand on her thigh.

The gesture made my stomach turn.

"Yeah, I'm fine. Don't feel that well. I think I probably caught whatever you had, Nat."

We were silent the rest of the ride.

MY DAD WAS out of town, again, and I was sitting on my couch watching TV when my phone buzzed. It was like I had been expecting it. A text from Aiden.

Still no plans for tonight?

I answered back immediately.

Nope, haha.

Why had I added the *haha?* It just came off as self-conscious.

I'm approx 3 blocks from your house sledding. You should probably come. I happen to know you like to sled.

Why didn't Brooke text me?

She's not here. Still not feeling good.

On her birthday, she must be pissed.

Sick/hungover/doesn't feel like hanging out. Whatever. hah.

Where are you guys sledding?

I'll walk over and pick you up. Dress warm!

I darted up the stairs, put in my contacts, applied mascara (a recent gift from Brooke), slithered on tight jeans, socks under my Uggs and a couple layers on top.

I didn't take a moment to wonder if this was a good idea until I had already gotten all the way back down the stairs.

Brooke wasn't going to be there. He was with his friends. He had invited me. It was eleven at night, and I was going sledding on Brooke's birthday without her. But with her boyfriend.

He was at the door in five minutes.

"Hey, you," he said when I opened the door.

There was that expression again. It felt different when he said it than when Eric did.

"Hey. I'm dressed as warmly as I can be."

"Should you blow that out?" He gestured inside, where I had left a Yankee Candle burning.

"Oh, right, yeah, hold on."

"Smells good," he said as I went back in.

"It's—" I looked at the label after snuffing it "—Apple Cinnamon Danish."

"Nice. My mom's always burning those things. Careful, it's pretty slippery," he said, holding out an arm when I almost fell on the steps outside.

"Thanks."

"You sure you didn't have a date going on in there? Got a candle goin', and a movie..."

"I like candles! And my dad hates the smell, so I don't really burn them when he's home."

"He's not home right now?"

"No." I ignored the skip in my heartbeat. "He's out of town for work."

He narrowed his eyes and smiled at me.

"What?"

"Your dad has been going out of town a lot lately, huh?"

"Yeah, kind of."

"I mean…in the almost two years I've known you, your dad has hardly gone out of town until the past couple of months."

"What are you implying exactly?"

"Nothin'…just that maybe he's got a girlfriend or somethin'."

"No…" My eyes widened and Aiden laughed. "Oh, my God, what if he does?"

"Hah! He's totally dating that Marcy girl."

"Oh…my God."

"Sounds to me like he is."

I covered my face. "Ah, how weird!"

"You are *not* wearing mittens."

"What? Why?" I pulled my hands away from my face and held them up.

He shook his head. "You're such a dork."

"Am not!"

"Natalie. You're in mittens. That's pretty much the definition of dorky. That and having day-of-the-week underwear that you actually wear on the right days of the week."

"Hey, I never get confused about what day of the week it is. I just lift up my skirt and take a gander."

He laughed and then looked at me. "You don't really have day-of-the-week underwear, right?"

"No, I'm just kidding. God, I have some limits to my oddness, Macmillan."

"It's probably only really dweeby if you wear them on the actual days."

"Agreed."

"So did you start *Bonnie and Clyde* yet?"

"No, I was about to make hot chocolate when you texted me. I was all kinds of cozy."

"Sounds like it. I love hot chocolate. But, I guess, who doesn't, really?"

"Yeah, but this is the best hot chocolate of your life. It's my grandmother's recipe and it's ridiculously good."

"What a tease you are, Shepherds."

He gave me a light shove on the shoulder and smiled at me.

"I am not!"

I heard it then. The flirtatious, girlie lilt in my voice. Was I flirting with Aiden? Hadn't I felt guilty about this once already? Why did I want to put myself through that again?

Whether or not I was flirting, my mental commentary was such a small part of my brain right now. My mouth, mind and batting eyelashes were acting of their own volition.

"Oh, you totally are."

"No, I just haven't been given the opportunity to share my hot chocolate with you."

"Ah, that's all it is. I gotcha. So after sledding, are you going to let me try it?"

My heart lifted a little at the idea of more plans with Aiden. What was going on with him? It seemed strange that he was trying to hang out with me alone. He'd never done this, really. We had been alone before. But not ever on purpose. Not like this.

I tried to reel myself in, telling myself that he was probably not thinking anything of it. I was Natalie. I wasn't a *girl* girl. He probably thought of us as two friends hanging out.

The logical part of my brain—which was shrinking rapidly—told me that I knew him. I knew Brooke. And I knew that he should be smarter than this. I knew that him wanting to hang out with me like this was suspicious and unusual. I also knew that there was no way I was going to be able to resist the prospect of him coming over.

"Of course." And then, before I could stop Flirtatious, Girlie Natalie: "You can even join me for my first viewing of *Bonnie and Clyde* if you want."

He looked at me, and for a second I feared he'd call me out for being completely inappropriate.

"I do love me some Faye Dunaway."

I wasn't sure if that was a blow-off or him agreeing to come. Before I had to figure out a clarifying response, I realized where we were.

"Oh, hey! I grew up sledding here!"

"Really? I guess that makes sense. It's the most convenient location for epic sledding near you."

There were some guys from the football team there, including Justin. I was glad that Reed wasn't there. Justin wasn't a whole lot better, but at least he was too stupid to say much. I was happy, too, to note that Eric wasn't there. Bethany was, however, sidling up to one of the guys in a way she probably considered sexy.

"Hey, Natalie," she said. "Where's Brooke?"

"She's sick," answered Aiden. "She hasn't felt good all day."

"That's too bad. Well…cool that you came out, anyway, Natalie."

I saw two figures trudging up the hill and realized one of them was Alexa.

"Eee!" she exclaimed when she saw me, dropping the rope on the sled. It started back down the hill, and whoever had been walking with her had to race down to catch it.

"Alexa!"

"I'm so glad you came," she said, throwing her arms around me. I could smell alcohol on her.

"You were able to drink again tonight? I would have thought the idea would make you sick after how you felt earlier."

"I got in a solid catnap earlier. Plus your burger and stuff at lunch helped a fuckton. Where's Brooke?"

"Sick."

"I guess someone didn't rally as well as someone else." She pointed at herself, laughed and then pulled me over to a spot in the snow where there were a couple bottles of liquor. "Pick your poison," she said.

"Um, whatever tastes best."

She handed me a bottle. "It's peach schnapps. Not super alcoholic, but you probably don't need something that strong. Go down the hill with me! Hurry up and swig that and let's go."

I took a big gulp, not minding the idea of a social lubricant, and then let her pull me onto the sled. She sat behind me. The guys started whooping.

"Now make out!" said one of them.

"Oh, shut up, Ryan," she said, but again, it was obvious she didn't mind the joke. Like Brooke, this sort of teasing was her rocket fuel.

I could have stayed there all night. It might have been freezing cold, and snow might have found its way into my boot almost immediately. But it was worth it. Worth it to laugh and feel clever and charming and—for the first time in a long time—part of a group.

I had forgotten that these people weren't merely—or at least weren't always—airheaded junior alcoholics. They were pretty fun.

Aiden and I went down the hill on the sled together, and the feeling of his body behind mine sent a thrill through me. We were then alone at the bottom of the hill, well out of earshot from everyone at the top.

"Nice braids by the way, Dorothy," he said, flicking one of them.

"It's sensible, since I'm in a hat, jerk." I pushed him, and he tripped backward into a mound of snow.

I cracked up.

"You asshole!" he said, and sat up to pull me down into the snow mound, too.

I squealed, and fell next to him.

"Hey, at least *I* didn't mean to!"

"Uh-huh, sure."

"I didn't!"

I looked past him and saw that one figure was standing away from the rest, watching us.

"We should go back up, I guess," he said. He groaned. "You want to go pretty soon?"

It was so weird to be making this decision together. Like... a couple or something.

I became aware that my desire to stay there all night had changed the second Aiden wasn't going to be there anymore.

"Yeah, sure."

The figure watching us turned out to be Bethany. I wondered what she would make of what she had seen, and if she— notorious gossip—would realize enough was going on to tell anyone. I got a guilty lurch in my stomach.

Aiden was clearly not that worried about how we came off.

"All right, guys, I'll meet up with you tomorrow. Gotta make sure this one gets home without cracking her head on the ice."

"It's a distinct possibility," I added in.

We said our goodbyes, I tried to calm my pounding heart and we set off toward my house. It was Aiden who spoke first.

"It's so weird how the sky gets like this in wintertime. Back home, it didn't really do this."

"What, how it's kind of light out?"

"Yeah. It's like a dark orange instead of pitch-black. I like it."

I looked up at the sky, at the white snow still coming down. Aiden stopped and looked up, too.

"It's pretty beautiful, I guess."

I laughed at his phrasing. "Yeah, pretty magnificent or whatever."

"Hey, you better watch that mouth, missy."

"Uh-huh. Hey, thanks for walking me home."

"No problem. Can't be letting you do it on your own."

"Hey, I'm a pretty self-sufficient girl."

"I definitely know that. But you need a little saving, I think."

"I most certainly do not!"

He shrugged. "I think you must need some."

"Hey, don't jump on that train, acting like I need a boyfriend. I don't."

I noticed, and I wondered if he did, too, that I didn't mention Brooke's name.

"Right. Well. I still think you could do with a little white-knighting."

"Maybe. Maybe I just don't know it."

It felt like a three-second walk, but we were already at my house.

"Um. Still want some hot chocolate?"

"Of course."

Plunge in my chest. This was a moment of truth, and I knew it. I might not have had a full-on understanding of what was going on, but I knew I was making a Choice. I wanted to spend time with Aiden, particularly this sort of illegal time, in the middle of the night with no one watching us. I opened the door and let him in.

CHAPTER TEN

"THIS IS THE best part about freezing your ass off for hours," said Aiden. "The part where you go inside and get to be warm."

"Definitely."

He took off his coat and sweatshirt, and I told him I'd be right back, I needed to change.

I shut the door to my bedroom and took a deep breath. Aiden was here, without Brooke. Just with me. Alone in my house. Why was he here? Did he like me? Was he trying to prove something to Brooke? Did Brooke even know I had gone sledding tonight?

Then a horrible thought struck me: What if he had heard I'd hooked up with Eric, and now thought I was just easy?

"Pfft, no," I said aloud.

That didn't add up. He knew me better than that. And I was pretty sure I knew him well enough to say he wouldn't be that guy. But then, everything he was doing right now was so unlike him.

And really…everything I was doing was so unlike me.

I went to the mirror to see just how windburned I looked. I decided that I didn't look terrible. I tossed on a little tinted chapstick and changed into a pair of yoga pants and an Abercrombie & Fitch tank top I'd gotten for six dollars once. It hung loosely, making it look like I wasn't trying, but it was low cut on the chest. I paired it with the bra Brooke had made me buy from Victoria's Secret. I hadn't worn it yet. I had to rip off the tag.

"Whoa," I said aloud to my reflection. It looked like I had boobs. The bra was actually a little tight. I didn't remember it being so tight when I bought it.

I headed into the kitchen, where Aiden was standing, now in long athletic shorts and a blue Hurley V-neck. I'd always liked that shirt. In fact, I had helped Brooke pick it out. I remembered feeling how soft it was on the hanger. I knew it would be just as soft on him now.

His eyes flickered for a split second to my chest. I suddenly regretted my clothing choice. What was I doing? Why was I trying to look good for him? I should have put on a sweatshirt and called it a day. I didn't want to look like I was trying.

"I see you lit the candle," I said, glancing at it.

Aiden cleared his throat. "Hey. Say what you want, but I like candles just as much as the next gal."

I laughed.

"So what's the trick to this hot chocolate?" He leaned against the counter and crossed his arms. My own eyes flickered to his arms for a split second.

Dammit.

"I can't tell you that!" I opened the fridge and retrieved the Tupperware filled with the whipped chocolate.

"Aw, come on."

"I can't! It's secret."

He nodded. "All right, I can respect that. Family secrets are family secrets."

"Mmm-hmm."

He considered me for a second. "I think you'd like my family."

"I've met your mom, she's really nice."

"Nah, I mean my cousins back home and everyone. I know they'd love you. But I think you'd like them, too."

"That's nice." I smiled. "Why?"

"Because you're fun. And real. And it doesn't matter where you are, you are always you. They'd respect that. I think you'd like them because they're a bunch of crazy rednecks who are actually a lot smarter than they seem." He got a fond look in his eye. "They're a hoot."

"They do sound fun, I'm sure you're right."

"Do you mind me asking…about your mom? You never talk about her and I know you're just here with your dad."

I shrugged. "There's nothing to say, really."

He must have sensed that this was not true, because he stayed silent.

"It's not one of those real tragic stories or anything. My mom was not made to be a mom. Like, at all." I gave a small laugh as I heated the saucepan. "She got knocked up at sixteen and never had a chance to grow up. She was a wild child, apparently. Very Brooke-like. And nothing like me."

"Was she good to you when you were a little kid?"

I shrugged. "It's more that I was an exceptionally easy child, and I made a cute accessory for her until I got older and more challenging."

"I doubt you've ever been challenging."

"Eh. I had my argumentative years. So when I was ten, she and my dad started fighting all the time. Mostly about how to raise me and how to deal with me. They disagreed on everything. Plus my mom still wanted to go out and party half the time. She was only twenty-six, so...I guess I get it. But he came home once and she was drunk—not like sad, alcoholic drunk, but had been drinking with girlfriends—and they got in a fight. My dad ended up telling her that she needed to get her shit together, and that if she couldn't, then she was in no shape to be a mother."

"Were you...there? Did you hear all this?"

"Yeah...my dad didn't know I was home. Actually, he didn't know that Brooke and I were both here. He knew we were having a sleepover, but he thought we were at Brooke's."

"Jesus."

"Yeah... So once he found out we were there, he got even madder. And basically, she had the choice to be better or to get out. And she got out. They weren't married, so it was a pretty neat ending."

"I can't picture your father mad."

"Me, neither, usually. But yeah. He was furious. And I get it. I think that he thinks that I resent him for it, sometimes. He'll bring it up every once in a while, and start to apologize. I don't think he gets that I truly understand why he was mad and that I mean it when I tell him that he's been enough for me."

"That sucks. But, man, I respect your dad so much for that. It's amazing that he was so strong for you."

I smiled proudly. "I agree. I think it all worked out just how it should."

"I think things have a way of doing that."

The pot of milk was steaming now. I took a couple of scoops of the chocolate and mixed it in. I stirred it, watching the brown swirl with the white.

"So where's the movie? I can go set it up."

"It's upstairs in my room. When you go in it's on your left on the bookshelf."

"Gotcha."

He went up the stairs, and then returned a minute later to

put it in the DVD player. He changed the channel and even got
the surround sound to work in about five seconds flat, which
impressed me. Even though it was my house and I watched
movies here all the time, I always had to crawl around for
about twenty minutes trying to figure out which was the right
input and how to make the surround sound work. When my
dad was home, I'd sit helplessly on the floor and call for him
and he'd do it for me.

I poured the hot chocolate into two mugs, topped them
with whipped cream and cinnamon sugar and brought them
over to the couch, where he was already sitting.

"It's probably pretty hot, so let it cool for a sec."

"You're basically a professional barista."

"Oh yeah."

When he tried it, he confirmed that it was the best hot
chocolate he had ever, ever had.

I was glad to find out that he wasn't one of those people
who stayed completely silent throughout an entire movie. I
didn't like watching movies with people who chatted the entire time, either, but I liked being able to comment.

I was completely comfortable with him, too. He sat with
his feet on the coffee table—I had already told him that was
fine, we were not the kind of house that cared about that kind
of thing—and I was lying on my side. My feet were tucked in
between the cushions. He got up to refill our hot chocolates
once, and when he sat back down, my feet ended up against his
leg. Neither of us readjusted, and so I made sure not to move.

My phone buzzed at one point, and my stomach plunged
when I saw that it was Brooke.

Did you have fun sledding? Sorry I couldn't go. Too sick :/

I started to answer, but then decided against it. If I answered and didn't say that Aiden was here, I was avoiding

the truth. I didn't know yet if I should feel guilty about this. I didn't even know if she would be mad about it. Either because I didn't seem like a threat, or because there was no reason to be concerned.

"Don't text through the ending! The ending is the best part," said Aiden. I glanced at him, and then at the screen. I had a feeling he knew it was Brooke texting me.

I watched what happened. It was a great scene that I was suddenly having trouble appreciating, because I was stuck in my head. Because something was eating away at me. A thought that I had been pushing out of my head since the party. No, not since the party. Since it had happened, last year.

I liked him first.

I had liked him first, and she had taken him. I had always rationalized that she hadn't taken him, that there was no chance he would have fallen for me, anyway. But lately it didn't seem so crazy an idea.

It had never become a big thing between Brooke and me. He had been new at school, and everyone thought he was cute. When she'd told me he was coming out to get coffee with her and some others, I'd asked if she would find out if he knew who I was, and if she might talk me up a little bit. But next thing I knew, she was going to the movies with him and asking me where the best sushi was for a person who didn't really like sushi, because she wanted to take him somewhere that would make her seem cultured and show him what it was like to date a city girl.

"Isn't that one of the best endings?"

I snapped back to reality. The credits were rolling.

"Yeah, wow."

"It's sad, but it's awesome. Did you like the movie?"

"I did, you were right—it's different than I thought it would be, but it was really good."

He nodded, looking proud to have gotten it right. "Yup."

It occurred to me only then that we were at the end of our night. It was that moment of truth where we would either say goodbye...or he would stay.

I stood up and looked out the window. "Holy crap, it's really snowing."

He came over next to me, so close I could smell him. I felt the same chest-shuddering feeling I'd had when we were on the sled together. He smelled like clean laundry and that body wash.

"Definitely no school tomorrow," he said.

"Not safe driving conditions at all," I added, it striking me how bold that was only after I said it.

But he didn't argue. "Definitely not."

I thought for a split second, and then asked, "Hey, have you ever seen *Vertigo?*"

"You know, I haven't. I've always wanted to. You have that poster in your room, don't you? The orange one."

"That's the one."

"Do you have the movie?"

"Of course."

"Let's watch it."

I thought momentarily about telling him that this was inappropriate and weird and that it made no sense for him to be here spending time with me. But, as I knew I would, I pushed the thought from my mind and succumbed to the temptation of having more time alone with him.

Part II

Brooke

CHAPTER ELEVEN

First Semester, Junior Year

THE NEW GUY was hot. People had been talking about him all day long—well, all right, girls had been talking about him all day long—but I had yet to see him. I knew everyone in the school except the new freshmen, so I was sure that when I saw him, I would know it was him.

It would have been impossible to miss him, even if I hadn't been keeping my eyes peeled for hours. I was sitting at my usual lunch table holding court with my friends, as I generally did, when he walked through the doors. I was struck speechless—something that was verifiably difficult to do. I stared at him and was instantly infatuated by his good looks and charmed by the nervous way he looked around the cafeteria.

I almost stood up and invited him to come sit with us, but resisted. I was glad I did when a girl named Kylie went up to him and did, and I saw how pathetic she looked.

"Brooke?" asked Alexa.

"What?" I responded dumbly, not able to take my eyes off him.

"You just…stopped talking."

"Right." I snapped my gaze back to her and tried to look unrattled. "The point is, everyone should watch the 1968 version of *Romeo and Juliet* and the '96 one back-to-back at least once in their lives. You'll never look at love the same way again."

God, would someone else come up with something to talk about for once? Why is the burden of conversation always on me? This was fine except for when I didn't feel like it.

The next day, I was lucky enough to be standing in the right place at the right time in the hallway.

"Excuse me."

I turned to see Hot New Guy behind me, holding a schedule and looking lost. And still superhot.

"What's up?" I tossed my hair to one shoulder.

"Can you tell me where to find room 324? It jumps from 318 to 400…."

"It's down this one weird hallway. Here, I'll show you."

"Are you sure? I don't want you to be late to class."

I was almost always late to class, but I liked that he thought I might be the studious kind of girl that hated tardiness.

"It's fine," I said. "My teacher will understand when I say I was helping the new kid."

He gave an adorably timid laugh. "Thanks so much."

"No problem. So…are you a junior?" I asked, like I didn't know damn well that he was.

We started making our way down the hall.

"Yes, ma'am." Was that an accent? "And you?"

"Yes, I am. And you just moved here from…"

"Texas."

We were already almost at his classroom. "Wow, Texas. Must be a big change for you, then."

He breathed in and nodded slowly. "It definitely is. But I'm excited to be here. I knew all the same people back home for most of my life. Pretty small town. So I'm lookin' forward to meeting new people."

There was definitely a slight accent, and I couldn't help but smile at it. "Here's 324."

"Yeah…I would never have found this."

"It's a tough one. Well, hey, if you want to, then look for me in the cafeteria at lunch, and you can meet some new people."

"Sure, I'll look for ya. Thanks again. What was your name?"

"Brooke."

"Brooke. I'm Aiden Macmillan. Pleased to meet you."

IF THE ACCENT, RUGGED hotness and politeness hadn't been enough to give me a blind crush, then him actually following through on finding me in the cafeteria did it. I was slightly nervous in front of him, but luckily he wasn't as shy as I'd first assumed. He jumped into conversation with everyone and seemed to be able to talk about just about anything.

"Brooke, by the way," Alexa started, looking excited. "My mom has been working constantly for the past two weeks, and she said she'll probably be going out of town next weekend. We'll have to do something. Hopefully it stays warm like this and we can use the pool."

"What's your mom do?" Aiden asked.

"She's a lobbyist in D.C." Alexa rolled her eyes. "Boring."

"Is she really? That's so cool. I guess this thing with the vice president is what's got her so busy, then, huh?"

So he kept up with politics and everything. I would have to ask Natalie what the "thing with the vice president" was so that I could sound knowledgeable about it next time I talked to him.

"Yeah, I guess," said Alexa. "If I ate only grapefruit for the next, like, month, do you think I could lose ten pounds? I love grapefruit, and I'm pretty sure I could do it. As long as I could still have coffee."

Aiden laughed, not knowing Alexa well enough to know that this was a serious query. He seemed to realize it quickly, though. "Run a mile a day and cut down on carbs. Don't starve yourself, or you'll put weight on faster next time."

Alexa stared wide-eyed at him. "Really?"

He seemed to resist another smile and patiently answered, "Yes."

He sounded like Natalie every time I suggested that I should do some extreme diet. When I'd mentioned that whole cayenne-maple-syrup-lemon-juice fast, she had calmly told me that it was a terrible idea, and that I should ride my bike more often.

When the conversation shifted to events coming up, Aiden asked if anyone intended to go see the Avett Brothers when they came to Baltimore in November. I knew the name of the band but didn't listen to them. Natalie was always putting them on in the car when I gave her DJing privileges. Since I drove everywhere for us, I mostly got to pick, but every once in a while I would let her put on her weird folky music.

I started to say that my friend would probably be going, but stopped when I realized that I would likely be edged out of the plan or end up feeling left out with the two of them. For some reason, I already felt like I could predict how the night would go. They would sing along to the songs and chat about boring stuff happening with vice-president-type people. God forbid I bring up a fad diet.

It was then that it struck me that what I should really do was to hook the two of them up.

But he's so hot, my simple, romance-obsessed brain said. *There's no way I'm that generous.*

The challenge came when, two days later, Natalie turned down the music on the way home. "Have you talked to that new guy at all? Aiden Macmillan?"

"Some," I confessed. I hadn't mentioned our interactions to her for some reason. Ordinarily, I told her everything from the inane to the gossip-column-worthy.

She hesitated, and then said, "I think he's really cute."

"Obviously he is. Everyone knows that."

"Yeah, I know…but he was wearing an Alabama Shakes T-shirt the other day. I don't know, I'm thinking maybe he isn't just another dumb jock like Justin and Eric and all those guys. And especially nothing like fucking Reed."

I shrugged, suddenly feeling a little territorial over the new guy, who I had decided I wanted.

She went on.

"He's also in AP Statistics, which is pretty cool. And I heard him saying he was going to apply for an internship at a vet clinic next year." When I said nothing and started singing along with the song again, she said, "Do you think you could put in a good word for me? Or like…introduce us? Something like that?"

"Sure, whatever. Hey, can you hand me my lip stuff? My lips are still sunburned from the other day."

THE NEXT DAY, I asked Aiden if he was doing anything on Friday, and if he wanted to go get coffee. My sudden competition with Natalie—and the irritating notion that maybe I would lose if he was given both of us as options—had given me confidence and made me feel like I had better hurry if I wanted to snag him.

When I was texting Natalie and told her I was going to get coffee, she immediately asked if he was going to be there. She seemed to assume that there was a group of us going, and I didn't correct her.

Yeah, he'll probably be there.

Awesome! Good word for your bff over here don't forget. :)

You're being so weird, you never go after guys, haha.

I know. I mean, I don't even know him or anything, maybe he sucks, but it'd be cool if he was...cool.

Hahah lewzer. I'll do my best to drop a line for ya.

Oh, come on, you're YOU, you can talk anyone into anything I'm pretty sure.

Yeah yeah yeah.

K, have fun! You would hate this movie I'm watching btw. It's in french, and it seems obvious that the english subtitler, like, barely spoke french. Haha. Text me when you get home and lemme know how it went.

K

The entire way to the coffee shop, I felt guilty for my white lie. I didn't know why I hadn't just told her I thought I might like him, too.

That wasn't true. I knew why. It was because I had guys pounding down my door half the time, and she didn't. Not because there was anything wrong with her, she just didn't put herself out there like I did. And it felt like a shitty-friend thing to do to decide that I wanted everyone, even the one guy she had ever expressed interest in. Once I realized that, I knew what I needed to do.

I needed to make this a platonic get-together and try to hook the two of them up.

I rationalized away my own interest as I wound out of my neighborhood, onto the main road and into downtown to where we had agreed to meet.

They really were probably better for each other. If I were to date him, he'd probably talk about boring stuff half the time, anyway. And make me go to concerts to see, like, the Avett Brothers and stuff. My talk about Bravo TV shows would probably make him think I was stupid. He would think I was a product of mainstream when I expressed interest in seeing someone like Justin Timberlake instead.

Yes, I decided. I would hate dating him. AP Statistics? He would absolutely think he was smarter than me. But he and Natalie would get along swimmingly.

So I sat there in my car, still worried about how I looked and everything, because, duh, but feeling sure that I would do a good job of talking her up. I would be the wingman. Fun! I never got to do that. I would be good at it. I envisioned myself confidently schmoozing him and talking about my friend and maybe not even sitting up perfectly straight or pulling my sexiest expressions. Maybe even gaining him as a friend. That would be fun, an actual guy friend.

Ooh, I could ask him for advice on other guys and everything!

He walked up at seven on the dot, and I waited until 7:02

to get out of my car, straighten my black tank top and scarf and head inside.

Aiden turned out to be the kind of guy who made you feel at ease immediately. Being alone instead of in a crowded lunchroom with other friends could have been real weird, but he was so easygoing that it wasn't hard at all.

He told me about his old town, what his parents did, where he intended to go to school if he could, what he hoped to do—generally speaking, he was perfect. He was going to be a vet, which I took to mean he was going to be saving the lives of puppies all day long for the rest of his life.

When I voiced this summary of his job, he just smiled and said, "Yup, I am a puppy saver."

I laughed, and then noted that that was the kind of response I got from Natalie all the time—the detached and indulgent kind that meant they had given up conveying the facts to me. I then remembered the choice I had made. Talk up Nat. Don't try to take him for myself.

He gestured at me. "What do you want to do?"

"When I grow up?"

"Yeah, when you grow up." He leaned back, and I could tell I was charming him. Eh, he probably knew he was charming me, too.

Shit! I was being charmed and being charming! Abort, abort, abort.

I cleared my throat. "Probably something in fashion. I know that, like, every girl wants to do that, but I love it."

"Yeah, God, why are you such a girl?"

I glared at him and then smiled. Ugh, but how was I supposed to not be into him when he was being so cute and charming?

"You'll regret alienating me when I'm the talk of Lincoln Center at fashion week."

"I...have no idea what that means."

"Hey!" I kicked him under the table. "You'll regret it. I'll be rich and famous and I won't give you any free clothes."

Dammit. I was flirting again.

"That's okay. Give them to someone who will appreciate them better. I can see you being famous. You don't seem like the kind of girl who sits on the sidelines."

"And what kind of girl do I seem like?" Full-on flirtation mode.

He gave a small flick of an eyebrow that almost derailed me and said, "Oh, I'm not telling you that."

"Aiden!" I tried to look offended, and surely failed. *God, stop flirting. Bring up Natalie.* "So...anyway. My apparently awful personality aside...have you met my friend Natalie?"

He wrinkled his brow in thought. "Natalie. The brunette?"

I hadn't heard her referred to that way before. It sounded so sexy. The brunette vs. the brown-haired girl.

"Yes, the one who dresses like a new-age Mary Poppins." That had come off slightly disparaging, and I really hadn't meant it to....

He gave one laugh. "I didn't see her in any stupid little hats or slide up any railings."

"No, but she's all skirts and jackets and little boots and stockings." Ugh! Why couldn't I stop?

"All right, what about her?"

I shrugged and smiled. "I don't know, what do you think?"

"What do I think?" he asked. I nodded and he gave a help-less look. "She's hot, I don't know. She seems like a smart girl. I haven't talked to her hardly at all."

"Right, well. She doesn't really talk much. She does with me, but she's, like, socially backward. In a good way!" I added the last part at his raised eyebrows.

"Socially backward in a good way, okay. Why are you asking?"

"I think you two might hit it off if you actually hung out sometime."

I leaned forward, hoping I looked clever and unattached. I privately loved that I got to come off as uninterested in him. You might say that that meant I was in fact interested in him, but when it comes down to it, I'm at least a little bit interested in almost everyone, and I certainly want them all to be interested in me.

"You think so, huh?"

"Yeah, she's smart like you. You're similar, I think."

"I'm not necessarily looking for someone a lot like me, you know." The bait he was dangling made the butterflies start. He then squashed them. "I'm not looking for anyone, period."

"Well, maybe she'll find you."

"Who, Natalie?"

I shrugged and smiled. "Or whoever."

He didn't seem interested in her, I decided. I took this as permission to go after him myself. Hey, I had done my best.

A few minutes later my phone buzzed with a text inviting me to Alexa's. Her mom had ended up going out of town, it turned out. I asked if he wanted to go, and the next thing I knew, I was in his Jeep for the first of many, many times.

THAT NIGHT, AIDEN and I did everything we could to drive each other crazy. Whether he realized it at the time or not, that was what was happening. He was perfectly able to meet new people and engage with them without my assistance— something that was very sexy to me.

I was proud to be arriving with him. He felt suddenly like my property. People would now attach us together and be jealous that I had already gotten the attention of the most eligible guy in school.

I had a couple of glasses of André Brut, choosing not to drink so much that I would lose my wits, but enough to loosen myself up and blame any overconfidence on the alcohol. When beer pong began, we played together, and I was delighted by the fact that I was having an "on" night, and that I seemed cool, popular and with it. Particularly once the girls around me started to drink too much. I became a standing statue of a goddess while all the others were crumbling.

Aiden at that party was the drunkest I would ever see him.

He was a little flushed and a little more flirtatious than I had expected him to be.

We were outside, and some people there were smoking a joint, but we weren't. I remember how dark it was, and how there was a bluish light coming from the side of the house that lit us just enough. We were silhouettes. I could feel the light hitting my hair and my eyes in just the right way, and I stared up at him, smiling and teasing him. He was playful back at me.

"So do you think I'm going to fit in here at...what's this school called?"

I laughed and took a step back and then forward again. "Winston Churchill High School?"

"Winston Churchill. That's right. Sorry."

"Don't apologize." I smiled. "You're cute, if a little dumb."

His expression dropped a little, but I could see that he knew I was teasing him. "I am not dumb."

"Yes, you are." I pushed him backward with one finger, and he stumbled just a little into the wall. I stepped back, laughing at him.

"Are you laughing at me?" he asked, stepping forward, a grin on his face, voice lowered.

I nodded and looked up at him. "Mmm-hmm."

"Laugh at me again." He grinned wider and took me by the waist. It tickled and I laughed even harder. He picked me up until he was holding me up with my arms locked to my thighs.

"Ahh, Aiden! Put me down!" I didn't mean it, of course,

and he knew that. I was aware of how we must look to everyone out there. We were like the two characters in the movie who were about to fall in love. I knew the girls around were jealous. I gazed down at him and bit my lip. "Put. Me—"

"I'll put you in the pool, Brooke, I swear I will." His accent slipped out, something I was loving.

"Don't you dare throw me in that pool, Aiden Macmillan!"

He was still holding me effortlessly. My tank top had ridden up just enough that I knew he could see my flat stomach, still tanned from the summer. I worried for a moment about what he'd think of my belly button ring, but decided he'd think it was sexy. It was tasteful and small.

He walked over to the edge of the pool and stood right on the edge so the water was behind me.

"Aiden!"

"Ask nicely."

"Put me down!"

He looked like he was considering it. "Hmm…that wasn't nice enough."

"Please? Please put me down?" I put on my best Bambi eyes and a little pout.

"You want me to put you down?"

I nodded.

He slid me down slowly, one of his hands gliding up the back of my shirt. He placed me so that the balls of my feet were barely standing on the edge of the pool. I had complete faith he wouldn't drop me. And then he kissed me for the first time.

Natalie's interest in him became a distant thought.

THE NEXT NIGHT, Natalie and I were eating Chinese food and watching *Bar Rescue*—a strange and shared guilty pleasure of ours—when she finally brought it up. We had been together for hours, and I had sensed that she was trying not to.

"You never texted me last night after you got coffee. Was it fun?"

"Um, yeah."

She cocked her head at me knowingly. "Okay, what's that tone?"

"What tone?"

"You sound weird. Did you ask if he knew me? I talked to him for, like, two seconds, he probably doesn't."

"No, he knew you."

"Oh, God, did he say something awful?"

"No! Of course not. It's just…well…I mean, we kind of hit it off. It was just the two of us when we got coffee…and then Alexa was having people over. I would have texted you and told you to come, but I know you don't care about parties."

"I would have gone to coffee, though," she said quietly.

Shit. That's totally what I should have done. If my intentions were really as pure as I had convinced myself that they were, I would have told her to come.

"I'm sorry, Nat—I won't, like, date him if you don't want."

But we both knew it was already too late, and we both knew that she would never take such a stand.

"No, of course not! I mean, I don't even know him. It was dumb. You guys will look totally cute together." She gestured at the screen. "It's the big reveal, watch. I really don't think this show is fixed."

I felt awful. But it was in the past now. It had happened. And all I could do now was tell myself that she wasn't that into him, that the two of them never stood a chance and that this would definitely be worth it once he and I got together for real.

Eventually, I would forget that she had ever had any sort of interest in him at all.

CHAPTER TWELVE

Beginning of Winter Break, Senior Year, December 22

I WAS LYING on my stomach on my bed with a pillow over my head.

"This sucks," I said, my voice muffled.

"Oh, stop it." Natalie pulled the pillow off me. "This is such an obnoxious problem for you to be having. Poor little Brooke, accepted to *too* many schools."

I groaned. "It *is,* though. I would gladly trade places with you and take some time to figure out what I actually want to do."

I said it in an effort to make her feel better about the fact that she had no solid plans for the next year, but realized immediately that it probably came off as patronizing.

"Okay, stop. Let's go through each school one by one." She grabbed the pile of acceptance letters. "You give me the pros and cons, and I'll write them on the back of the letters. At the end, we'll take a look and see what we end up with. Sit up like a big girl."

"Fin-*uh*." I sat up and leaned against my headboard.

"Okay, first up, University of New Hampshire."

"Hippies."

"Is that a pro or a con?"

"I don't know."

"We aren't playing the word association game, Brooke."

"Okay, okay, okay. Um. I don't know, I could, like...be all Jennifer Aniston/Kate Hudson-y there, and stop brushing my hair and rock that for a while. I can kick around in the autumn leaves, you know I love doing that."

"It makes you feel like you're in a commercial, I know."

"Uh-huh. And then I'll meet some cute boy with good bone structure hidden under a beard I'll talk him out of."

"Mmkay, Brooke? This isn't really what I meant."

"No, no, this is helping, this is helping. Cons are...hippies are gross and I hate when people bitch about the environment and carbon footprints and all that."

She let her head fall back in exasperation, but took a deep breath and said, "Boston University."

"I would invest in some vintage glasses like yours...stock up on scarves and hats. It's a really pretty city. And everyone's supersmart there. I'm not actually sure if I'd call that a pro or con. Probably lots of pretentious guys...maybe I could date some prodigy musician from Berkeley with perfect hands and fingers. Ooh, I could go see him play at little open mics, and he would write me songs...."

"Anything else?"

"It gets really cold and my cousin goes to BU and I hate her."

Nat sneered. "I'm actually with you on that one. Okay, UCLA."

"Fake bitches everywhere."

"Reasonable."

"But! I could tan year-round, and my hair would be super-blond. I could date a surfer guy."

"Georgia Tech."

"Ooh, I could be a Southern belle and wear pearls and become the type of person who raises an eyebrow at another person for having bad etiquette. But there's a lot of racism there, I hear, and that's not cool."

She shook her head, laughing at me, and said, "University of Pennsylvania."

"Kill myself."

"Brooke."

"I have no pros for that school. The only thing is that that's where my parents want me to go." She looked expectantly at me, like I was going to go on. "That's it. I literally hate the idea of it. Like I legit might throw up."

"Okay, then, Towson."

"Blech. It's only an hour from home. That's a con. But Aiden will be here, and that would be nice."

"Brooke."

"What?"

"You cannot pick a college based on where your boyfriend is."

"Why not? What if we get married?"

She blinked one long blink. "Brooke, it's dumb and you know it."

I shrugged. "I dunno."

She set down the papers. "Yes, you do. You know where you need to go."

"I can't go to New York."

"Yes, you can."

"No, I can't. That's the one stupid place my parents won't stupid pay for."

"I know that. But I am one hundred percent sure it'll be

worth it. Fashion Institute accepted you. That is so crazy awesome I can't even wrap my head around it. Here, I'll do your pro-con list. It's New York. Your dream city. It's fashion. Your dream major. And it's a whole three and a half hours away from your mom and dad. But! It's only a short bus ride to see Aiden or have him come up there, if you guys stay together."

I pouted. Of course she was right. It was where I belonged, and I knew that. "But paying for it all on my own sounds a lot less appealing than letting my parents pay."

"Would you rather pay for your dream life, or have your parents buy you one you're going to hate?"

I rolled my eyes. "I mean, when you put it that way..."

"That's the only way, Brooke! Come on. This is stupid. You know I'm the sensible one of the two of us, and yet I'm telling you not to take the safe bet. And that's because I know you, and I know what you should choose in order to be happy."

It turned out that the decision had basically been made for me as far as my parents were concerned when I unwrapped one of my presents on Christmas, and found that I had been gifted a U of PA hoodie, which now sat in a dark corner of my closet. The rest of my winter break was tense with my parents.

I finally lost it on New Year's Eve. The argument started about my plans for the evening, and worked its way around to college, like everything did nowadays.

"This is exactly why I'm not paying for you to go to New York," my mother said.

"Oh, my God, this is so stupid!" I yelled at both of my parents. My dad was sitting in his usual chair, glancing at the muted Fox News behind me, and my mom was staring me dead in the eyes and looking furious, but irritatingly calm.

"Because I want to go to a party on New Year's Eve, you won't let me go to the college I want to go to."

"No, Brooke, this is a symptom of the problem at hand.

You would rather party than do almost anything else. You are going to go to Pennsylvania, get yourself a real degree and then decide what to do from there."

"Fashion Merchandising is a real degree, Mom."

She laughed, and I wanted to hit her.

"Mom, it is. Seriously. And I'm not going to party all the time in New York, it baffles me why you think that."

"I am not allowing you to waste my money on a useless degree, in a city filled with bars and clubs and crime!"

Oh for fuck's sake.

"You sound ridiculous right now, I hope you know that."

She raised an eyebrow and looked blankly at me. I hated that I had inherited that look from her.

"Whatever, this is so stupid," I said.

"I don't know how I feel about you going into D.C. tonight, Brooke."

Oh, good! My dad had finally decided to join the discussion. He always brings a fun, new way to say no to the conversation.

"You are kidding me."

"No, it's not a safe city, the roads are dangerous, people are out drinking and driving, and I—whose party is this, anyway? I've never heard of 'Sam.'"

"He's a friend of a friend, Dad—"

"Oh, that sounds really safe, Brooke."

"A friend of a friend?" My mom piped up again.

"Yes—oh, my God. I'm going. This is stupid. Alexa's parents got us a hotel room and everything—we'll be safe, Jesus."

"Don't take that tone, Brooke Marie, and no, you are not going. I didn't realize that you were going to a stranger's house."

Fury rose in my chest. This was always the problem with talking to my parents for a few sentences too long.

"Is Aiden going?" asked my mom.

It was a sore subject. Aiden and I had hardly been talking lately, and he'd gotten all pissed off about me wanting to go tonight. He wanted to stay in and watch the ball drop and order in dinner.

Natalie and her dad were watching the ball drop and staying in, too. I would never understand why Natalie—and Aiden, for that matter—would rather do that than get all dressed up and go out.

Once I had refused Aiden's plan and insisted on going to the party, Aiden had said he didn't care. At this point he was having a bunch of people over to his place. If that had been the original plan pitched to me, I might have considered it.

"No, he's hanging out with other people tonight."

"And what's Natalie doing tonight? I'm sure she's not partying."

An opportunity for a lie. "She's going, too, Dad."

"Really," he said.

"Yes, God, do you feel better now?"

"John okayed this?"

My dad had always respected Natalie's dad and his opinions. "Yes," I lied.

He looked thoughtful, but also like he knew that if he didn't allow me to go, then I would go, anyway, but I would lie about it, not keep in touch and ultimately make things worse.

"I want you to leave sooner rather than later, then," he said, ignoring my mom's look. "Leave before it gets dark."

"Okay. Thanks." I took my lie and ran with it, right to D.C.

It was a roof party at a mostly-stranger's house. My mom had been kind of right on that. I pretty much knew that his name was Sam, and that he was a freshman at Georgetown, loaded and having a blowout. Not just anyone was invited, and Alexa and I were thrilled to be part of the few. We arrived, both of us five inches taller than normal, rocking pumps. Mine were brand new from Nordstrom, and I had spent the past three days walking around the house in them to be sure they wouldn't blister me or cause an embarrassing stumble.

As we knew it would, our entrance turned a lot of heads. We had left early, as my dad insisted, and killed time by going to a blowout hair salon for Victoria's Secret Angels–type hair, and we looked awesome. We had heard there'd be a professional photographer, so we'd decided it was worth the forty-dollar blow dry.

We ran into other girls we knew, and once we stood together, we were a force to be reckoned with. Each of us was approached by guy after guy, but no one more than me. In that nasty, girlie way, I loved it.

But the night didn't matter until around eleven-thirty on the roof.

I was sitting in the corner of the concrete patio on a stool, surrounded by some dumb girl and two dumb guys, basically holding court, when Reed walked up.

I have to explain Reed. Before high school, I didn't know him. His real name was James Reed, but no one ever called him James. It didn't really fit him. He needed something just a little more off-kilter.

When I met him in ninth grade, we barely spoke. He was a cocky little shit, and it was obvious. Our relationship was pretty much him not talking to me, or hitting on me when he did, and me rolling my eyes a lot and telling him how shitty he was.

We "hated" each other. But it was that flexible kind of hate. I was supposed to hate him because he had had sex with Natalie without any intention of dating her. But she hadn't really wanted to date him, either. So really, there wasn't much to hate about him. On her behalf, anyway.

If I was honest, I had always thought he was kind of hot. But I wasn't honest with anyone about that, least of all him. I had confided it once to Natalie, who had absolutely no feelings for him anymore, and she had merely wretched and told me that it wasn't her job to prevent me from getting herpes.

Thinking he was hot was embarrassing, and not something I could ever confess to anyone but her. Not because he was, like, butt-ugly or anything. He was not. He had pretty eyes. Really glorious, sharp cheekbones, actually. And this endearing grin that I hated because it usually meant he was being a dick, but that was just so boyish and charming it was hard not to smile back. Or if you're me, groan exasperatedly and walk away before he caught you finding him anything but revolting.

I was supposed to be immune to him. If I wasn't, then I was just like every other girl.

I didn't even know he was at the party until he sidled up. He had a glass—most people had plastic cups—holding what I assumed was whiskey on the rocks. That's another thing. If you knew Wild Reed, you knew that he was drinking whiskey. Not only in favor of other liquors, but in general. If he wasn't, it was an off day.

I locked eyes with him, suddenly feeling like the people around me were not nearly as interesting as before.

"Happy New Year's, Skinny."

Oh, yeah, that's the other thing. *Skinny.* Since day one, that's what he's called me. On many occasions he's grabbed me somewhere on my hip or ass and told me I needed to fatten up and that I looked like shit. It occurred to me once a long time ago that there was actually a good chance that he didn't know my real name.

He was really a charmer.

"You look like a fucking waiter." I sipped champagne from my solo cup, surveying his black pants and white shirt. I dropped my gaze to the hand he was extending to me. It held an actual glass of champagne.

"And you're looking a little trashy—wanna switch to crystal?"

I wet my lips and narrowed my eyes before setting down my cup and taking the glass. "Thanks."

"Anytime."

Then he just fucking looked at me. Like, not saying anything. What was I supposed to do with that?

"What?"

He shrugged and took a sip of his drink. "Nothing. How was your past year?"

"Great. Thanks for asking."

"Now you're supposed to ask about mine."

"I don't really care about yours."

"Don't be a bitch, I brought you a glass of champagne."

"Yeah, that's a huge accomplishment on *New Year's Eve*."

"You didn't manage it."

True. Shit. "I didn't care all that much. What are you even doing here? How did you get invited?"

"Sam's my best friend. Thanks for the shock, though."

Oops.

"I thought you were crashing, as you are so wont to do."

"Well, I'm not. In fact, you are, more than I am."

"Hey, I was invited, thank you very much."

"On Facebook?"

"Yes."

"Yeah, you're welcome."

My jaw dropped. "Excuse me?"

"I told him to invite you. So you're welcome for the invite. I think 'thank you' was what you meant. You really have terrible manners for such a snob."

Oh, the embarrassment of realizing I was only at the party because of freaking *Reed*.

"Well, it's a very nice party."

He nodded, looking smug. I wanted to hit him.

"It is a nice party. There's a couple having sex in one of the bedrooms and everything."

"Ah, great." I nodded and took another sip.

"Want to copy them?"

I choked a little on the bubbles. Once I cleared my throat, hand on my chest, I said, "First of all, I never copy anyone. And second, you're disgusting."

"Yeah. That's what I hear." He gave me that crocodile grin, and got distracted by a pretty girl. "I'll talk to you later, Skinny."

The feeling I got then was weird, unexpected and completely offensive to the not–idiotic part of my brain. I was jealous.

Of whoever that porn–star–blonde girl was, whose dress had been short enough or tight enough or whatever to divert his attention from me. Bitch.

And then I was alone. I hadn't even realized the others had drifted away.

Wellll...this just got embarrassing.

I collected myself, feeling weird and stupid, and found Alexa. Thank God she was with a panel of guys. One of them might even have been the one just talking to me earlier. I was barely paying attention.

A small while later, we all gathered to watch the ball drop

on a big projector screen that had previously been playing music videos. Then the countdown started.

10. Alexa and I cheers'd our champagnes, mine glass and envied, hers plastic.

9.

8.

7. I dabbed my bottom lip to make sure I wasn't spilling.

6.

5.

4. I realized the midnight kiss was coming, and I didn't have anyone.

3.

2. I realized I wasn't thinking about Aiden, I was thinking about…

1. Reed put his hand on my waist, pulled me into him almost too forcibly—but not quite. My lips tingled from the champagne, his were warm from the whiskey, and before I knew what was happening, I was kissing him back harder than I have ever kissed anyone. Like, we should have been in private. It was *not* classy.

His hands were in the right places—my hip bone, then my lower back, the other in my hair and on my neck and jaw. I bit his lip, and he kissed me harder before biting back—not as hard as I had.

My legs seemed to fill with the bubbles from the champagne. I suddenly wanted him to throw me against the wall and do whatever he wanted.

But instead, he kissed me once more and then pulled away. "Happy New Year's, beautiful. I'm outta here." He winked at me, that stupid smile on his face, and walked out of the crowd, down the steps and away from the party.

Gahhhhd. That was my only thought.

I turned to see Alexa, doe-eyed and smiling in shock at me.

"What the hell was that?" I asked, my fingers gravitating to my lips.

She shook her head, eyebrows still raised. "I was going to ask you!"

We had invited the other girls to stay in our hotel with us, but they had all found guys to hook up with and sleep uncomfortably on a floor with, so just the two of us left not long after midnight.

Alexa and I talked about the Reed kiss from the time we left, all prettied up, to when we were in the hotel room in glasses, tank tops and boyshorts. I knew I could trust her not to tattle on me, but of course I was beginning to wonder who else had seen. Because if someone had, I couldn't explain why I had kissed him back like we were on a plane about to crash. I wouldn't be able to explain that to Aiden, Natalie or even myself.

Of course, I found myself asking Alexa what she thought it meant. Did he like me? Was he into me at least? Was he being an asshole? Had he won—or lost—a bet? There was no telling. The only thing I knew was that I had annoyingly not hated it. Or…to be more honest with myself, I had fucking adored it in a way I never had before.

The only thing we were able to come away with was that he was just being Reed. Manwhore that he was. Player. He liked to fuck with people. He liked to acquire people. He was basically me.

And that is the last person in the world that I would ever allow myself to be into.

CHAPTER THIRTEEN

Day of the Stupid Cupid Rager

"STOP."

"Stop what, Brooke? I'm merely asking you if you can maybe not flirt with a bunch of dudes tonight."

"You're saying that like I'm some kind of huge slut."

"No, I'm saying it like you're Brooke."

I gaped at Aiden. "What in the fuck is that supposed to mean?"

"What, does it offend you that I called you by your name?"

"Um, it does when you're basically telling me I'm a whore, and acting like my name is like…fucking…whatever the word is."

"Synonymous."

I took in a deep breath. "Jesus, yes, whatever."

He paused. "I'm sorry. I didn't mean it like that."

I shrugged. "Whatever."

"Brooke."

"No, it's fine, I'm so glad you chose to pick a fight with me tonight, though, thanks. This party will be really fucking fun."

He shook his head as we turned onto Natalie's street.

"Don't shake your head at me."

He looked over to me. "Really, Brooke?"

I gritted my teeth. This was how it had been with Aiden lately. Nonstop arguing. Over nothing. Absolutely nothing!

"Look, Natalie's coming out tonight, I know you're pumped about that. I didn't mean to pick a fight with you. I don't want tonight to go south, that's all. I want to have fun, too. And you know I never do when you're flirting with a bunch of guys."

"I'm never flirting with a *bunch of guys.*"

"You know what I mean." He parked. Natalie was sitting outside.

"I do not."

"Lately you've been doing it more, and I don't know why."

I shrugged. "Me neither."

Natalie opened the back door and climbed in, suspending Aiden's and my conversation and setting the tense tone that I knew would stay with us for the rest of the evening, whether we liked it or not.

I was better at faking it than he was. I was capable of acting like nothing was wrong. But Aiden would stew and be mad, and the only time he acted like he was all right after that was once he had stopped caring. This was not a good thing. It meant that he cared less about fixing it, not that he cared less about whatever the problem was. It wasn't long into the party that it became obvious he didn't feel like patching things up with me.

Because I am my own worst enemy, I went out of my way to do some shots, become the life of the party and flirt with

Justin. Drunk, this seemed like a perfectly fine plan! I knew it would get Aiden's attention, and of course it did.

"Brooke, what the fuck?"

"What?"

And the next thing I knew, he was talking to me again. Drunkenly, this seemed like a victory.

"You can't keep doing this shit, Brooke."

"You are so fucking controlling!"

He pulled me away from the many listening ears.

"No, I'm not. I'm your boyfriend. You can't keep doing this, and you can't keep doing it to me. Do you know how you make me look when you do this?"

"So that's the point, is it? How you're coming off to other people? Not because it makes you feel bad—just 'cuz you're embarrassed?" I was giving him the nastiest snarl.

"Do you *want* to make me feel like shit? You are, don't worry."

"I'm sorry, baby...I didn't mean—"

"I'm reaching the end of my rope, Brooke. No. You know, I have reached it. That happened a long fucking time ago. I really don't think I can keep doing this."

"No, no, please, babe, I'm sorry. Fuck," I muttered. "I was just trying to get your attention. I don't know why I did it like that. I'm so sorry."

"You're always sorry. I should record you sometime and crop together all your apologies so you can hear how many you say in any given week."

"Yes, yes, I'm—" I started to apologize again.

"Look. We won't decide anything now. We've both been drinking. We'll just...we'll deal with it tomorrow."

"Aiden, you know I hate having this kind of thing held over my head."

"What do you want me to say, Brooke? I can't make you feel better about this. And I don't owe you that. We have this talk now, and you know how it ends. Or we talk tomorrow and try to deal with it. Up to you."

I couldn't meet his eyes. "Tomorrow, then."

"That's what I thought."

And he walked away from me.

I resisted the urge to immediately succumb to tears. As I knew she would, Natalie came over.

"You okay?"

AIDEN AVOIDED ME for the rest of the night. It infuriated me to hear him having fun in the basement while I sat upstairs talking to girlfriends and trying not to feel like shit. I didn't even want to talk to Natalie, really. She had a way of making me feel the full measure of guilt that I'm due. And right now that wasn't going to help.

I was actually surprised at how well she was holding up on her own. On one hand, I was glad everyone liked her. But on the other, annoyingly childish hand, it made me feel like old news. She was the new hot thing. All of my guy friends were asking about her or trying to talk to her. I felt irrelevant. I wasn't worth hitting on, because I was with Aiden. Either they wouldn't hit on me because they knew I was taken, because they liked Aiden too much, or because they were too busy kissing Natalie's ass.

Earlier in the night, when she had been talking to a group of guys, I'd had the stupid stab of jealousy that had driven me to start flirting with Justin to begin with. I wasn't even that attracted to him. But I knew he'd flirt with me. I knew it would make Aiden talk to me again. And—and this was where it got really twisted—I thought Reed might notice me flirting with his cousin and pay me some attention.

But no. Even Reed, piggish Reed, wasn't paying attention to me.

I ended up alone. I wanted to cry. And I wanted to talk to Natalie. So I walked downstairs. And to make all matters worse, Natalie was making out with Eric Hornby, the best-looking guy in our class besides Aiden.

Like. *What the fuck.*

So...I was completely irrelevant. I had no boyfriend, probably, no one lusting after me, and now everyone with a penis wanted to bang my best friend. Fucking fantastic.

I went back upstairs. Almost everyone was asleep, and I was wide awake. I poured myself a double shot and downed it. Maybe it would help me pass out.

"Hey, Skinny."

Reed was shirtless and walking toward me.

Maybe it wasn't too late for a little attention, after all.

"Hey, asshole," I said, but my heart wasn't in it.

"What's up with you?" He could tell.

"I'm never going to fall asleep."

"I have something that'll help."

I raised an eyebrow. Finally. Someone at least making a sexual joke in my direction.

"Oh, yeah?"

"Yeah, hold on." He ran back down the hall to whatever room he was staying in, and then returned with a small pill. "Xanax. Put it under your tongue and you'll be asleep in no time, love."

He smacked me on the ass, took the bottle of Kentucky Gentleman from the counter and left again.

So he had some girl back there. I really was all alone.

I wandered over to the couch where Alexa had passed out and lay down on the other end of it. I put the Xanax under my tongue and let it calm me into sleep.

It was possibly the most pathetic moment in my whole life.

WHEN WE DROPPED off Natalie the next morning, I had been sure that the second we were alone, Aiden would dump me. I was eager now to get it over with.

"So…do you want to talk about last night?" I asked when he didn't say anything about it.

"What about last night?"

He flushed.

"What do you mean, what about last night? The horrible fight we had?"

"Right. Don't worry about it. We were drunk."

I stared at his profile. "Are you serious?"

"Yeah. It doesn't matter. You didn't mean anything by it, you were drunk. Shit happens."

This was completely unlike him. But I wasn't going to push him. "All right, then…"

The rest of the ride was utterly silent. No radio or anything. He kept looking like he wanted to say something, but then saying nothing. I kept wanting to ask, but then also saying nothing. So I just stared out the window.

OVER THE NEXT weeks, things stayed kind of tense and awkward between us. He was busy, so we didn't see each other all that often. I had been sure that he would use my birthday as an opportunity to try to make up. To get back on track to being Us again.

"Whoa, Brooke!" exclaimed Natalie, who had just opened my locker for me. "What the hell?"

"What? What the fuck…"

"Why is there a bottle of liquor in your locker?"

"I have no idea. Whaaaat…wait." I knew exactly who it was from. Only one person would do it. My heart jumped a little at the sight of the note. What would Reed say?

Happy birthday, let's see how much you can handle.

"Holy crap," said Natalie, "do you have a secret admirer?"

"I guess. That's really weird." I tried to deflect. "Maybe Aiden…?"

"Aiden would never risk getting you in trouble like that."

"No, no, you're probably right." Of course she was right.

"Then…any idea who it is?"

"Lotta people like drinking and a lotta people like me, Nattie." I didn't know why I didn't want to tell her anything about Reed. It was embarrassing that I had this stupid crush on him. And I knew she'd get all preachy about Aiden again, anyway.

"Well. At least you know it's a guy. No girl has handwriting that bad."

"Truth. Uh. Well, I should go to class."

NEXT THING I knew, I was blowing off my boyfriend—the one I had just been so desperate to fix things with—for the opportunity to see what might happen with Reed.

CHAPTER FOURTEEN

I HONESTLY CAN'T say what possessed me to do it. Except maybe the memory of the kiss on New Year's. But whatever it was, the second I saw the bottle in my locker, and knew who it was from…it shook me.

I'd been getting ready for dinner with Aiden, a dinner that I knew would be expensive and delicious, and fun if he was in a good mood. I had just put on my mascara, the last step of my makeup, when I looked at myself. In a pink dress. Perfect pink lips. I stared at myself for a long moment, and it was as if my reflection made the next move. I sent a text. My nerves went through the roof as I waited for the answer. It wasn't five minutes before I got it and sent my reply.

Then I called Aiden.

"Hey, babe."

"Hey…" I said. "I feel like shit. I don't think I can do anything tonight."

"Feel like shit? How?"

"Like puking. Natalie was sick recently, too. I think I caught whatever she had."

"Natalie was puking?"

"Yes, duh, remember at lunch she was sick?"

"Yeah, but I thought she was just...I didn't realize she actually threw up."

"Yeah." Why was he so stuck on that? "Well, anyway, I'm sick now, too, I guess the bug is making its way back around...I'm sorry, can we reschedule and do it some other day this weekend?"

My heart was pounding with the lie, and with my new, exciting plans.

I expected him to call me out on being hungover that morning, or on the fact that I sounded like I was lying. But he didn't. "Yeah, that's fine. It's your birthday."

It occurred to me that this was also the moment where he would usually offer to come take care of me. It would be an obstacle if he offered...but he didn't.

We really weren't the same anymore.

"Thanks for being so nice about it...."

"Yep. Well...feel better."

"I will. Just need rest probably."

"Probably."

Awkward silence.

"Okay...well, I'll call you tomorrow or something."

"Yup."

"Okay, bye."

And he hung up.

I texted him immediately.

I hope you're not mad...

It's fine. A couple of people were going to meet up to hang out later with us, so I'll do that.

Cool. Tell Natalie not to get me sick anymore! I assume she's going right?

I hoped the light tone of the last text would undo some of the guilt of me blowing him off and whatever he had planned. He didn't answer right away, but finally he said, I'll check.

Next thing, I was pulling off my dress, standing in my room in a black strapless bra and matching lace underwear, looking at my texts to Reed and his response.

So. What are we doing with this bottle?

Supposed to drink it, stupid. You wanna do that together?

Yep.

My nerves twisted with excitement as I saw a new message.

Don't you have to meet your boyfriend?

I hated how he was unafraid to bring up Aiden—the last subject I wanted to discuss with him.

I don't have to do anything i don't want.

I'll come get you in forty.

My stomach churned like snakes slithering through gravel. I retouched my makeup, making my eyes a little smokier. I picked out a new outfit. Black, almost completely see-through tights, a black skirt and dark red bralette top. I topped it with a cropped leather jacket.

I gazed in the mirror. I looked hot.

What was this nervousness I was feeling? When I sat, my foot shook anxiously. I was biting the lip plumper right off my bottom lip. My stomach felt concave with tension.

I opened my bag and pulled out the bottle I had found in my locker.

I unscrewed the lid, put the bottle vertical to my lips and gulped a couple of times. I took one more than I knew I should. But screw it. I needed to toss my nerves out the window.

It felt like three days before I heard the roar of his car outside. The asshole didn't come up to the door, or even text me to let me know he was there. I waited a couple of minutes before realizing he was fully aware that I was watching for him.

What a dick.

I passed by my mom, who was working on her laptop. She and my dad had no plans tonight. Typical. The exact, lifeless marriage I wanted to eventually avoid having. My mom was tired from her business trip, and my dad had worked all day, so my birthday had barely been acknowledged beyond the promise that we'd do something for it in a few days.

"Mom, I'm going out with Aiden."

She finished typing and then looked up at the clock. "It's pretty late, Brooke."

"It's Aiden, does it matter?"

I could tell she was too tired to really fight with me.

"Don't get back too late, all right? I have to get some rest tonight, and I can't stay up all night worrying about you."

These sentences from my mom always threw me for a loop.

It was almost affection, but dripping with such irritation that it fell short.

"Got it. 'Night."

I walked down the pathway in front of my house, making sure I didn't teeter in my wedges, and climbed into the passenger seat. He took a drag from his cigarette and then tossed it out the window.

"Hello, Miss Sweet Eighteen."

He sped off, so loud it probably would have concerned my parents if they hadn't so confidently thought I was going out with Aiden.

"Let's not even talk about my birthday, shall we? It's not like it matters."

"Guess not. Why aren't you with your boyfriend or your BFF, though? Would have thought you would be."

I shrugged. "It's just not a big deal to me. I'll celebrate with them this weekend."

"Gotcha."

"Where are we going, by the way?"

"McShul's."

"Isn't that a bar?"

"Yep."

"And…we can get in?"

"Yep."

"How's that?"

"I know everyone who works there, and you are my hot plus-one. We'll be fine."

I got the slightest, Natalie-ish butterfly of nervousness in my stomach before playing it cool. "Sweet. Who are we meeting?"

"Some of my friends."

The implication was that I was not going to know them. I did well with groups of new people, but something about being charming ol' Brooke in front of Reed made me feel slightly silly.

He turned up the music and lit another cigarette.

Why had he even wanted to see me tonight? Was it a joke? Or a test to see if I would ditch my boyfriend for him? Was I doing exactly what he expected?

I really didn't want to seem like one of the girls he lassoed in before letting them go. The dumb little ninnies who let him walk all over them, bending to his every whim. Except Natalie, who had really needed the break from logical thinking.

"Let me get a jack," I said, extending my hand.

Finally, a note of surprise on his face. But he said nothing about it, just pulled out a cigarette and handed it over. He flicked his lighter and lit it for me.

It was pretty far from Cary Grant, but this is a new age.

This wasn't the first time it had been valuable to me to fake it with a cigarette, so luckily, I knew what to do and how not to start coughing and turn blue.

Hating the way it made my head immediately spin, I asked, "So, why aren't you with some girl tonight?"

"I am, aren't I?"

"You know what I mean. One who will actually bang you at the end of it."

He looked at me and gave me that genuine, boyish grin. "I am, aren't I?"

I gave a laugh and inhaled. "Um, not even kind of."

The small lilt in my voice made me sound—even to me— kind of like a little girl saying, "Ew, boys are so gross."

He looked back to me, giving a quick glance from my knees to my eyes, and then said, "That's okay. Wasn't banking on it."

I rolled my eyes, my tongue in my cheek.

We got to the bar, got in with no problem and met his

friends. I tried to be confident, but found myself taking a slight backseat. Something I never do.

Reed left for a few minutes. I saw him talking to another girl, and then he vanished and returned with two shots and two drinks.

He handed one of each to me.

He raised his shot. "To your birthday."

"To just another Thursday."

He smirked and then we both downed them. He went back to talking to his friends, leaving me alone to find my own way with these people.

I ended up in conversation with a nice enough girl, Kelly.

"So are you guys, like, dating?" she asked, indicating Reed.

"Oh, God, no. Why…would you even ask that?"

"Because." She shrugged. "He doesn't really bring girls around that often."

"Right. Well, I mean, he's not even talking to me right now."

"That's how he is. It might even mean he likes you more. If he didn't, I bet he'd be trying to fuck you in the bathroom."

"Man, am I flattered." I laughed, and we cheers'd with our drinks.

A while and a few more finished cocktails later, I went to the bathroom and snuck in another shot order on the opposite side of the bar. Some nasty-ass old man hit on me, but I shrugged him off with a thank-you and a smile.

As I waited for my shot, I was struck by a sudden pang of guilt—my first one. What was Aiden even doing right now? I was off with some other guy—not only another guy, but someone Aiden really disliked. He had hated Reed ever since finding out about his treatment of Natalie. He was very cut-and-dried about how girls should be treated by guys. And he'd always been pretty great to me.

Guilt guilt guilt.

I paid for my shot, drank it and went back toward our table.

Reed intercepted me before I got there and pulled me over to his bar stool. I stood between his knees.

"I thought you left."

"Would you blame me?"

"What's that supposed to mean?"

"I mean, you're over talking to whoever, and I'm all by myself!"

"You were talking to Kelly."

"So? I don't even know Kelly."

"So, why does it matter where I am?"

I shrugged. "Guess it doesn't."

His smile faded a little and he dropped his gaze to my lips before pushing back a little by my hips. His hands remained there.

"Sorry I wasn't paying you enough attention, princess."

"Totally fine, asshole."

I couldn't help but smile back, despite my narrowed eyes. That's what we were. An asshole and a princess. There was something I kind of liked about that.

As the conversation grew more flirtatious with Reed, and our faces grew closer, thoughts of Aiden went further and further from my mind. Would I regret doing something with Reed, or not doing something with him?

Part of me knew that I wouldn't hesitate if given the chance. I wasn't noble enough to say no.

He pulled me close to say something in my ear—my memory started to get pretty blurry here—and his lips brushed against my skin just enough to make my breath catch.

He said one thing, then put his hand on my spine under my shirt and pulled me closer. I responded and ran my thumb along his jawline. He spoke, and I found myself looking at his mouth. His teeth were white, and though a little crooked, they were good teeth. And his lips…I didn't even want to kiss them. I just wanted them on me.

I realized at one point that I was holding his hand on his thigh. I only noticed as he let go, moving his to my hip bone again with his finger on the inside of the top of my skirt.

"You are such a fucking player," I said, not stepping away. In fact, I moved my hips a little closer to his.

"Am not."

"Oh, of course you are. And you're trying to play me, which is illogical and ill-advised."

"I can't play you. In order to play you I would have to make you a promise first."

"That's not true."

"Yeah, it is. Other girls hook up with me because they think I'm going to give them more than I am. It's a promise, even if I never say anything."

"Right, and with me…"

"With you, you're already taken, aren't you? No chance here that we're going to be something, and we both know that."

I hesitated, trying to figure out his intention by the words. "Right. That among a slew of other reasons. The boyfriend thing…I mean, he may not always be my boyfriend, so that doesn't really count as an obstacle."

"And what are my obstacles as far as getting you to let me fuck you?"

I hated the excited chill the words sent through my heart right down to my thighs.

"Uh, mostly the fact that I would never do that?"

He looked up at me, standing in front of him, his eyes strangely and intriguingly intense. He pulled my hand up his own thigh to feel how badly he wanted me. It was the biggest I'd ever felt, and when you're me at a homecoming or prom

or you have snuck your way into a club, you have a lot of op-
portunities to accidentally find out what your dance partner
is packing.

I couldn't help but take a deep breath and let my lips part
as I looked back into his eyes. The intensity of them made
me want to see how serious he could be. Not all laughs and
jokes, but serious passion.

The facade dropped for both of us. It was obviously not a
game to get the other one to be into us. We didn't hate each
other. Or maybe we did, but either way, we definitely wanted
each other.

I didn't know what my next move should be. It definitely
wasn't to hook up in the bathroom. But before I had a chance,
he decided for us.

"We're leaving. Grab your jacket."

I'd never been told what to do before. No one dared. At
any other time, or maybe with any other person, I would
have argued with his brash tone. But I didn't want to. I kind
of liked it.

I did as he said, and followed him out to the car.

My vision was worsening, and I was definitely starting to
teeter in my shoes. I got into the car and boldly put my hand
on his thigh. He held it, and I squeezed his leg.

I wanted him badly.

I pulled my hand away and leaned my head against the seat
belt. The window was a little open, because he was smoking.
The air hit my face, cooling me off. I hadn't even realized I
was flushed.

To allay the guilt I was starting to feel, I texted Natalie.

We drove for about fifteen minutes, music pounding. We
finally rolled to a stop, and I opened my eyes to find that we
were at my house.

I turned to him.

He shook his head. "You should get some sleep."

The rejection hit me hard in the gut. Dammit. Was he serious? It was one thing to feel slightly rejected last time. This was a big one.

"Um. Okay?"

"It was fun."

I put my hand on the handle, but paused and turned back to him. "What the hell is your deal?"

He shrugged. "Nothin'."

I stared at him, looking for some sign of something in his face. But there was nothing.

I shook my head, a stunned smile on my face. "All right, then." I took a deep breath and opened the door. I turned back and leaned in the open window.

"You know you're a fucking idiot, right?"

He shrugged and messed up his hair.

"It seems a bit fucked to try to bag a girl on her birthday, just because she's blasted. Especially once she passes out."

Oh, so this was a nice gesture?

"Hah. Wow, well, okay. Thanks for looking out for me, then, Reed."

"Anytime, Brookes."

I wished I still had the door to slam as I turned away and went back to my house, feeling completely rejected.

At least he'd stopped calling me Skinny.

Part III

Natalie

CHAPTER FIFTEEN

March 21, the morning after sledding

When I awoke to the gray light and the repeating *Vertigo* DVD menu at 6:00 a.m., Aiden had an arm wrapped around my ankles. I didn't want to move. I savored the moment, watching him, and then tried to get back to sleep. I don't think I ever did, but still, I lay there until 10:00 a.m. with him. When he shifted, I...pretended, I guess, to wake up.

"Hey," he said. He looked slightly regretful. This caused guilt to rise in my own chest.

"Hey," I said back, and sat up. I ran my hand through my hair. It felt like a bird's nest, and I was sure it looked worse.

By the light of day, it seemed so obvious that we shouldn't have hung out like we had the night before. Nothing had happened. But that wasn't the most important issue. The important issue was whether Brooke would feel weird about Aiden staying over.

We both knew she would.

He picked up his phone and rubbed his face. I watched him read something and mutter, "Dammit."

I remembered my own phone and looked to see that I had a text from Brooke asking if I wanted to come over in a little while. She had only sent the text half an hour ago.

"She texted you, too, huh?" he asked.

"Yeah. She wants to know if I want to come over later."

He nodded slowly. "Guess she's feeling better."

"Hangovers go away. Amazing, huh?" I gave a small laugh.

"How, um…how are you feeling? Brooke said you were throwing up a little while back."

"Oh…yeah, I'm fine. Must have been a bug or something. I don't know, maybe stress? My body handles stress in weird ways."

"Well, as long as you're feeling fine now, I guess it's all good."

The truth was that I hadn't been feeling my best lately. I almost never got sick, and when I did, I usually felt kind of crappy under the surface. It never turned into anything that stopped me from going to school or anything. No flus, colds, sinus infections, nothing like that. I was exhausted and listless, but was mostly fine. I didn't want to tell my dad or he'd make me go to the doctor, which would be expensive and pointless. I was one hundred percent sure I would get blood drawn and they'd tell me it was just stress and to drink more water. That happened every time I gave in and went to the doctor.

"Yep, I'm good."

"All right, cool…well, I should head out."

"Right, right. Um. I'm sure I'll see you soon. Monday at least."

"Yeah." He looked at me for a second as he stood, and then his tense expression softened. "Last night was fuckin' awesome by the way. *Vertigo* is a crazy movie."

"Long. But crazy, yes."

"Yeah, it is really long. Probably why I'm exhausted this morning."

I stood to walk with him to the door. "That's probably due to the fact that, this time, you actually did sleep on the couch."

He took a second to realize what I meant, and then said, "Ah. Right. I guess…this is another thing we don't mention to Brooke?" He made a wincing face.

"I guess not…just…I don't want her to feel weird."

"No."

"We should probably stop doing things that she wouldn't want to hear about," I said.

He bit the inside of his cheek and nodded quickly. "Probably a good idea."

His gaze locked on mine for a second and a half too long, and my heart swelled.

"Bye, Nattie."

"Yep, bye." I turned quickly and closed the door.

SATURDAY, BROOKE AND I were sprawled on her living room couches watching TV. She had never asked anything about her birthday night, and I hadn't gone out of my way to bring it up. She was acting a little weird, asking me to come to her house instead of coming over to mine as was our tradition.

"So," she said, turning to me suddenly, "I was thinking… about what we should do tonight…"

"What do you think, *Romeo and Juliet* or *Moulin Rouge!*? Also, are you sure you want to do nachos? I don't know that I'm in the mood."

The idea of cooking ground beef for nachos, much less eating them, had been turning my stomach all day. I wasn't in the mood to make them at all. Especially not in Brooke's mom's pristine kitchen.

"Actually…I was thinking we could do something else."

"I really don't feel like going to a party."

"No, no, God, no. Me, neither."

We both knew that wasn't true.

"Uh-huh, so what, then? What are you going to beg me to agree to?"

She sat up and directed herself toward me. "I was thinking, tonight we should go out to dinner."

I stared at her, waiting for the catch. She knew I loved going out to eat, so there was no reason that this should be something she had to get me to agree to except financially.

Brooke gave me a rectangular smile and put up her sunglasses. "With Aiden and Eric."

Oof.

"Oh," I said, without meaning to.

"I know you're not that into Eric, but he's such a cool guy, and I think if you got to know him a little more and hung out some…I'm not saying you guys are going to get married and have little Eric-Natalie babies or anything, but he so wanted to take you on a date, and you haven't let him…so I thought a double date was a good way of hanging out with him but having it be comfortable."

My heart was pounding, and I was torn between the want and the dread of seeing Aiden. Especially with Brooke. Especially with someone else who was supposed to be my date.

The temptation was strong.

"Come on, Nattie…it'll be fun! The boys will pay, it will be awesome. You're going out with your best friend in the whole wide world to celebrate her eighteenth year, how can it be all that bad?"

I knew it was asking for trouble, but I didn't think I would ever be able to give up an opportunity to see Aiden.

I scooted my glasses up my face and rubbed my eyes. "I hate you."

"Eee!" she squealed, and drumrolled on my stomach. "It's gonna be fun. Promise."

WE BLASTED MUSIC, pigged out on the Costco-size bag of Sour Patch Kids Brooke had unearthed in her pantry and felt like the old Us. We danced around in our underwear, knowing all the words to our favorite songs that we loved and that we loved to hate. She was just finishing straightening my hair and we were seductively singing one of our most beloved hate-to-love songs: the one and only Bieber's "Boyfriend."

We laughed our whole way through it, even while trying to take it seriously.

As I'd known she would, she pulled me into her room to find something to wear. She tossed me a pair of dark denim skinnies, a black strapless bra and see-through white shirt.

"Isn't that a little skanky?" I asked, holding up the black-and-white.

"Yeah, but you're not, so it's ironic." She stared at the outfit, the fashion-sense wheels in her brain working. She nodded at her own thoughts and then told me to flip my hair upside down. Next thing I knew, she had put it in a big chic bun, high on my head. She told me to close my eyes as she enveloped my head in a cloud of hairspray.

I put on the outfit as she shimmied into a high-waisted white skirt and paired it with a loose, turquoise chiffon shirt. She accessorized with a rose gold watch and pinned up one side of her hair, which she had curled a little.

"I'm going with the good-girl look, since it's also ironic. I gave you the bad-girl outfit. You're welcome."

"Oh, you're a good girl at heart...kind of."

"And maybe you have a little bad girl in you! I don't know, I'll leave it to Eric to find out. Oh wait! He already did!"

"Brooke!"

I looked at myself in the mirror and couldn't help but see it. She came over and looped some earrings through my piercings. Dark metal, thin chains. Oddly they worked, even though I would never pick them out for myself.

The brief moment of self-admiration faded, and I remembered I was not a bad girl. Just a terrible person. I looked good tonight, and the only reason that was true was because Brooke had helped me. And the only reason I cared about looking good was to look as hot as possible in front of her boyfriend.

Her phone buzzed on top of her dresser, making the music dip out.

"Oh, they might be here." She went over and looked. "Yup! Toss on those shoes, and let's go."

She pointed at a pair of strappy black sandals with dark fixtures the same color as my earrings, and slipped into a pair of wedges she'd bought with me at Aldo, and which she had only just now taken out of the shoebox.

I followed her and the butterflies in my stomach down the stairs and into Aiden's Jeep.

"Hey, boys," she said. "No, Eric, stay shotgun, we're going to be all BFF back here. But I insist on playing at least two songs of my choice. Hey, baby."

She popped up, wrapping her arms around Aiden's shoulders and kissing him on the cheek.

"Hey, how are you?"

"Good." She lingered by his ear and whispered something.

He laughed a little and gave her a pat on the arm. "All righty…sit down now. Before I make you."

"Ooh," she said, sitting back. "So demanding. I love it."

She gave me a little wink and buckled her seat belt. I had

to hurry and arrange myself into something passable and not horror-stricken and nauseated. It didn't work.

"Nat, what's wrong?" she asked.

Aiden looked back at me.

"Nothing." I smiled, trying to convince them both and myself. "I thought I left my wallet upstairs, but it's here. So. Nothing to worry about."

"It's on me tonight, anyway. Finally got a date with the elusive Natalie Shepherds!" said Eric, turning to Aiden for a high five.

He gave it to him, and I laughed a laugh that wasn't my own.

I hated myself for wanting to crawl back home like I wanted to now. I suddenly didn't know why I had agreed to this. It was a terrible, terrible freaking idea. If it was anyone else, and Brooke was able to give me advice, like she always did, she would have said, *You have got to be fucking kidding me. Why torture yourself?*

In fact, she would have managed to talk me out of the whole thing to begin with. Months ago, she would have detailed the reasons Aiden wasn't all that attractive, anyway, or why I wasn't in love with him so it wasn't worth the risk, or anything like that to cool my burning desires for him. If only it was anyone but Aiden, her boyfriend.

We got to Bethesda, where we were apparently eating.

"Where are we going?" I asked.

She gave a sweet look and shrugged. "I don't know!"

I should have guessed we were eating at Chin Chin. It was a pretty warm night, and their patio would be open, with heaters on. The restaurant itself was an awful off-white with hospital-cafeteria seating. But in the spring and summer, the patio opened up on the back alley, which was supernice. It was like a Zen garden, with lots of candles and nice plants and flowers.

She squeezed my arm. "It's been too long since we ate this crap. God, I am going to punish some dumplings."

We sat in the corner of the garden and started looking at the menu, as if we didn't know what we would be ordering. We were all laughing and making polite conversation when a voice came from behind Brooke.

"No facking way. Is that Natalie and Brooke? My two dream girls?"

I looked up. Oh, God.

Brooke didn't turn. She just got wide-eyed and looked at me. "Tell me it's not Reed."

I cringed at her, and she sighed before tossing her hair and turning to him.

He came over, his arm around Bethany. She smiled big at us. She bothered me, so much.

"I can't believe you guys are here right now!" Bethany sounded genuinely excited.

Eric stood to give her the hug she held her arms out for, then the same for Aiden. Brooke didn't stand, but let her embrace her as she leaned back in her chair.

"What's up, my bitch?"

"Nothing, we just had a bunch of sake at the bar—" Bethany dropped her voice. "They didn't card us or anything! How awesome is that?"

"Superawesome, as long as it's chilled. Hot sake is like fucking piss," chimed in Reed.

"Dude, come sit with us, pull up some chairs," said Eric. He sat back down.

I felt Aiden looking at me, his eyes asking if this was cool. I had always found his aversion to Reed kind of…sweet. It wasn't hard to be averse to Reed, of course, but Aiden seemed to hate him purely because he had been a dick to me when we'd hooked up. I gave a good-natured eye roll and he looked away again.

"Don't mind if I do take a seat." Reed scooted in, basically on top of Brooke.

She rolled her eyes and looked to Aiden. "Are you kidding me right now?"

Aiden waved away her concern. "You're harmless, are you not, Reed?"

"Absolutely harmless. Hey, Lin, let me get a round of chilled sake for my friends."

The small girl he spoke to smiled coquettishly and nodded before going over to the bar computer and putting in the order.

"Loves me." He fanned himself with both hands.

"You ever hooked up with her?" Eric asked indulgently.

"Nah, you never hook up with the girls at restaurants and bars, you get them obsessed so they'll hook you up."

"Right on," said Brooke sarcastically, holding her hand up for a high five. "God, you are so fucking cool."

"I know you don't mean it—" he smacked her hand "—but you should, so I'll give you that."

"You're just awful to know."

He shrugged.

Brooke looked at me and mouthed, *Sorry.*

I waved it away. Honestly, I didn't mind. Reed was a blustering mess of entertainment and kept the night from being quite so double-date-y as it was.

The sake arrived a second later, and the girl named Lin couldn't keep her eyes off Reed, who gave her that annoying grin of his. I guessed it was the crooked smile and rakish hairstyle that had her sweating. I felt like I should warn her. But I knew it would do no good.

"To being at a table with three possible prom queens, and all the tits we're going to see later!"

Eric and Bethany alone laughed.

"Um, no," said Brooke, putting down her shot.

"I'm just kidding, babes, get your panties out of a bunch. Or are you wearing any?"

Aiden looked at me. Brooke just glared at Reed, but I could see something in her eyes that made me seriously concerned.

The signs of an enamored Brooke:

1. Her eyes are narrowed in a mean but sexy way.
2. Her tongue is in her cheek.
3. There's a smile playing at her lips that she doesn't realize is there.
4. She's zoned in on the guy, less aware of everyone else than she should be.
5. She's acting like he's the last person in the world she wants to be around.

Maybe it was the mood she was in or something. She had always said she hated Reed. On my behalf and on her own. But maybe that was number five in action.

"How about to the lucky guys who get to spend a meal with us?" Brooke corrected his toast.

"I can be down with that." Reed held up his glass. He winked at her, and I caught her wink back.

"Much better!" Bethany laughed, and held hers up, too.

"Definitely lucky." Eric pulled me a little closer by putting his hand on my waist. I stiffened.

"Can we just drink this shit?" Aiden said, putting up his own.

"That!" I said, joining.

We all clinked glasses. Aiden mouthed, *It's not that bad,* at me as I looked fearful before taking it.

He was right. I could see how people could drink a lot of that and regret it later.

We did another round almost immediately. I didn't really mind. It was a breezy and light-blue evening, and Aiden was driving. I knew he would stop after two and not do any more.

I declined after the two shots myself, however, when I started feeling sick from them. The queasiness passed pretty quickly, and I caught Aiden's eye again. Being sober and having everyone around us grow increasingly less so proved to be pretty annoying.

At one point, when Reed and Brooke were in conversation and Eric and Bethany were semiflirting (weird), I did the hand gesture of shooting myself in the temple. Aiden laughed silently, put his hands over his mouth and glanced at Brooke. She wasn't paying attention.

Reed insisted that we do a round of hot sake at the end of our meal, despite advertising it as tasting "like piss."

"Yeah, but you have to try it at least," he said.

"Jesus Christ," I screamed after taking a half a sip. Everyone else but Aiden took theirs. I shook my head. "I'm not drinking that."

Everyone laughed, but we had all clearly hated it exactly that much. Even Reed was looking regretful.

"All right, all right, that wasn't worth it. I apologize for that."

He threw down a bunch of money on the check holder and said, "Let's get out of here."

"How much is the check?" asked Aiden.

"It's on me, don't worry about it."

Aiden looked at the check, and then looked at him. "It's only forty bucks, how is that possible?"

Reed stood and gestured at Lin. "Loves me."

I could see why. There was at least eighty dollars lying on top of the check.

I walked next to Brooke. "Gotta give him some credit, I guess."

"Guess so." She shrugged and gave a quick smile, but seemed uninterested in talking to me. She didn't even look at me when I spoke. She quickened her step and walked next to Bethany. What the hell?

"So what now?" Reed asked, his hands behind his head, stretching. He seemed unselfconscious about inviting himself into our evening.

"Oh, my God, I know." Bethany perked up unexpectedly. "Let's go to freaking laser tag. Is that crazy?"

"That," said Reed, pointing at her, "is the least crazy thing I have ever heard. Laser tag it is."

Fifteen minutes later, we were signing up for laser tag and putting on the ridiculous outfits. Five minutes after that, we were in the dark room, which was being pumped with dry ice and lasers with colored lights everywhere.

We did girls against boys. Though I barely knew how to play, I found myself laughing and enjoying myself.

I turned a corner and ran into Eric.

"Don't shoot!" I said. "That wouldn't be very nice."

He laughed. "All right, I'll let you go. But it's going to cost you."

"What will it cost me?"

He walked toward me and tapped his cheek for me to kiss him.

My confidence was brimming, but I still wasn't into the guy.

It happened faster than I could even track. One second I was leaning in to kiss him on the cheek, the next, Aiden was running up behind me and using my own trigger to shoot Eric in his target.

"Dude!" said Eric, visibly annoyed.

"Hah!" Aiden kept running.

"What an asshole!" he said.

I grinned and ran. "Sorry!"

CHAPTER SIXTEEN

"Hey, Daddy, I'm going to school."

My dad glanced back over the couch at me. "What's that now? It's almost eight o'clock at night!"

"I'm—Daddy, I've told you this, like, thirty times."

"Oh, right. Working on the project with Aiden."

"Yes."

"Do you need a ride?"

"No, he's picking me up."

He hummed the tune of "K-I-S-S-I-N-G" at me.

"Shut up! And hey, speaking of, I'm pretty sure you're dating Marcy and not telling me."

"What makes you think that?"

"Um, probably the fact that you have never in your life had more conferences to go to, and you guys are, like, all flirty now at the diner."

He was eating his favorite at-home dessert, a scoop of vanilla ice cream with whipped cream, chocolate syrup and sprinkles. It was always an adorable process to watch him make it. All finicky, and making sure he added just the right amount of each ingredient.

"I want you to date her, you know that. I've been telling you to ask her out for how long now?"

He sighed, and I knew Aiden had been right. "Yeah, I know, but it's not the most normal thing in the world. Old dad, having a girlfriend."

"In this day and age? Are you serious?" My phone buzzed and I saw Aiden had texted to tell me he was outside. "I gotta go. But, Daddy…it's fine. I'm glad you guys are dating."

He gave me the sad-Dad eyes. "Really?"

I laughed and went over to him and gave him a hug. "Yes, dummy. I'll be back in a couple of hours."

"All right, have fun."

"It's homework."

He turned back to the TV. "Doesn't mean you aren't going to enjoy yourself."

As I walked toward his Jeep, Aiden leaned over and pushed open the door.

"Nattie, what's goin' on?"

"Nothin'…thanks for picking me up."

"No problem at all. You're on the way, anyway. I'm pumped to start making this thing happen!"

"Dude, me, too, we've been doing such boring work on it for so long, I can't wait."

"I got the posters printed, and they look really good."

"Really? That's awesome. Can't wait to see."

It started raining halfway there, so when we arrived we had to dash from the car to the doors of the school so we didn't ruin all of our stuff.

We got everything inside, nearly dropping all of it in a puddle at one point, but then recovering. Our station was in the center of the school, in a big open square where people spent their time between, before and after classes. It was the perfect place. It was weird to see it at night like this, completely deserted. We had waited until after most practices were over so that we would have the space to plan out the project. The only reason we were allowed in quite so late was that play rehearsal went until ten at night.

An hour later, we were into it. We had used Command strips to put enormous foam boards up on the wall—his idea, to avoid the crappy look of general craft paper.

He was using a yardstick and a pencil to mark the areas we would be renting out to people. In the end we'd decided to charge one dollar per person to be part of it, and a nine-dollar upcharge for each specifically rented block.

I was sitting in the middle of a circle I had made of piles of papers. We'd had some contributions turned in already, due to the project being mentioned on the morning announcements. I held up a stack of movie tickets (a surprisingly high number of people collect them), and looked around for somewhere to put them. I finally reached behind me and started making a second ring of piles around myself.

I looked up to see Aiden laughing.

"What?" I looked at him through my glasses.

He leaned on his yardstick, smiling a little, and then it faded. "Nothing. You're funny."

"Hey, I'm just trying to stay organized here."

He gestured at the speakers I had set up, playing Cold War Kids, by my backpack. "Are you ever not listening to something?"

I shook my head. "Not ever by choice. I can't stand silence."

"Kind of weird for someone who stays home most of the time."

"I've gotten out plenty."

"Can I grab a sip of that?" He held out his hand and I gave him the soda I had just sipped from.

"I don't know how Brooke does it so often, though. The parties and stuff. She's going to burn out halfway through college."

"Probably for the best."

"That's actually true. Better now than when she's a little older and ought to start worrying about real life, I guess. Unlike my mom, who did it all once she had a kid."

He handed back my soda. "Thanks. Should we go hang these posters up? I'm about finished measuring this stuff out."

"Yeah, sure, I could definitely stretch my legs."

Aiden grabbed the pile of posters. They were white, all with different colored print. They advertised the wall, gave the costs and suggestions for what to contribute.

We wandered down the halls, him handing me the posters, me sticking them to the walls, doors and bulletin boards.

"So let me ask you," he said. "Brooke said you're going to be here next year. And you haven't talked at all about your plans for college. I haven't thought I should ask, but…what's the deal there?"

I breathed deeply and puffed out my cheeks. He was a fan of asking the loaded questions. "I didn't figure it out in time. I didn't know what I wanted to do or go to school for. And my dad isn't exactly loaded, so I didn't want to send out a bunch of applications to random places for no reason."

"Couldn't you go somewhere with an undeclared major and start getting the lame general ed classes out of the way?"

"I could, but I don't even know where I want to be. What if I pick somewhere, and then figure out what I want to do, and they don't offer it as a major?"

"What would that be?"

"I don't know…who knows? It could be anything."

"You're still not sure about what you want? Not at all?"

I glanced at him before putting up another poster. "No."

We started up the stairs. "Well…what do you like to do?"

"Um…"

"You like to watch movies. Listen to music. Cook. There it is!" He pointed at me.

"What?"

"Cooking. You like cooking."

"I do, yeah, but—"

"Have you ever thought about culinary school?"

I took another poster. "I mean, I have thought about it. In a way…but I can't go to culinary school."

"Why the hell not?"

"I don't know! It's so specific. I'm supposed to go to *college* college."

He stopped dead. "Natalie."

"What are you doing?"

"You're not 'supposed to' do anything. You have to do what's going to make you happy. Cooking makes you happy?"

"Sure, yeah. I like it. I'm good at it."

"Do you like anything better, that you can think of?"

I shook my head. "I guess not."

"You don't want to teach, or act, or be a scientist, or become a doctor or lawyer or anything?"

"Hah. No. I do not."

"Can you see yourself being a chef?"

A smile crept across my face involuntarily. "It would be pretty cool."

It felt freeing. Imagining becoming a chef felt like getting away with something. Someone would pay me to do it?

"I guess it doesn't feel like something I could really do. As if it isn't a real job or something. But I know that's dumb. I know it's a real job."

"It absolutely is."

I bit my thumb. "It would be pretty awesome to cook for a living. Every time I ever think about all the other things people are going to school for, I get so stressed, and so discouraged."

"That's because none of those jobs are right for you. I could never become a chef. Same way you probably don't think you would ever want to become a vet."

"God, no."

"There you go. All right, let's hurry up and hang these posters."

"Oh, sorry, I didn't know you were in a hurry."

"I'm not," he said, grinning. "You are."

ONCE HE DECIDED we needed to go fast, we pasted up all the posters within fifteen minutes. Then we were in his car, on the way home, and then walking into my house.

"Hey, Daddy," I said as we walked in.

"Nat, I didn't expect you back already." He muted the TV and turned to us. "And Aiden, too, huh?"

"Yes, sir, how are you tonight?"

"Good, good. Watching a little SportsCenter here."

"Did you see what they were saying about the Redskins this year? The draft is going to be crazy. My buddy and I have a bet going on who we'll land as quarterback."

I made a face at Aiden and then at my dad.

"We're boring Princess Natalie, I think," said my dad.

"Really? Five seconds of football, that's your limit, huh?" He and my dad laughed.

"You kids got some more homework to do?"

"No, actually..." Aiden nudged me. "You want to tell him what you figured out?"

Dad looked at me, intrigued.

"Um, I was thinking about applying to culinary school."

His mouth fell open. "You serious?"

I nodded. "I think so."

"I think it's a great idea, personally," said Aiden. "She likes cooking. She's good at it. And there are a bunch of culinary schools in D.C. I bet she could end up working at a really great restaurant down there somewhere."

"You know, I suggested this to her once and—" he held up his fingers in a circle "—nothing."

"I needed to think!" I said.

"Yeah, yeah. Well, I think it's great, honey. Seriously. Didn't I tell you I liked Aiden?"

Oh, my god. Embarrassing.

"Uh-huh, okay, so we're going to go use my computer, is that fine?"

"The door stays open. And here—" He reached into his back pocket to retrieve his wallet. "Here's my Visa, in case there's an application fee."

"Okay. Thanks, Daddy."

We started up the steps.

"Your dad likes me?" Aiden whispered, smiling brightly at me.

"Don't get too full of yourself, he likes almost everyone." But I smiled back, feeling happier and more settled than I had in as long as I could remember.

"And...submitted." Aiden double-clicked, and then turned around in my desk chair. "How do you feel?"

I was sitting on the edge of the bed, right behind him. He had sat with me for two hours, him on his phone and me on my computer, finding places to apply to. Then he'd helped me fill out applications to two nearby schools and kept me company while I completed dull financial aid forms.

"I feel awesome," I responded. "Really good. It's crazy. I've had no idea at all what I wanted to do. For the longest time."

"Yeah. Sometimes things'll hit you. You figure them out, all of a sudden."

"Apparently."

He snapped his fingers. "Just like that."

"I guess so. It feels right."

He nodded and gave the sides of my thighs a light tap. "Good. I'm glad."

A few seconds of silence. "Yep. Me, too."

His eyes landed on mine, and he held my gaze. My chest lit on fire, and my skin started to tingle.

"I'm glad you finally know what you want." He looked very serious.

I nodded, and when I spoke, my voice was a little quieter than I had expected it to be. "I'm, well…I'm glad you know, too. Being a vet…is so cool…"

He nodded. I wasn't even sure when or how it had happened, but we had grown closer. If I leaned forward, I could kiss him.

I had to resist the strange and crazy impulse to do just that.

The silence suddenly felt so loud. One more nod, and then he dropped his gaze down to his hands. "Fuck," he whispered.

"What?"

He tilted his head and narrowed his eyes at me. He wanted to say something. I didn't know what, but I wanted him to say it.

"Natalie, it's getting pretty late, you gotta wrap it up." My dad's voice echoed up the stairs and into my room.

"'Kay," I yelled back.

When I looked back at him, the moment where he was going to say whatever it was…was gone.

"I should go."

"I guess so…thanks so much for…" I gestured at the air. "Everything, you know."

"Anytime. I'll, um…I'll see you."

CHAPTER SEVENTEEN

AIDEN STARTED ACTING completely weird after that. Even weirder than he had before. Two weeks passed, and I got nothing. No explanation of what he might have been about to say, or why he'd seemed upset when he left, no explanation for why he wasn't talking to me now. He wasn't giving me the silent treatment exactly, but he was in no way trying to start or keep up a conversation with me.

In our class together, he was all business. He even put in his headphones when we met to put things on the boards together.

Self-deprecating as I could often be, I was sure this time that I had done nothing to deserve this. The change in his behavior was so obvious that for once I was sure it wasn't in my head. He had acted one way, something had happened and now he was completely different.

It's upsetting to know you made someone mad with your actions, but it is arguably more infuriating to know this but not know what your actions were. Brooke seemed normal enough. She, too, though, seemed not to be talking to me as much. She said it was because she was studying for her final exams, but I just didn't know. She was normal when we did talk, but it wasn't normal to talk as little as we were.

Today was the day of the prom rally. It marked three weeks exactly till the last day of school for seniors and two weeks until the end of classes and beginning of exams. It also meant prom was two weeks away.

Brooke always got pumped up and excited during this time of year. Weird as she might or might not have been acting over the past couple of weeks, you would never know it from how she flew over to me when she saw me.

"Nattie! I am so excited. But freaking out. What if I don't get nominated in my senior year? I will be humiliated."

"Freshman and sophomore years you were nominated for Homecoming princess and won the second time. And last year you were nominated for Homecoming queen and beat out the senior girls. You only lost prom queen last year because Lauren Hottinger was on crutches with a broken leg from when she was building a house for Habitat. How can you possibly be worried?"

"I'm still convinced that bitch was faking."

"Well…that might be going a bit far."

She shrugged. "I don't know, I don't want to not—ugh, can you imagine?"

No, I couldn't. Because no part of my life had ever been about homecoming or prom court, except in relation to Brooke and all of her anxiety about it every year.

"Well, I voted for you."

"Aw, you did?" she asked, like it wasn't obvious that I would.

"No, I voted for Alexa." I gave her a look. "Obviously, Brooke."

We started making our way to the football field for the rally.

"Oh, there's Aiden," she said, pointing. She held a finger to her lips in a "shh" motion—as if I have ever or would ever scream his name or shout or something.

She snuck up and then jumped on his back. He buckled almost imperceptibly, but then grabbed her under the knees and said, "Hey, babe." He set her down and looked to me. "Natalie."

I noticed now that Eric was with him. I waved with a tight-lipped smile at them both.

"Anyway," Brooke said as we all walked together. "I voted for you, too."

I actually looked around me to see who she was talking to. "Who?"

"You!"

I scoffed. "What a waste of a vote!"

"I don't know." She shrugged. "Everyone talks about you, whether you like it or not. Especially with, ya know…" She glanced up at Eric, who was now back in conversation with Aiden.

I rolled my eyes. "Bull. But that's cute of you to nominate me. Thank you."

"Did you nominate Aiden?" she asked quietly. "Or did you have to vote for Eric?"

It honestly hadn't even occurred to me to do otherwise. "Yeah, I voted for Aiden."

"Okay, good, I want to make sure. Can you imagine how awkward it'd be if, like, Eric won? Or if someone else random did? I do not want my dance to be with someone else."

At the entrance of the stadium, there were a couple SGA students handing out class T-shirts. We gave them our sizes and years and took them. We made our way to the best seats we could get in the bleachers.

It was finally hot out today. It had been an exceedingly

long winter, with an infuriatingly frosty spring. But for the past few weeks it had been warming up nicely. Even without stepping outside, anyone could have guessed it from Brooke's dark, short Daisy Dukes.

"Put on your shirt!" said Brooke, who was pulling hers on over her tube top, and then tugging the tube top down and off. "Come on, don't make me the only loser with school spirit. Why are you in a sweater, anyway, you masochist?"

"I'm always cold in the classrooms." I stood and pulled off my sweater.

"Whoa, where the hell did those come from?"

"What?"

She pointed at my boobs. I hadn't even worn a padded bra today, but they looked big under my tank top.

Aiden stared at me from beyond Eric, who was still talking about...whatever he was talking about. As soon as my eyes locked on his, he looked back to Eric, but I could tell he was not listening. Apparently neither was I, since Brooke punched me in the arm, and said, "Natalie."

"Sorry, Brooke, what?"

"I said let me do your face paint. A little school color under each eye."

I allowed her to put a streak of blue and green under each eye like football paint, and then did the same for her. She immediately whipped out her phone to snap a picture, which was shared within seconds in every available way.

"So." She dropped her voice and put her phone back in her purse. "I think Eric is going to ask you to prom."

"Oh." I guessed I should have seen it coming.

She gave me a look. "Nat! You just need someone to go with."

"I really don't know...that I want to go."

"Oh, hush your face. Me and Aiden will be there and everything. It'll be fun."

A few minutes later, the cheerleaders started their first routine.

Aiden got up and left the bleachers with Eric a few minutes later.

"Where's he going?" I asked. "I mean, they, where are they going?"

"They're doing the next cheer routine with a bunch of the school's jocks. Didn't Eric tell you? It's hilarious."

And it was. All the guys came out a few minutes later in cheer uniforms and wielding pom-poms. It was funny to see the linebackers in belly-exposing shirts, and it was kind of sexy to see the guys being confident enough to pull it off. And, of course, Aiden had those abs and that sexy muscle-V by his hip bones that I was so transfixed by. I stared at him for a second, then looked at Eric. He did, too. His body was pretty incredible. And yet, looking at his did nothing for me.

After all that and a couple of competitions between grades that Brooke and I mostly chatted through, it was time for the prom court nominations. Aiden had returned by this point, and Brooke now gripped one of each of our knees. Eric was sitting next to me, and I was glad he wasn't touching me.

First the underclassmen nominations. Then junior year. Then seniors.

"Nominations for prom king are…" Principal Wallace opened an envelope. "James Reed. Eric Hornby. Matthew Heimer. And Aiden Macmillan."

"Whoo! Yeah, babe!" Brooke put her arms around him and then went back to squeezing my leg. Twice as hard, now that Aiden was making his way to the field.

"Prom queen nominations are Alexa Roberts. Bethany Rogers. Brooke Harris. And Natalie Shepherds."

I felt my insides turn to slush. *No way. No freaking way.* I had heard wrong. I was going to stand up and realize I had totally made it up and make a complete ass out of myself. I was in a haze as Brooke's elated face turned to me and she pulled me up from my seat. Everyone was clapping and whooping. And I felt like I was in a dream.

They blasted some hugely overplayed, up-tempo song I always skipped over on the radio as we went to join the rest.

There we all walked, down the stadium steps, a league of us, nominated by the people we were passing by. The other girls were long, lean, with shiny hair and smiles that showed just enough teeth. They laughed as they stepped confidently down the aluminum steps, seemingly in slow motion. There wasn't much surprise on any face—their own or our audience. I looked at Brooke, who was holding one hand in the air and reaching back for me with the other. I took it. I was one of them. One of the four. Making my own way down the steps.

It had never even seemed like a possibility. Never something I would have expected or even wanted, because it was so crazy. I had spent so long in hiding.

We walked onto the field, and I felt more alive than ever. It was like I was in someone else's shoes. Someone who didn't get awkward when people talked to her. Someone who didn't stay home and watch Netflix most nights or rewatch all the seasons of *Gilmore Girls* instead of going out and drinking or whatever else I had been missing out on.

Maybe I had wasted the past few years. Maybe I could have had a real group of friends that I would have cried about leaving at the end of the year. Maybe I had missed out. Maybe now I recognized what the value was in being a girl with a signature scent and a parking spot, and an effortless, breezy smile that told the world I was not surprised to find myself nominated. Maybe I always could have been this way.

We walked toward the boys. Aiden smiled at Brooke and me, and we all stood together and posed for a yearbook picture.

I imagined how we must look. I was in a shirt that bore the letters *WCHS* written big over the word *Senior*. I had my hair swooped to one shoulder, and school colors under one eye. To someone browsing through the class yearbook in a few years, they would look at us and take us in without ever knowing that I didn't fit in.

And maybe, for once, I wasn't so out of place. Maybe I never had been. Maybe I had always been this girl, hiding under glasses and big sweaters. And if I had realized it a little sooner, there was a chance that maybe I wouldn't have given up Aiden so easily to begin with.

CHAPTER EIGHTEEN

THAT WEEKEND, ERIC had a get-together at his house for the prom court and a few other random people.

Eric's place was a lot smaller than Alexa's, and so was the party—something I actually didn't want for once. It was easier to hide in a big group of people. And to avoid looking at Aiden, who was still acting like I had run over his cat or something.

Despite becoming a little angry with him for his sudden indifference, I was still pitifully fixated on him. Every time he moved, I was aware of it. When he spoke, I listened but tried not to look him in the eyes. Not that he was looking at me, either.

We were about two hours in and a couple of card games deep when Eric asked if he could talk to me. I said sure and followed him outside into the chill of the night.

"What's up?" I asked as I pulled the door behind me.

"Uh…" He bit his lip and—anxiously?—cracked his knuckles. "You wanna help me get this fire pit going?"

It was a little chilly tonight, a fire pit sounded nice. "Sure."

"Cool. Why don't you wad up some of that newspaper there by your feet and toss it into the middle."

"Okay…"

I did as he said, and he gathered some twigs and got a Duraflame log from the shed. Once we had the fire lit, he got around to it.

"So, um, I know I've made it clear I like you. I guess maybe you don't know how you feel about me, or maybe you're not into me…." He looked nervous, and I wondered how many girls in the world had ever seen him like this. I only ever saw other girls acting like nervous twits around him. "But I wanted to know if maybe you would be my date to prom. As friends or as whatever you want. I know that I want to go with you."

I felt almost nothing when he asked. No real disappointment. No excitement. Just apathy.

"Sure. Yeah, that sounds fun."

"For real?"

"Yeah, of course." I put on a smile.

We went back inside after a hug that made me feel equally nothing at all, and he announced it to the room at large. Brooke, Justin, Alexa, Bethany and some others sitting around all gave a cheer for us.

Aiden finally gave me a shimmer of a glance. I literally shook my head in irritation at it. What was his deal?

Eric gave me a squeeze on the shoulder, looking at a text on his phone. "It's Reed, I'll be right back. I gotta show him where to park."

Brooke stood from the couch. "Kitchen?"

She held open her arms once we were out of sight. "Well?

"Well, I got a date!"

"I know! You are not happy. You do not look happy."

I put on a big smile.

She grimaced. "Nope, that didn't work. What's wrong? Why aren't you excited? So many girls would kill to be going with Eric."

"Maybe I should let one of them go, then, and stay home."

"Stay home? You are nominated for prom queen."

"We all know you're going to win, anyway, what does it matter if I'm there or not?"

"That is not true, you have a very good chance, too! And because of everything we have talked about! I have been very generous not forcing you to go out in the past couple of weeks. But going to prom is important!"

"I know," I said, leaning against the fridge, "but...what's the point if it's not going to be...I don't know."

She narrowed her eyes at me and smiled. "You like someone else, don't you?"

"What? No!" My heart was in my stomach. Dark flashes went through my mind.

"You totally do. Otherwise, you wouldn't care either way! You like someone. Who is it? Tell me tell me tell me."

"No one! I don't like anyone. I don't like Eric that way, that's all."

"I don't believe you."

"Okay, don't believe me, fine." Upon seeing the wounded look on her face, I added, "I'm sorry. I don't know what my problem is."

"Well, I think if you do like someone else, you should go for it. You can't sit around wanting someone and not doing anything about it. And if you want to tell me who it is, then you can, but I won't ask again." She looked innocently at the ceiling.

I suddenly hated myself for any private thoughts I'd been having about Aiden. All day for, like, ever. And here was

Brooke, the movie character who had no idea what had happened right under her nose.

"Meanwhile," she said, pouring herself a shot from a bottle in the freezer. She held it toward me and I shook my head. I was already feeling a little woozy. "I think Aiden is cheating on me."

Lurch. "Why?"

"I don't know," she said before taking the shot and making no face at all. "I have a feeling. He's acting a little different lately. Not as affectionate. Doesn't get jealous. Barely cares if I can or can't hang out. Like, it's been for a while. I don't know, maybe he's mad at me about past stuff. But he didn't seem that mad. And then…the past couple of days he's just been basically silent."

Why would he be giving *both* of us the silent treatment?

"Sure you don't want some?" she asked.

"No. I'm pretty sure that stuff is making me fat. I feel like a tub of lard."

"You're fine," she said, but in a way that made me think maybe she agreed with me. "It does add weight, though. I have to be all salads and stuff now most of the time. Remember when I put on that, like, ten pounds last year after only two months of drinking beer and stuff?"

She poured herself another shot and took it.

"Brooke…"

"What?"

"Two shots in a row?"

She snorted. "Oh, Nat, it's seriously not a big deal." She looked at me. "I'm just…I don't know, I'm not feeling all that drunk yet. Just kicking myself into gear."

"Why do you need to be drunk?"

"God, Mom, shut up." She laughed, but it didn't meet her eyes. "But…listen, you don't know anything, do you?"

"Know anything?"

"About Aiden. You guys have gotten tighter in the past couple months…."

What was she implying? My heart was pounding. Did she have a feeling I liked him?

"What would I know?" I asked.

She shrugged and then laughed. "I'm sure nothing. But who knows, he might have confided in you or something. Like maybe something happened, and he asked your advice. And maybe you would tell him not to tell me…"

Before my feelings for Aiden, I would have found this whole conversation insane. Of course I would tell her.

"It was a stupid question," she said, waving away the conversation like it was a cloud of gnats. "I'm being dumb. Come on, let's go have fun."

BROOKE GOT DRUNKER and drunker. Everyone else was pretty intoxicated, too, but she was on a whole other level. For a long time, she seemed fine. Her usual hammered version of herself. Then, around one in the morning, as the party started to die down, I watched as she faded into a much darker type of intoxication. She was outside with a few people, then came back in, looking kind of upset—and then she hit her rock bottom for the night. We were almost alone in the living room when she fell backward into a wall.

"Brooke! Shit…" I went over to her and kneeled on the ground where she had ended up.

"I'm fine!" She smiled and batted my hands away. "That was a clumsy thing, not a drunk thing."

"Right, I know, but I still want to make sure you're okay."

"I'm good. Maybe jus' help me up and into that room I put my stuff in?"

"Okay." I stood and pulled her up.

In a dizzying few seconds, she fell backward again, and then spilled her bright red drink all over her favorite white Nordstrom blouse. I knew how much she had spent on it, and that it would kill her in the morning to realize what she had done.

"Jesus, Brooke." I covered my own face in horror.

"Ohmigod, ohmigod, ohmigod…" She was whispering to herself. I watched the tears start to come. I recognized them as her embarrassment tears.

"Come on, stand up, let's get you to the bathroom."

It was a struggle, but I finally got her up and out of the living room.

I tied up her hair in a messy bun on top of her head, then pulled her shirt off, trying not to get anything on her face. I took off the shirt I had over my tank top and set it aside to put on her after getting the sticky crap off her.

She was crying and telling me how much she loved me and how sorry she was. I gave nonanswers back as I wiped her face and chest with a washcloth, telling her it was okay, not to worry, I wasn't mad. We'd been in there for about fifteen minutes when someone knocked on the door.

"Brooke? You in there?"

"It's both of us, hold on," I called, then asked Brooke, "Do you want Aiden to come in?"

She nodded.

I opened the door.

"Throwin' up?" he asked, taking a seat next to me on the side of the tub.

"No, she spilled her drink. Not a big deal."

He reached over and rubbed her back. "You okay, Brooke?"

"Yeah. I'm dizzy, though."

I worked the red out of the shirt as well as I could, and then hung the damp fabric over the shower rod. I helped her into

my shirt. She agreed that it was time for her to go to bed, so
Aiden led her into an empty bedroom.

As soon as her head hit the pillow… "I love you both…so
much…" she muttered as we left the room.

Aiden and I went outside. I did not want to talk and wake
people up now that they were passing out.

It was slightly chilly, but still warm by the fire pit. He lit it
up again, and we sat in two of the cushioned chairs surround-
ing it. I wondered what we could possibly have to talk about
after the way he'd been acting.

"Does she do that a lot?" I asked. "Get that blasted, I mean.
I know she gets drunk, but…"

He ran a hand through his hair, looking tired. "Enough
that it's a pain in the ass. It's one thing to do it every once in
a while. I can't feel sorry for her anymore, when it's her own
damn fault. She's going to feel like shit tomorrow, too."

"I don't know why she's doing that."

"To be cool? To have a problem for someone else to fix?
Or maybe because she doesn't learn? Could be any of that."

He still wasn't looking me in the eyes. After almost a full
minute of silence, I'd had it.

"All right, Aiden, what is your deal?"

"What do you mean?"

"I mean, you've been acting totally weird. I don't know
why, or what I did." A stupid impulse to cry took me over. I
wasn't usually a crier. I breathed through it. "You helped me
with my culinary school stuff, and then got…mad or…some-
thing. I don't even know what happened. You left, and you
haven't acted normal at all since then."

The expression on his face told me that he knew exactly
what I meant.

"It's not…" He ruffled his hair. "You didn't do anything
wrong. It's not you."

"Well, what the hell is it, then?" I had never yelled or spoken so familiarly with him.

He took a deep breath and then leaned forward, elbows on his knees. He bit his bottom lip and stared at the logs. "I have to break up with Brooke."

I hadn't been expecting that.

Just then, she pulled open the back door and came out.

"What the fuck are you guys doing out here?"

Aiden sat up. "Talking, Brooke. I thought you were asleep."

"You're out here, like, arguing like a…like a fucking couple or something. Seriously, what the fuck."

Her eyes were a tiny bit out of focus, and I could tell she was having trouble standing completely upright.

"We were just talking, Brooke." I quickly realized I should say nothing else. I sounded like I was lying. My heartbeat was in my throat. I was dying to ask Aiden more. Why had she wandered out just then?

"Aiden, what's your damage exactly?" She slurred a little. "I fuckin' I told you that your lil' friendship with Natalie made me feel weird. I told you that. And yet you're filling out applications with her, sledding with her, sittin' out here just talking…and I just heard you yelling." She pointed to me.

Neither of us spoke.

"Fucking. Whatever, guys. Why don't you guys get married? I don't fucking care anymore."

She looked to each of us, waiting for us to say something.

"Brooke…" I started. She raised her eyebrows and leaned toward me.

"What, Natalie?"

I didn't know what.

She threw a hand in the air. "Natalie, will you come inside and sleep with me? Aiden, I think you should go home."

I resisted the urge to look to him, and instead wordlessly

followed her inside. She didn't say anything else, either. We went into the dark room, crawled into the bed and the night was over. She probably fell asleep immediately. But I felt like I was up all night.

I listened to Aiden close the front door, to the sound of his car starting and pulling out, and then silence for hours.

"I'M SO SORRY," said Brooke the next morning as we drove out of Eric's neighborhood. "About last night. It's so humiliating... I don't even remember what I was upset about. I just remember yelling at you. For talking to Aiden, I guess? I'm so sorry."

"No, it's fine."

"God, he's gonna be so pissed."

I didn't know that he would. Not after what he had told me. How he wanted to break up with her. I hated knowing that he had said that and not feeling like I could tell her.

"I'm sure it'll be fine," I said, going with the pat answer.

"I hope so. If he breaks up with me over this..." She shook her head, and I felt a stab of sympathy for her. Until she kept talking. "If he breaks up with me, I'll have...like, what, six days to get a date for prom?"

I WAS IN a relatively irritable mood for the next week. For the first time all year, I was busy. Some of my stress came from the fact that I knew I would hear back from the culinary schools this week, some of it from the tests I had to study for, some from the fact that I never heard another word about Aiden and Brooke's potential breakup. From either of them. She had been busy, and we had hardly chatted except in the morning when she drove me to school. Aiden was too swamped to drive us. According to Brooke.

Friday afternoon, I finally got a chance to sit and do nothing. Everything had been turned in. The only thing left between me and graduation was prom, a couple of exams and the ceremony itself.

My dad came home from running errands a few hours after I got home from school and surveyed the scene.

"What on earth is happening here?"

I was curled up in a ball on the couch, tears streaming down my face watching *Titanic,* with half of a box of Oreos and an empty popcorn bag in front of me.

I sniffed and had a sip of the lemonade I was drinking. "It's the saddest movie, and you know the whole time that they're going to reach a tragic end!"

"You girls and your crying over movies." He put down the two bags of groceries he came in with.

"Hey, I never usually cry over movies."

He gave me a look, and then came over and sat down in the armchair next to me.

"Is there anything you want to talk about, Nat?"

"What do you mean?" I wiped a tear from my cheekbone.

"I mean that…I want to know what's going on with you. You're—" he did the so-so motion with his hand "—off."

"Off?"

"You're not yourself. You've been getting sick, and now you're crying…."

"I'm fine. It's a really stressful semester, that's all. Everyone's busy and stressing out. It's not only me. Seriously. Girls who usually dress nicely for school and wear jeans and cute boots and stuff, they're all showing up with their hair up and glasses on, looking like they haven't slept in a month."

"You don't seem to be having that problem. You're sleeping half of every day away lately."

"It's normal senior year stress, Dad, it's fine."

He sighed and then glanced at the coffee table. His eyes locked on my cup. "Is that lemonade?"

"Yeah?"

He blinked a couple of times and then leaned forward in his chair. "Natalie, I'm just going to ask…there's no way you're pregnant, is there?"

My immediate response was to laugh. "God, no. Are you kidding? Me. Hah."

But then something started to prickle under my skin. My heartbeat quickened. My eyes blurred.

My dad's voice sounded miles away. "When your mom was pregnant with you, she couldn't get enough of lemonade and cookies."

"I think I hear my phone ringing upstairs." I stood up quickly and darted up to my room.

CHAPTER NINETEEN

OH, MY GOD.

Oh, my God.

When was the last time I had had my period? I hadn't even thought about it. I had been so entirely consumed by the Aiden and Brooke thing, the "next year" thing and our senior project...I hadn't even noticed.

Hadn't I had it last month? No...not really. I'd bled for maybe an afternoon and that was it. I hadn't really thought anything of it.

It was like watching a reverse video of a mirror being shattered. Everything was suddenly flying into place, and I was stuck staring at my own reflection and thinking, How the hell did I not realize this, and what the hell am I going to do?

I'd been sick constantly. I was tired all the time. My boobs had been looking, as Brooke put it, "seriously awesome" in bras. And now I couldn't remember my last period. I started crying and collapsed onto the floor.

My dad knocked lightly and then pushed the door open. I

was too horrified to stop him or to hide my tears. I fell into deep sobs, and allowed him to help me off the floor and into the edge of the bed, where I fell into his side and cried. I felt him take in a deep breath, but he said nothing.

I was in a blind, red-eyed haze as I buckled into the passenger seat in the car and was driven to CVS Pharmacy. He didn't make me come in, and returned after a few minutes with a bag. I had resumed crying while he was inside, and cried even harder when I saw that he had purchased a bag of my favorite candy as well as three different pregnancy tests.

I couldn't look at him. I couldn't even think about the details of what this meant. Even as I did the tests, I knew what they would say. Positive. And then positive again. And then once more. Positive.

My dad let me stay alone in my room and didn't force me to talk about it right away. He always knew what I needed. He was such a good father.

After an afternoon in shock and hiding in my room, my dad called me downstairs, where we sat down at the kitchen table and had a talk.

"Natalie, how did this happen?" He spoke softly.

I shrugged. I couldn't look him in the eye. "I don't know. I went to one stupid party."

"The one…that was a while ago, back in February, right?"

"The day after Valentine's Day."

He did the math in his head. Three months. In this context, it was not simply three months. It was a trimester.

"I guess you didn't use protection then, or did you?"

"I don't know." I shouldn't have said that. The expression on his face made me immediately regret it.

"You don't *know?*"

"No. I drank a lot. And you know I don't drink, ever. So I kind of…blacked out and don't remember."

"Do you remember...sleeping with..."

I didn't think it was possible to feel worse than I did, but confessing all the sleazy, classless details out loud and to my father was doing the trick.

"Eric."

"Eric? I've never even heard you talk about an Eric."

"That's because I don't really have much to say about him."

My dad exhaled. "Have you thought about what you want to do?"

Neither of us looked at the other. I knew this was going to be a sore subject because of my own mother.

"I haven't...I mean I didn't even realize until today..."

He nodded and massaged his jawbone. "All right. Well." Finally I met his gaze, and the disappointment and sadness I saw there made my throat tight and my heart hurt. I knew exactly why he was mad. Exactly why he was upset.

"Daddy, I'm really sorry."

"You don't need to say sorry to me, Natalie, you have no one to apologize to." The volume of his voice was rising. He rarely yelled or got angry, but I knew that this was the one thing that could do it.

"I'm not the same kind of person as Mom."

"No, you're not. But this is how it happened to us."

"How *it* happened? How *I* happened. I made the same mistake as you guys."

"No." He said it loudly as he stood and crossed to the kitchen sink. "I did not say mistake, Natalie."

"Yeah, okay, but she did. Didn't she? I know you remember when I was ten years old, sitting right up there." I pointed at the top of the stairs. "I remember you telling her to shape up or ship out, and I remember that she blamed you for me, because you were the one that didn't let her get an abortion."

"Oh, sweetie..." He put his hands on his hips and stared

at the floor. "This is why I'm upset with you, Natalie. Not because you're a teenager who got yourself into trouble. But because I hate that you're going to have to wrestle with this choice. And that it's so loaded, because of your mom. And me."

My eyes were filling with tears. "That's why I have no idea what the hell I'm going to do, Daddy. Because I was almost... well, I was almost never born. And...that would have been Mom's choice. And now I have that choice."

He came to my side, pulled me up and hugged me as only a daddy can. "We'll figure this out, Natalie. It's going to be okay."

CHAPTER TWENTY

THE NEXT MORNING, it took me a minute to remember the very real truth.

I was pregnant. I, Natalie Shepherds, notorious good girl, was *pregnant*. I was a pregnant teenager.

I climbed out of bed and looked in the mirror. It took me a full minute to get up the courage to really survey myself. Finally, I picked up the edge of my T-shirt and looked at my body from the side.

Yes, I had been feeling bloated and fat. But I had also been eating constantly, and—though not anymore—been drinking. I'd figured it was bad habits that were making me feel bad. It was clear now that I had been in some serious denial. The small bulge that had formed in my lower abdomen made the whole situation undeniably real.

I dropped the edge of my shirt, feeling a little faint. I had no idea how I had let this happen. The inarguable reality of it made me feel numb.

And today, not twenty-four hours after finding out that I

was pregnant, I had to go to prom. Where I would not only be a pregnant high schooler, but a pregnant prom queen nominee.

IT WAS FOUR in the afternoon, and Brooke had just led me upstairs and dropped her robe. She was standing in her bathroom in nude stockings and a bra, looking a hundred pounds thinner than I felt. Her hair was back in a sleek, tight, Heidi Klum–ish ponytail. Even without makeup, which she hadn't applied yet, she looked gorgeous.

"So your hair," she said, "what are you going to do to it?"

"I figured I'd leave it up to you."

She popped her hip and looked thoughtfully at my hanging, straight black hair. "I'm thinking controlled-messy—loose tendrils and side bangs. It's going to look good. Especially since your dress is so retro."

I had been really excited about my dress. Brooke had picked it out for me online last week and insisted I get it. My dad had approved, and it had arrived a few days ago. It was ivory, with a formfitting top and a loose skirt. I was glad of this, since I was now overly aware of my stomach.

Brooke's dress was a tan–gold color. It was strapless and tight on top, very tight on the waist, with a mild-tutu-type thing happening on bottom. It was one of the many things that might look bad on a hanger but looked incredible on Brooke.

I allowed her to do my hair, as I always did, and then she started in on my makeup. She was in high spirits, laughing and chatting as she applied subtle fake eyelashes to my eyes, buffed foundation into my skin, stood back and looked at me, did a few more things…and this went on and on.

Finally she turned me toward the mirror.

I almost didn't recognize myself. I had let her do my makeup a million times, but never to this extent. Usually just eye shadow or eyeliner she wanted to try out on me. But I looked…like someone not pregnant. Someone who looked like they might be nominated for prom queen and possibly win.

The type of girl boys fall in love with, and the kind that Brooke had told me I could be.

"You look hot, right?" she said proudly. "I like the hair the best, you look like a 1940s movie star. Okay, now stop admiring yourself, I only have half an hour to do my makeup and that is really pushing the limit."

I sat down on the toilet lid and watched her start in on her own fake eyelashes.

"Okay, so I need to tell you something," I said.

"What's up?" She held a set to her upper lid and let it dry.

I watched her for a second, feeling the tears start again in my throat.

"What are you doing!" she squealed. "Nothing can be worse than ruining all that work I did!" But she seemed to see on my face that, yes, something could be worse. "Natalie, what's happening?"

I couldn't summon speech at first. She waited patiently until I finally sputtered, "I'm f-fucking pregnant."

I fell into a sob and heard the words echoing around the room.

Brooke's voice was soft and quiet. "You're what?"

I nodded into my own hands.

"Oh, my…oh, my God, Natalie. How is that possible?"

"That one night…the S-Stupid Cupid party at Alexa's."

Brooke kneeled on the ground next to me and pulled me into a tight hug. "Eric?"

I nodded, and she let me cry into her shoulder for minutes on end.

When I finally composed myself, she pulled away and moved my face so that I could look at her. "It's okay, Natalie." She still seemed stunned, but like she knew she needed to be the dependable one for once. "It's going to be fine."

I nodded. I had no idea how that was possible, but I had to believe she and my dad were right.

She got me dressed and ready like I was a doll, lifting my feet to put them into heels, fixing my hair and makeup again, putting my jewelry on me. She tore her stockings kneeling on the bathroom floor with me, I noticed. She took them off without saying anything, and tossed them before finishing her own final touches.

It was going to be a long night.

WE ATE AT Maria's Cucina, an Italian restaurant, where I could find almost nothing that sounded appetizing to me. I usually loved Italian food, and I wasn't sure if it was the stress of the night or a symptom of my current condition that was doing it. I ordered fettuccine Alfredo, since Brooke agreed to have some. She was only getting a caprese salad, because she didn't want to feel bloated.

Eric was deep in sports talk with Aiden across the table from us. Bethany was with Reed, who was about the last person I felt like spending time with. Really, I could do without either of them. Alexa was with Sam, Reed's friend. I guess they had worked things out.

While everyone was talking, Brooke kept tossing glances my way, then looking at Eric. I avoided her gaze each time, but people started to notice that we were both quiet. Alexa nudged me and asked if Brooke was okay. It was more noticeable that she was being quiet.

"She's fine," I said, and then turned to Brooke. "Bathroom."

"We'll be right back," she said to the table.

We went into the big stall, and I crossed my arms at her. "You can't be quiet and weirded out all night."

"How can I not be?"

"Because it's not your problem."

"Of course it's my problem. If it's your problem, then it's my problem. You know that. It's always that way."

Aw, Brooke.

"Yeah. I know. But look, I'm really...I'm okay about it." This wasn't true at all, but I needed to say it. "This is prom. I intend to have a good time. And frankly, you're bringing me down."

"Nattie..."

"I mean it!" I tried to look as genuine as I could.

"It's...it's too weird! Are you going to tell him?"

"Later. Maybe on Monday. Or tomorrow. Or any other time. But tonight is prom. And you've been dying for this night your whole life. So stop worrying about me. We have plenty of time after tonight to do that."

She nodded and then unzipped her clutch. "Okay, well, if you're sure, then I'm pretty sure this is a night that calls for a drink or two. For...for me anyway." She withdrew her silver flask and took a long, multigulp swig.

Ordinarily, this would have been annoying to me, something I would try to stop her from doing. But tonight, for once, I would rather she be buzzed and not thinking about real life. I wanted her to have fun...and not stare at me all night.

AT THE TABLE, Brooke poured more of the flask's contents into her Sprite, downed it in about five minutes, then ordered and refilled another. It didn't take long to see the effects. She was back in the conversation, talking loudly and cheerfully. By the end of dinner, she had emptied her flask, and she and everyone else were having a ball.

Aiden, Eric, Brooke and I took Aiden's Jeep. When we

pulled up to the school, Brooke reached into her overnight bag and pulled out the rest of the bottle.

"Brooke," I said, pushing it out of sight. "Drink, fine, whatever, but we cannot get caught with that shit here!"

"Oh, come on, it's completely dark out." She held it up to Aiden. "Want some?"

He shook his head. "I'm good."

Brooke sneered. "Of course you are. Can you do me a favor and not judge me for once?"

He said nothing and looked away. I could almost see him bite his tongue. She was verging on that tipping point into mean Brooke.

Reed whipped into a parking spot across from us, his headlights on. He, Bethany, Alexa and Sam spilled out of the car.

"Guys. Let's relax and have a little fun." Brooke turned up the speakers in the Jeep, blasting "Kids" by Sleigh Bells. "Stop being so concerned about everything. Nothing is really that bad. Seriously, chill out!"

She kicked off her shoes and took down her hair, which had miraculously not gotten crimped in the ponytail band. She ran over to Reed's car and turned on the brights. Aiden and I flinched in the glare.

Brooke bounced up to Alexa, and they danced in the middle of the street. They were silhouettes, both perfect, thin cheerleader-quality bodies. I thought, as I watched her, that she had lost weight lately.

Brooke held up the bottle and let Alexa drink from it. Reed came over to them, smoking a cigarette. He grabbed Brooke's hips and grinded on her from behind, and then laughed at Eric, Aiden and me. Eric went over.

Brooke and Alexa danced together, and I watched all three of the guys and Bethany watch them. Aiden looked like he'd rather be anywhere else. Bethany just looked mad.

Eric grabbed the bottle. "I'll take some."

"See, Aiden," she shouted, "some people like to have fun besides me."

Eric took a few hearty sips from the bottle before handing it back to her. "Damn, that is sweet."

"Oh, get over it, at least it's something."

"You want some?" She held it up to me. "Come on, have some." She shimmied her shoulders at me.

"I don't—"

"What are you, afraid of Eric's cooties? I think it's too late for that!" She whispered the last part and then burst into giggles with Alexa.

Aiden didn't acknowledge her at all. I didn't know what to say, since the reason I was saying no went beyond my own prudishness. The mood she was in now, I didn't trust her not to say something to give me away. I could imagine her thinking she was whispering or making a thinly veiled comment.

"Aiden—" she smiled "—you and I used to have so much fun. When did you get all stiff?" She gave him a look that I understood meant that she was aware of her slightly sexual phrasing.

He stepped back, and away from her.

"Gahhd," she said before walking away again. After they finished dancing, she grabbed her clutch from the front seat.

"I'm sure they're going to check bags at the door," Aiden snapped at her.

"Yeah, maybe, but not inner thighs!" She lifted her dress a little, exposing a garter on the inside of her leg. It was barely covered by her dress. I watched everyone's gaze go to her thigh. "I only need to get in with it, once we're in there I can put it back in my purse. Come on, let's go!"

She slipped back into her heels and skipped off with Alexa, Sam trailing in their wake.

Eric smacked Aiden on the chest. "Dude, not to be weird? But your girlfriend is fucking badass."

"Damn right I am!" Brooke answered from fifteen feet ahead.

Aiden looked at me. "Maybe it's just me," he said, "but fuck that."

I resisted the urge to ask when and if he still intended to end it.

Instead, I let Eric take my hand and followed Brooke. I watched her, backlit by the lights of the school, wobbling a little in her pumps. Reed walked with her, Bethany clinging to his other side, and though I couldn't hear the words Brooke said, I heard a tone I recognized well. Charming Brooke. Witty Brooke.

Fall-in-love-with-me Brooke.

God. She really would turn it on for anyone.

Aiden, Eric and I walked in silence from the car to the school, all of us seeing but not saying a word.

Brooke did get into the school with no problem. She strutted into the gym, which was dark and loud and hot, already filled with sweating bodies. Kanye and Jay-Z's song "Why I Love You" was blasting and making the room shake. Every five words there was a censored swear word. Why even bother playing it?

Looking around at everyone gyrating on one another, I guessed I understood why.

Brooke spun around and pulled me to her. She had looked so put together earlier, and she still did, but her dark eyeliner had melted down a little. Typical for Brooke, it only made her look sexier.

She left Aiden and Eric to find their own way and led me to the center of the dance floor.

Soon we were surrounded by her many friends. I could see

now that she had been right. Everyone was either drinking or already drunk. I really didn't feel like dancing, of all things, right now, but she kept pulling me to her and making me.

After a few songs, she yelled something at me, and I couldn't understand her. I made the motion for *I can't hear you,* and she just laughed and held the flask to my mouth. I shook my head and pushed her hand away, but she said something else and tried again. Everyone nearby was looking at me.

Suddenly the heavy bass seemed louder and more intrusive. I tried to regain my composure even as I felt myself sinking into my old position: Brooke's un-fun friend.

For once, I didn't really give a damn. Especially with what was going on with me, I wanted the safety of home and my own bed. I didn't want to be out here masquerading as a normal teenager. If I ever had been one, I was certainly not one now.

I didn't know where Aiden was, but I could see Eric dancing with Bethany, Alexa and Sam. Brooke had drifted away from me a little, and I had to search for a few seconds to catch sight of her.

She was obviously drunk. Dancing with…who was that? Reed.

He had his face on her neck, and she had a hand on his jaw. Just as I saw them, though, she broke away from him, looking nothing but wasted, and went back to dancing with other girls. He stared at her, looking annoyed, and then stalked off.

I broke away from the group, feeling dizzy and burning hot. I burst out into the hall, which was fluorescent-lit, and which I knew probably made me look exactly how I felt— sick. I realized I had gone out a side door. I was by the math classrooms. I took a few deep breaths, grateful for the emptiness of the hall.

A moment later, I heard the door open behind me. I turned to see Aiden.

"Shit," I whispered to myself, sniffing and trying to adjust my makeup under my eyes.

"What's going on? Are you okay? You ran right past me. I don't even think you saw me."

I leaned against the wall. The cold felt good on my back.

"Yes, I'm fine. Too hot."

"Wait here, I'll get you some water."

"No, Aiden, really—"

But he was already gone. I slid down the wall and sat on the ground with my eyes shut. It felt like hours until he came back, but I knew it had been only a few minutes.

He sat down next to me. "Here, drink this."

I did. It felt good.

"Were you drinking with Brooke?"

"No."

"I didn't think so."

"Yeah. I think I hate prom."

"Oh, yeah. Tell me about it. What wouldn't I give to be back at your place watching more Hitchcock movies." He tossed me a side glance with a tight smile.

I remembered what I had wished for when Brooke and I had had our spa night. I had wished for a guy to leave parties with. To watch movies with. I had thought of Aiden then. I would give anything to leave with him and do just that.

Meanwhile, Brooke was inside doing whatever the hell with Reed. Yes, I had meant it when I'd told her I would never care if she was ever stupid enough to hook up with him. But it did bother me that this seemed only to endear him to her more.

I mean, I did lose my virginity to him.

Meanwhile, Aiden was out here being a good guy to her best friend. They didn't have a real relationship anymore.

He was a placeholder until she went off to school. A way to spend her days.

"Yeah," he went on. "I would love to get the hell out of here. Have some more of that hot chocolate."

"It's May," I said with a laugh. "It's not hot chocolate season anymore."

"Anything, then. Whatever you wanted to make me."

I bit my tongue and turned to him. His eyes scanned my face. My heart swelled. I didn't just want to spend time with him. Or flirt with him. I didn't even just want to kiss him or put my hands under his T-shirt. I wanted him to be my person. The one I could call when I was upset, happy, angry, any of it. And I wanted to be the person he needed.

My swollen heart sank as I realized that now there was even more of an obstacle thrown into the mix. Not only was he Brooke's boyfriend—even once they were no longer together, he'd still be Brooke's property—but now I had the whole pregnancy thing thrown in. With Eric.

I remembered how I had felt almost nothing when he'd asked me to prom. And it hadn't even occurred to me to be jealous to see him dancing with Bethany just now.

I shook my head without even meaning to.

"What's wrong?" Aiden asked.

I covered my face and spoke into my palms. "Oh, nothing. Nothing at all. The whole world sucks, that's all."

"No, it doesn't."

"Yes, it does." I sighed. "Because I fucking...I liked you when you came to this school. I liked you all along, and I still like you. And I hate how miserable I have to be about it."

I didn't uncover my face. Instead, I buried it in my arms and pulled my knees toward me.

A moment later, he put an arm around me and whispered, "Hey."

I lifted my face, expecting him to say something meant to be reassuring. But instead, he kissed me.

The kiss ran through my whole body. I never wanted to stop. I could have stayed in that half–lit math hallway, on the cold, dirty floor for my whole life.

His hand reached for mine, and our legs rested against each other. I wanted to move closer. I almost did, but then pulled away.

Oh, no…

Elation was lifting me off the ground and into the clouds, but guilt was creeping up my spine, wrapping around each vertebra.

"We should go back in," he said. This time, unlike before when our moments together had been unexpected, he didn't look guilty or upset. "They'll be announcing the prom court winners soon, and we can't miss that."

He helped me up and pulled me toward him. Not all the way, and I longed to fill the gap.

And just like that, we went back into the fray.

"Do me a favor," he said as we neared our group again. "Don't hook up with Eric."

His lips were so close to my ear when he said it, and I could feel his warm breath on my skin. I shut my eyes and pulled away.

The music faded, and Principal Wallace's voice came on to the speakers. "All right, attention please. It's time to announce prom court!"

Cheers and applause.

First he announced the underclassmen's prince and princess. I didn't know either of them.

Then the moment of truth.

"This year's king…is Aiden Macmillan."

I had known it, of course, so I turned to him and smiled

and clapped. He gave a small bow and smiled at me before going up to the stage.

The applause died down, and Principal Wallace allowed everyone to take a moment with baited breath. I looked at Brooke, who had collected herself and looked presentable again. She was staring directly at Principal Wallace until she felt my gaze on her.

I smiled at her excitedly, waiting for them to say her name.

"And finally, the queen. Natalie Shepherds!"

The applause lifted and rose again, but I felt my heart sink into my shoes. My eyes widened, and my smile faded. Brooke kept her face turned toward me and I watched her take a deep breath.

This was not happening. Brooke would absolutely lose it. It literally seemed like a joke. It might seriously be a joke.

Feeling sicker than I had in the hallway, I walked toward the stage. I had never fainted before, but I felt scarily on the brink. The noise and applause around me fell into a muffled hum, and my head spun. I looked at Aiden, who was looking as freaked as I was, but not quite as shocked. I looked for Brooke again but couldn't see her anywhere. I climbed the stairs and stood in the spotlight with Aiden. They put the crowns on us and said to smile. We each put one on for the picture but couldn't make eye contact.

Finally I spotted Brooke again in the audience. She was smiling, too, and trying to look genuine, but I could tell that it wasn't real. I would bet anything, too, that if I could see her eyes, they'd be brimming with unspent tears. Reed nudged her and pointed at us, whispering something to her.

I wanted to be sick. It wasn't until now, when I had won one of the most exciting honors a girl can win in her senior year and I had to dance with Aiden to the senior prom song, that it all really hit me.

I had never been more revolted by myself.

CHAPTER TWENTY-ONE

WE DIDN'T LAST the whole song. The second people stopped looking up at us alone, we pulled away from each other and stepped down off the stage. I went into the crowd to find Brooke. Everyone was grabbing me and talking to me, congratulating me and asking me questions, but I couldn't answer any of them.

I searched everywhere for her before finally finding her dancing with a bunch of people.

One second Brooke was stepping away from Alexa, the next she was looking horrified, and the next—she had her hand to her mouth and was sinking to the floor. She had just puked. At prom. Into her own hand. In front of everyone she knew.

Alexa looked helplessly at me, and then said, "She had a sip, and then this…"

It was almost worse than in the movies when the music screeches to a halt. Instead, the music pounded on, and people's gasps and laughter and comments made the din louder and more chaotic. Aiden and I immediately jumped into our roles. He scooped her off the floor and I took to his side to open doors and take her immediately outside and to the curb by the car. I ran back to the bathroom to grab paper towels and fill a cup with water and followed. He set her down and stood back. His hand was on his hip and he was pacing. Aiden was mad.

Brooke looked like a broken, dirty Barbie sitting there. The kind you might find in a spider-filled corner of a garage. She had her face on her forearm and I could see that she was crying. I took her hands in mine and cleaned them off as well as I could with my limited supplies, and lifted her face so I could make sure that was clean, too.

"Brooke, you have got to get your shit together as quickly as you can so we can get you home. The chaperones are going to figure out what happened, and we need leave so that they can't know for sure that it's from alcohol."

"Even though it's obvious," Aiden added.

"That's not going to help right now."

He leaned back on his car and muttered, "Sorry."

"Babe, please don't be mad at me. I'm so sorry, I didn't mean to get so drunk. I didn't even have that much."

He launched himself off the car. "Brooke, your bloodstream is probably about seventy percent alcohol right now, so save it. You did mean to get drunk. And you did have a lot, obviously, look at you."

I didn't want to stop him. He was right. And we needed to talk to her about it. But now wasn't the time. "Aiden. Seriously. Just give it a rest for now."

"Am I wrong, Nat? No, I'm not."

"I'm so fucking *sorry,* Aiden, that I ruined *your* special night. No, shut up. Do you think I wanted to do this? Do you think I wanted to lose out to my best friend, and then hurl onto my prom dress and into my own fucking hand? No! So stop yelling at me!"

"No, you didn't mean to, but you didn't mean not to! You're such an enormous pain in the ass. I can't do this with you, I'm so sick of it. You can't just be a mess that Nat or I have to deal with."

I was stunned and I didn't know what to say. She was staring up at him with so much hurt and hate in her eyes.

"Do you agree with him?" she asked, turning her glare at me.

I went red. "What do you want me to say, Brooke, you have to make a change—"

"Fuck you. Fuck you both. That's…just…fuck you both. I am so sick of this. I keep just turning a blind eye on you guys. You keep ganging up on me, and I'm sick of it! It's like I'm just this little idiot you both have the burden of having to care for." She was yelling now. "And I'm not! I'm not into the same crap as you guys, and I might like to go to parties and whatever but you two are the exception to the rule. I could be a lot worse, so stop judging me constantly!"

I looked around and realized that Eric, Reed, Alexa, Sam and Bethany had joined us.

Brooke railed on. "I dunno if you guys are flirting, or bound together in this little Hate Brooke Club or what. But, Aiden, seriously, you think Natalie's so fucking perfect. But everyone has shitty nights where they make a mistake or two. Natalie fucked Eric at Alexa's party when she was blackout wasted. Not the smartest move, right? But *I'm* the idiot who can't—"

"That's not true," interrupted Eric. "I heard that rumor, too, but I would have thought you'd know it wasn't true, Brooke."

She looked bewilderedly at him for a moment. The rest of us seemed frozen in time.

"You didn't hook up with Natalie," she clarified.

I couldn't turn to look at him. I just heard him say, "No. Absolutely not. I kissed her. That's it."

"Then…"

The pieces were coming together for Brooke. As soon as I heard Eric object, I knew the truth, too.

"Then you…" she started again. Her eyes narrowed into slits, and her chest heaved. She gave one humorless laugh and then shook her head at me with an ugly smile. "You fucking bitch."

I fell back from where I'd been kneeling next to her. "Br—"

"Oh, no. You do not fucking speak." She laughed again. I couldn't do anything but sit there on my ass, shocked. Numbed. Horrified. It was like a nightmare.

"Reed, you mind giving us all a ride? Home, or wherever?"

"'Course not."

Bethany and Alexa walked to Brooke's sides and helped her up. I felt like I had disappointed them, too. Like I wasn't who they'd thought I was, either.

Eric looked like he didn't know what to do and wasn't quite catching on.

"Eric, you're coming with us. Mom and Dad over there have a lot of shit to figure out tonight."

Eric caught my gaze for a moment, and must have seen something there that made him realize it was okay to retreat.

Another cackle from Brooke, and they were gone. For the first time, Aiden and I were seriously, truly alone.

"We should go somewhere and talk. Not here," he said.

"I agree."

We got in his Jeep and drove for a few minutes. The impending conversation was making my head spin. There were too many things to say. I now had the complete story. Brooke also knew. Judging by how angry she was—and how justifiable that anger was—everyone in that car would soon know, too.

And yet Aiden still only knew the half of it.

"Just pull off," I said, indicating an empty parking lot.

He did, and pulled into a space where we were kind of hidden. He shut off the engine and leaned back. He propped his head up on his hand, and swore softly.

When I could no longer take the silence, and the postponing of the beginning of this conversation, I said, "You remember that night, then, I'm guessing."

He paused, then nodded.

"You lied to me. You told me it wasn't us. I asked you, straight-up, if it was us."

"I know."

"Why would you lie to me?"

Aiden sighed deeply. "At first I didn't realize you didn't know. I thought you were just playing it off. But then when I came to talk to you about it at the diner…I caught on to that fact. And I started to tell you. I knew you needed to know… but I couldn't."

"You needed to. I deserved to know."

"I also didn't know you thought you'd hooked up with someone else."

"I had to assume. I knew I'd done something, and I never would have thought…I would never have done that with you—with Brooke's boyfriend. And a girl knows when she's done it, Aiden."

He winced. "I'm such a fucking idiot. It doesn't make any sense now. I should have told you. But I kept telling myself keeping quiet was the right thing to do. I knew you would hate yourself for doing that to Brooke, and I already did. I felt so fucking bad about it. I didn't want you to feel that guilt if you didn't have to."

That I could kind of understand. Because right now, I felt like the worst human being on the planet.

"Yeah. Well, I guess that explains why you've been acting so weird," I said.

"I'm sorry I was being a dick." He rested his head on his hands at the top of the steering wheel. "But I hooked up with you that night because I wanted to. Because I liked you. I shouldn't have, for a hundred reasons…but at first I was okay with it. I felt guilty, but since I was the only one who actually knew, it was like I had gotten away with it. And shit was rough with Brooke, anyway, so I kept justifying it. But Brooke didn't deserve that. And you didn't deserve how I started acting toward you." He rolled his head back and forth. "Fuck."

An arrow of empathy went through my heart, and I longed to reach out and touch him. To comfort him.

"It's…" he went on "…it got even harder as the weeks and months went by, because I still liked you. And at your house that one time…"

"After I applied to those places?"

"Yup…I wanted to kiss you so badly. I was so happy, simply to be sitting there doing applications with you and joking around. I looked at you and it hit me that the feeling wasn't going away. And that I would have to end things with Brooke. Then that became all I could think about."

"But you didn't."

He turned to me, and then gave a laugh. "I had a feeling she wouldn't tell you."

"Tell me… You broke up with her?"

"Yes. Last week. I promised to still go to prom with her and act like everything was fine. Usually, she would have told you."

"Yeah. Usually."

What had happened to Brooke and me? From the way she

had acted during the past couple weeks, I got the feeling that she had been uncomfortable with Aiden's and my relationship before I had ever known it.

My stomach clenched as I remembered that I, too, had a confession.

"Aiden…"

"Yeah?"

I took in his face at that moment. The expectant look in his eyes, no idea what was coming. It was the last time he would ever live in this world as he knew it. Everything was about to change for him. I'm sure I'd looked the same way right before my dad asked me if there was any chance.

"This is so hard to…I don't even know how to tell you this." He stayed silent, allowing me to find a way. So I just said it. "I'm pregnant."

As I knew it would, every millimeter of his face changed. But there was something there that told me that he wasn't entirely surprised. Instead of yelling or freaking out, he reached for my hand. I let him take it as he leaned back in his seat and stared straight ahead.

The pale blue parking lot light hit his face and eyes, and I watched him work it out in his head. And then he said possibly the only thing that could make this unbearable night better.

"We'll figure this out together." He shifted to look at me. "We're going to be okay."

Part IV

Brooke

CHAPTER TWENTY-TWO

Double Date/Big Mistake Night

"NO FACKING WAY. Is that Natalie and Brooke? My two dream girls?"

"Tell me it's not Reed," I said to Natalie.

It was. Dammit.

"I can't believe you guys are here right now!" said Bethany. I snickered as I watched Natalie's face. She'd always hated Bethany, for no reason.

I didn't care for her, either, but I also didn't mind her.

"What's up, my bitch?" I said, allowing her to come to me.

"Nothing, we just had a bunch of sake at the bar. They didn't card us or anything! How awesome is that?"

Typical night with Reed. I got an annoying pang of jealousy that she was out with him right now. Not long ago, it had been me.

"Dude, come sit with us, pull up some chairs." Eric invited them to sit down.

"Don't mind if I do take a seat."

He sat right next to me. I had to act like this was a huge annoyance, but in reality I was kind of excited that he was here.

"Are you kidding me right now?" I asked, looking at him, and then to Aiden, who used to care about this kind of thing.

"You're harmless, are you not, Reed?"

"Absolutely harmless. Hey, Lin, let me get a round of chilled sake for my friends." He looked back at us. At me. "Loves me."

Shots were had, and eventually we all got involved in our own conversations.

"I can't believe we ran into you tonight. What bad luck," I said, crossing my legs and leaning slightly toward him in my chair.

"I make my own luck, sweetie."

"Excuse me?"

"You checked in on Facebook, you dumb blonde."

I sneered at him. "So? Jesus, so you fucking stalked me? You're, like, the worst thing."

"Actually…" He leaned back, chewing on a toothpick. "I came to check that out." He gave a head tilt toward Aiden and Natalie, who were talking.

I was confused. "Wait, what?"

"This whole thing over there."

I lowered my voice. "Are you talking about Nat and Aiden?"

He nodded at me, smiling a little. "Yeah."

"What about them?"

"You're kidding me, right, Brookes?"

"Why don't you spit out whatever the fuck you're talking about, Reed, for real?"

"There's a little tension there, don't you think?"

"Um, no?"

"Watch them. Don't *watch* watch them, but keep your eyes out for it, and I promise you'll see it."

He stared into my eyes, and I cast a glance over at Natalie.

There was something kind of weird about the way she was looking at Aiden. I looked back to Reed, who knew I'd seen it.

I shook my head a little, and then glanced at Aiden. He was looking at her, too, and smiling about something. He rubbed his cheek, and I looked away again.

Reed raised his eyebrows at me.

I couldn't even smile back. I blinked, feeling hurt and shocked. My heart was pounding. There was no way. There was no fucking way, right? That they were, like, kind of flirting?

Reed saw whatever it was behind my eyes and dropped his grin to shout for our waitress.

"Lin, more sake."

ONCE WE STARTED playing laser tag, which I was seriously not up for, I felt a little panicky. Reed and I stayed in a corner, hiding from everyone else.

"You all right, Brookes?"

"Yeah. Fucking great."

He pulled a joint from a box of cigarettes in his pocket and lit it. It would go unnoticed because of the dry ice floating through the place.

"Want some?"

"No."

He shrugged. "Thought it might help you."

I pushed myself off the wall and looked for anyone else. I found them. I found Aiden using Natalie's gun to knock out Eric. I walked back to Reed.

"What the fuck is going on?"

He shrugged, eyebrows raised. "No idea. You're way too prime to be fucked around on."

I looked at him. "Are you really saying that to me?"

"Yes...?"

"Don't give me fucking lines."

He laughed. "All right, darling, anything you say." He inhaled from the joint.

"Oh, fuck it. Give me some."

He held out his hand first, and I took it. He spun me around like we were dancing, ending so that my back was to his chest. He then held the joint to my lips and let me inhale. He put his hand over my mouth, the noncigarette resting between his fingertips, telling me to hold it in. I did, until I couldn't, and he let go and unspun me.

"Whoo…" I said, looking at him.

His always-intense gaze bored into mine, and a smirk grew on his face. "Come here, sexy."

I stepped to him. He kissed me.

Fuck it. It seemed like I suddenly might not have anything to lose.

CHAPTER TWENTY-THREE

Four days until prom

I WENT IN Aiden's back door, as I had a hundred times before. It had always made for a night full of fun promise. We would watch movies, hook up, drink sometimes—that was always my favorite kind of drinking: the kind where it was just the two of us—or sometimes just sleep until our phone alarms went off, and I would sneak out and back home, no one's parents the wiser.

But things had been weird forever now. And I had a feeling I knew what was going to happen tonight.

I went downstairs and saw him right where I knew he would be. He was always waiting for me on the couch, ready to extend an arm and kiss the top of my head.

"Hey," he said, scooting over for me to join him.

I sat down. "Hey…"

No kiss on the head.

"How you doin'?"

The coolness in his tone freaked me a little bit.

We knew each other well enough that there were no words that needed to be spoken.

"Aiden," I said. "Please don't do this."

He wasn't going to deny what he was doing. I already knew that.

"We have to. It's already over, it's only a matter of saying it."

"No, please…I don't know why exactly it's been all messed up, but I hate it. Don't you hate it?"

"Yes, I do."

"So if we both hate that it's fucked up, let's fix it!"

"Brooke."

"Aiden?" I started crying. "I know I'm always flirting with other people and stuff and making you jealous—"

"It's not making me jealous, you're so…you have no respect for our relationship or for me as a person."

"Okay, but we never talk about it like this. That's all we need to do.…"

He breathed deeply, wetting his lips and looking away.

"It's not right. We aren't right."

Desperate, I shook my head. He let me lean over and kiss him. It was weird and seemed loud and unnatural.

"Brooke…"

"Don't say it."

"I have to. I'm sorry."

Tears stung my eyes, and I felt like I had dropped a roll of ribbon and couldn't catch it. "Aiden, no…please, I'm sorry, things have been bad lately, but I'm…I'm stressed about school, and everything. I…I'm sorry, please…"

He sighed, but I knew there was no arguing with him. "It's just not—"

"No, no…stop," I said, holding up my hands. "Fine. Okay, I get it. We're over. Just…please, I can't hear you say the words."

I wanted him to come to me, put his arms around me as he

had so many times and comfort me. Tell me I was being stupid. That there was no way that was what he wanted to say. But he didn't. He ran his hand through his hair and stared at the floor.

"Look, I still want to take you to prom," he said. "It's not like I hate you or anything. Let's go together and have a good time."

"Oh, there's nothing pathetic about that." I wiped the tears from under my eyes.

"It's not pathetic. We still like each other. It'll be fun."

It was completely pathetic. But nothing was more pathetic than not having anyone to go with at all.

"Okay. Don't...can you not go out of your way to tell anyone we broke up?"

"Okay." He agreed, as I knew he would.

Suddenly all of that embarrassment and sadness came back, and a new wave of stifled sobs engulfed me. I walked over to the bottom of the staircase and turned before leaving.

"Don't you love me anymore?" I realized only now how long it had been since he'd said it. And how pathetic I sounded asking.

"I care about you. That's not going to change. But we're different than when we got together. We're eighteen. There's no point in trying to force something like this."

I knew I couldn't reel him back in, and that was the worst part. Knowing that for once in my life, no matter how hard I worked or set my mind to it, there was nothing I could do.

Love is the one thing that, no matter how much you want it, if it's not there, there is nothing you can do to get it. No measure of hard work, begging, crying, wanting or needing; nothing in the world can make love happen out of nothing.

I could see this was hard for him, but I could also see that he had his mind made up. There was nothing left to say.

I climbed the stairs, away from the past year and a half of my life, and walked out the front door.

CHAPTER TWENTY-FOUR

Prom night

WHOA. NATALIE? PREGNANT? And I thought I had had a shitty week. *What the fuck.*

I felt like I should look up into the sky to see if any pigs were flying around.

I held her as she cried in my bathroom. It was selfish, I knew, but I was so incredibly relieved it wasn't me. I knew everyone would be shocked. Unlike if it had been me.

I was also pretty sure she was going to keep it. I knew all about her relationship with her mom. I knew that her mom had wanted to have an abortion. Even if Nat didn't know it yet, that was going to stop her from doing the same.

When we were at dinner, I couldn't stop looking at her. Knowing that she was in her last few months of childhood essentially. Well, her own childhood, anyway.

What? Like, seriously, *what?* She was going to have a baby. With *Eric?* That was too crazy. He was a good guy, though. He'd probably stick around and do the right thing.

Natalie pulled me into the bathroom to tell me to stop obsessing. I hadn't realized she'd noticed. But she was right. This wasn't my own personal problem. Ugh, the only way I'd be able to stop thinking about it, though, was to get shitfaced. So I got on with it.

I was used to Natalie not being a huge fan of drinking or… like, fun. But going out with her and Aiden was such an incredible drag. Neither one of them were drinking. Natalie, it made sense. But I couldn't stand being chastised for what I was doing.

Everyone gets drunk at prom. It's not the end of the fucking world.

We were in the parking lot about to go in, and it was so shocking that I would want to have some shots. I couldn't stand it.

I hated watching them together. I didn't know for sure if it was my imagination that there was something between them…but there absolutely was. They were awful little mirror images, being judgmental together. It's not like I needed Natalie or Aiden to get drunk with me, but you can have a good time sober and not judge or get mad at the rest of us. Eric, Reed, Sam, Alexa, Bethany and I were all down to get a little hammered.

Sorry, not sorry.

I just hated them for not loosening up for once and having a little fun. I don't mean to sound like the antagonist in a peer pressure video, but God.

Nat had some fun with me on the dance floor, but it wasn't long before she vanished from the gym. I watched in shock as Aiden followed her only moments later. I turned to Reed, who was dancing next to me.

"Natalie just fucking left and then he followed her." I screamed the words in his ear.

He responded by pulling me close to him by my ass and looking down at me through his brown lashes. This close to his face, I could see a scar on the top of his sharp cheekbone.

Reed slid his hand down my stomach, across my hip and then reached under my dress. He only gave one small flick of his finger, but he hit the bull's-eye. I let out a sound without meaning to, and hid my face in his neck, dancing with him. He reached his hand down a little farther and took the flask from my garter belt.

He didn't let go of my back, and opened the top of the flask with his teeth. I couldn't help but stare at his mouth and want to feel his lips on mine again. On me. Anywhere.

He took a swig, then pulled me closer again and put it to my lips. He stared at me, his mouth a little open, like I was doing something really dirty. I pushed it away after a few seconds.

I danced with him, feeling like I would do absolutely anything with him if he asked.

But then they made the announcement that prom court was about to be revealed. I felt sick. And it wasn't from the drinks. I was drinking, yes, but I was not even drunk yet. And I knew the difference.

The rest was a blur. A blur as I saw Natalie and Aiden return. As I watched him lean in and say something to her. As the whole court's names were announced, from Aiden…

To fucking Natalie.

The second they said her name, I wanted to run screaming from the room. But I couldn't. This was my best friend. I was being jealous.

Of her stealing my life.

No big fucking deal.

I clapped like everyone else as they took the stage together. I'm sure they'd have loved it if they'd realized that everyone was staring at me, not them. If they didn't see what was wrong with this picture, everyone else certainly did.

So I smiled and clapped, looking up at them like I just adored them and was so happy for them.

I didn't let anyone else see how I was privately noticing the overly intimate way they touched. The way the space between them was tight and not pushing them apart like it should be. They should be distant. They should even be dancing like stupid grandparents at a kid's party, not looking quite so much like they hated that they had to be so close, but that they'd better do it for the sake of appearances....

I felt Reed's eyes on me.

"Give me your shit," I said to Bethany. Hers was stronger than mine.

Without hesitating, she handed it over. I drank way too much in one go. But as I watched Natalie and Aiden leave the stage, it all became too much. If I had been a Victorian lady, I might have fainted, only to be roused by smelling salts, but instead I just got dizzy and puked. So freaking sexy.

How on earth did Pukey McGee not win prom queen? I mean, damn.

It was enough to lose the title of queen. It was enough to throw up on myself at my last and only senior prom ever. It was enough to hear my ex-boyfriend talking to me like I couldn't hear him as I tried to recover outside, and for me to hear in his words and in his voice how truly, deeply sick of me he was. It was enough for the world around me to be spinning, and for me to see that once again I had gotten too drunk and embarrassed myself in a hundred different ways.

I sat there, outside of the school where I had once been so popular and liked and where I had once been more than a sad story my peers would tell later on in life. "And then this one girl lost prom queen, and puked all over herself. It was hilarious," I imagined them saying in freshman year of college when people still talked about high school events. And later in life, being a tragic *beware* tale for fathers to tell their daughters about the pretty girl who had lost it all because she drank too much and so desperately needed attention.

But no. The worst part was that that was the flattering outcome. In all reality, they probably wouldn't remember me at all.

I listened to Aiden and Natalie talk to each other while I sat, crying and trying to breathe and not feel the full weight of the humiliation I knew I would carry for the rest of my life. It was different lately. With both of them. Each of them. If I had been this embarrassed and upset only a few weeks ago, either one of them would have been by my side trying to make me feel better. But now they were treating me like a badly behaved dog who couldn't understand anything they said but who had made a huge mess.

"Babe," I tried to say to him, "please don't be mad at me. I'm so sorry, I didn't mean to get so drunk. I didn't even have that much."

It was a lame excuse, and we all knew it. But it was all I had.

"Brooke, your bloodstream is probably about seventy percent alcohol right now, so save it. You did mean to get drunk. And you did have a lot, obviously, look at you."

"Aiden." Natalie chimed in. "Seriously. Just give it a rest for now."

It was like Mom and Dad yelling at me. *Really, Natalie?* Um, a) when did she get so comfortable with him that she could say anything independently to him at all, b) when did he start listening to her, and c) what was with "for now"? Just yell at me later? That was rude.

"Am I wrong, Nat?" he asked her. "No, I'm not."

Nat? Since when was he calling her Nat? Fury brewed in me.

"I'm so fucking sorry, Aiden, that I ruined your special night. No, shut up. Do you think I wanted to do this? Do you think I wanted to lose out to my best friend, and then hurl onto my prom dress and into my own fucking hand?" Seriously. And he was going to yell at me more. "No! So stop yelling at me!"

"No, you didn't mean to, but you didn't mean not to! You're such an enormous pain in the ass. I can't do this with you, I'm so sick of it. You can't be a mess that Nat or I have to deal with."

You are kidding *me. Oh, man. I'm such a fucking* burden.

I glared at Natalie, who had the nerve to have big puppy-dog eyes right now.

"Do you agree with him?"

"What do you want me to say, Brooke, you have to make a change—"

Wrong answer. That was not the way to be a best friend. She was supposed to have my back, even if she told me later how she really felt.

"Fuck you. Fuck you both. That's…just…fuck you both. I am so sick of this. I keep turning a blind eye on you guys. You keep ganging up on me, and I'm sick of it! It's like I'm this little idiot you both have the burden of having to care for." I was yelling now. "And I'm not! I'm not into the same crap as you guys, and I might like to go to parties and whatever but you two are the exception to the rule. I could be a lot worse, so stop judging me constantly!" My eyes felt red from the anger in my heart. "I dunno if you guys are flirting, or bound together in this little Hate Brooke Club or what. But, Aiden, seriously, you think Natalie's so fucking perfect. But everyone has shitty nights where they make a mistake or two. Natalie fucked Eric at Alexa's party when she was blackout wasted. Not the smartest move, right? But *I'm* the idiot who can't—"

"That's not true. I heard that rumor, too, but I would have thought you'd know it wasn't true, Brooke."

What...? What did Eric just say?

"You didn't hook up with Natalie," I clarified.

"No. Absolutely not. I kissed her. That's it."

"Then..."

Who was it? But I knew who it was. Of *course* I knew.

"Then you..." I wanted to cry. Or hit someone. Or jump off a bridge. "You fucking bitch."

Natalie was pregnant. With *my boyfriend's* baby. And I already knew she'd keep it. They'd had sex. I'd been in the same house. No one had told me. She had told me it was Eric. She...how long would she have let this go? Lied always, and said the baby was Eric's?

"Br—"

"Oh, no. You do not fucking speak." I turned from her so she couldn't see my quivering chin and reddening cheeks. "Reed, you mind giving us all a ride? Home, or wherever?"

"'Course not."

"Eric, you're coming with us. Mom and Dad over there have a lot of shit to figure out tonight."

I had a pretty ferocious second wind gusting in. I felt more sober than I ever had in my life.

I took shotgun and let the others load in the back. For once, Reed didn't make a joke. We exchanged a serious look before he put a hand on my thigh, and said, "Anywhere you want to go, Brookes."

Dread and comfort filled my bones and guts.

"Wherever people are getting fucked up."

Everyone was silent in the backseat. They would go with

me, I knew they would. They wouldn't ask to be dropped anywhere else. Because they were good friends.

I shut my eyes and cracked the window.

"You feeling a little better at least?"

"I'm not going to puke in your car, Reed."

"I'm not asking you that because I'm worried you're going to ruin the interior on my pristine '01 Cavalier. I'm asking if you're feeling better, to see if you are feeling better."

My phone buzzed on my lap. Natalie.

I declined the call, and she called back immediately. Rage lit my insides on fire. "Jesus fucking Christ."

I rolled the window down farther and hurled my phone out of the car.

She could call all fucking night and I wouldn't care.

"Yeah. I am feeling better," I said.

WE PULLED INTO a neighborhood I had never been in before, up to a small, one-story house with a covered driveway. We all unloaded out of the car, and a dog started barking like his tail was on fire on the other side of the chain-link fence that enclosed the side yard.

"Don't worry," Reed said, "he's friendly."

"Oh, that's obvious."

He pushed open the gate and shouted, "Back!" at the huge black lab. He grabbed him by his collar and scratched his ears. The dog wagged his tail and Reed let him lick his face before saying, "All right, enough, enough."

I smiled a little. "What's his name?"

"Maverick. He's my mom's dog, but I'm watching him while I stay here."

"Where are we?"

"My buddy Nick's."

"You don't live with your parents?"

He scratched the top of his head and put his hands in his pockets before shaking his head. "I can't say I expect you to have all that much fun here."

"I'm hardly expecting to. We are with you, after all."

I was so tired and emotionally drained that my tone didn't even match up with the words. I could barely even be mean.

We followed him inside. The living room was littered with people lying and sitting. The house was more well-lit than I wanted it to be. I needed a dark corner to crawl into, or a sea of people to drown in. Not a glaringly bright living room filled with a bunch of strangers. Well, actually, now that I looked at them, I could see that I had met some of them.

Reed kicked one of the guys off the couch, saying, "I pay rent here, you don't, get the fuck out of my way." But in that charming, Reed-ish way that makes you not mad.

My vision began to blur. I was dizzy, and a headache was kicking in. The guys sat up a little straighter when we three hot girls walked in. The lazy-looking chicks all touched their hair and fussed with their shirts when they saw Eric and Sam.

People started passing around a joint, and Reed held it out for me.

"Do you smoke?" he asked, his breath held. "Besides once at laser tag?"

"Uh. Whatever." I took it and inhaled.

The smoke was thick and sharp and felt awful. I held my breath for a moment but then collapsed into deep coughs. I couldn't breathe back in without it burning.

If I'd thought I was spinning before, I was wrong. This was spinning. It didn't kick in right away, but when it did, I realized that everyone's voices sounded incredibly far away. I envied Reed, who was laughing and talking animatedly to everyone around, clearly not in the nightmarish land my mind was in. I felt like my heart might stop at any moment. At least if it did, then it wouldn't ache like it did right now.

Bethany and Alexa were laughing and flirting. Of course they were. Their worlds had not imploded. Eric was starting up a game of Madden with one of the other guys. Sam was calling a cab.

I felt detached from my body and realized I was sitting with my legs wrapped up, mermaid-style, facing Reed and the back of the couch. I wasn't in control as I lay a hand on Reed's ribs, where I knew one of his bigger tattoos to be. He lifted his arm, and I fell horizontal onto his lap, facing him. He lifted me and tossed a pillow under my head.

I looked up at him for a moment, the music around us deafening. He didn't smile or anything. He just gazed at me. I was struck by a sudden urge to cry. I stopped myself but shut my eyes tight.

He hopped back into the conversation, talking loudly and excitedly again. Arguing about something. Some actor on a TV show. "No, no, dude, are you kidding me, he's the worst...."

But he let me lay my head there, and during a couple moments where he wasn't speaking, he even ran his fingers through my hair. I guess I had pulled it out of its ponytail. I didn't even remember doing that. Hopefully it didn't look like shit.

I fell asleep at some point. When I woke up briefly, hours later, I was alone in a bed. I could hear everyone else, still out in the living room. I rolled over and fell back asleep.

CHAPTER TWENTY-FIVE

I ROSE FROM the dead the next morning at nine. I opened my mascaraed eyes to see Reed, lying on his stomach. I was down to my strapless and my thong, but nothing had happened, I knew that much.

I crawled out of bed, moving the mattress as little as possible, and grabbed my dress from a chair in the corner. There was no way I'd walk out looking like this much of a Walk of Shamer. I went to Reed's dresser as quietly as possible and took a T-shirt and a pair of running shorts. I put them on, and thought how short they must be on him if they were this short on me. He was probably only five-eleven or so, but still.

One of Reed's interesting quirks: he was one of the fastest runners in the district. I never knew how he managed it, considering that half of his diet was whiskey and the other half cigarettes. I looked at him, sleeping soundly, not being an asshole or bragging about his latest fucks. Despite myself, I cracked a tiny, fond smile. I then got my mental shit together and realized I was possibly going insane.

This was Reed we were talking about. I had once been at a party with him, watched him go off with a girl and then come back because she was talking too much. Which I knew, because he told this loudly to everyone at the party when we watched him emerge so quickly.

Of course, the girl had been White Girl Wasted, and was definitely annoying. Still, he was a rude dick.

I scribbled a note and left it on his bedside table.

I took a shirt and some shorts. They're really fucking short for a dude. FYI. Thanks for last night. xx Brooke

The doorknob was locked, and I walked out to find that Bethany, Alexa and Eric had left. Why hadn't they texted me and asked if I wanted to leave when they did? I understood not knocking on the door, but—

And then I remembered throwing my phone out the window.

God. My mom was going to kill me.

I found Reed's phone on the coffee table and called a cab. I then sat on the front stoop waiting for it to arrive.

ONCE HOME, I took a shower, tamed my hair, did what I could with my gaunt and bloodless face and went downstairs. I had snuck by on my way in so as not to be seen wearing a boy's clothes. My mom was at the kitchen table with her laptop.

"Hey, Mom," I said as I made my way to the fridge. Maybe that chicken fried rice was still in there from the other day. That'd be good.

"Morning, Brooke." She sounded mad.

"Working on a Sunday?"

"Yes. How was prom?"

Ha.

"Um. Pretty fucking awful."

No chicken fried rice. I pulled some chicken tenders from the freezer and turned on the oven.

"Did you win?"

"No."

"Who did?"

"Oh, Natalie did." I slammed the bag on the counter.

She took off her glasses and looked at me for the first time. "Did she really?"

"Yup."

"That's wonderful for her. I'll have to write her an email to congratulate her. I haven't seen her in a while, how's she doing?"

"Applied to culinary school. She'll probably get in. I don't think it's the same as getting into a regular school."

That meant that she and Aiden would be in the same zip code most likely. Great. They could be one happy little fucking family. Literally.

I couldn't bear to tell my mom about her and Aiden. On one hand, it would be satisfying to tell her that her beloved Natalie was as big a fuckup as I was, but if I told her, I knew she would tell me that this was a bigger deal than stealing my boyfriend. She would tell me to "get over the pettiness, Brooke Marie" and to be there for my friend, in what was about to be the biggest change of her life.

"That is so good for her. I'm glad to hear it."

"Yeah."

"Well, I'm sorry you didn't win. Now, come sit down."

There was an air of me getting in trouble, and I couldn't imagine why. Had someone gotten in touch with her about my—cringe—self-vomit last night? It was only a matter of time, I supposed.

I sat down in one of the chairs across from her. She tossed

an envelope over to me. I picked it up and looked in the left-hand corner.

"University of Pennsylvania." My gut sank.

She nodded, setting her mouth on interlaced fingers.

I flipped it over, knowing. "It's already open."

She nodded once more.

It was a bunch of brochures and paperwork. "What...I don't..."

"It's your welcome packet. There's log-in information there for your student portal. You can start looking at courses and picking out which ones you want to start with next fall."

My eyes were wide and dry. "What the hell are you talking about right now?"

"Brooke, the decision has been made. Your father and I are sick of sitting around here waiting for you to make a decision. You are going to the school that is going to bring you the most success."

"Wow, thanks a lot for all the support, Mom."

"How am I supposed to support you when you're doing nothing? You were so smart once. I don't understand what happened to you! You don't apply yourself in any way, as far as I can tell. This program might bring that girl back a little bit. I'm not going to sit by and allow you to mess up your future even more. You are a mess, and I can't allow you to go to New York, where you'll stay out all night and forget about school entirely."

"That is not true! I want to go to New York because I want to do that program, not so I can stay out all night and party."

"I really don't think you'd enjoy being cut off financially, Brooke."

"No! Obviously not!"

"So, how about you do as your father and I say?"

I shook my head and stared at a spot on the table. "This is so messed up."

"It is not messed up, Brooke. It is your future, and it's a good choice. Stop being a petulant child."

"I am not being a child, I just don't want that life! I want to enjoy the next four years, and the ones after it."

"Brooke, once again, the world has not wronged you in any way. This is a good thing."

"I would be a success doing the program I *want* to do."

She gave me a look. "Brooke."

"God, have a little fucking faith in me! I am not a stupid little kid. New York is where I want to be. All I want is for you to help me to do that!"

She took her glasses off and rubbed her face.

"All right, here's what you're going to do. Go to Pennsylvania. Start this program. If you do well, don't party all the time and take some business classes, and you still want to go to New York…I'll help you pay for it."

This was an enormous change. "Seriously?"

I was careful not to get too excited and make her take it back.

"Yes. But I am saying that you have to be on the Dean's List at least. No 'barely getting by' on these classes."

"Got it. I will. That is…amazing, Mom."

"Okay, go take a look at those brochures. And don't eat too much. We're having a big dinner tonight. I've got chicken marinating. Invite Natalie over if you want to. I'd love to talk to her about her plans next year."

The comment brought me right back down to earth.

CHAPTER TWENTY-SIX

Winston Churchill High School Graduation Party,
located at Black Hills Recreational Park,
basically hosted by Aiden and Natalie

THE YEAR HAD not turned out anything like I had hoped it would. I'd wanted a last hurrah of a semester. Parties, senior skip days, and kill me for wanting my best friend and my boyfriend along for the ride.

I had thought it would be fun. I had thought we could forge a few more memories together. I wanted Natalie to not waste her time, youth and last high school months sitting at home. And what did I get for it?

I got to find out that my best friend was an insane, boyfriend-stealing bitch. I got to find out that she got knocked up by *my* boyfriend.

If I didn't know better, I might have thought I was pregnant from how sick I had been ever since prom. I'd hardly eaten anything. I had been drinking what was probably the equivalent of my recommended daily caloric intake, but that was about it.

I had aced my finals, except for chemistry—that I only got a *C* on—and was headed to University of Pennsylvania in the fall. I had faked it with my parents and acted like I was looking forward to it. Anything that would get me to New York.

I had started wearing the school sweatshirt my mom had given me for Christmas to replace stupid Aiden's stupid football one, which was now long gone. I was doing what my parents wanted. Everyone at school seemed to believe the act that everything with me was okay. In fact, I think they thought I was better than ever. I had played up feeling like I'd been dragged down for the past few years, and that now all I wanted was to have fun.

Never mind that my stomach was a constantly twisting knot of snakes and that I was dreading the coming fall, and that I had no idea how I was going to get through this summer without the people I used to love the most.

I was angrier with them than I had ever been with anyone. Not merely for the fact that I could picture them together. Going over to each other's houses. I hated imagining Natalie talking to Aiden's mom, who used to love me, and Natalie being so much sweeter and less foul-mouthed than I am. I hated imagining Aiden talking to Natalie's dad. He had always liked Aiden. I hated imagining—oh, the terror—of them going out to eat at the diner. Where he would fill the spot next to Natalie, ordering meat loaf and mashed potatoes while she ate her patty melt.

And how awful that I knew that I must come up in their conversations. They must sit there, in their happy little world, and think, *Oh, poor Brooke…we really hurt her. We really shouldn't have done what we did. And continue to do. Oh, fuck it, let's do it anyway.*

I hated the idea of their pity. That they thought they were the cool pair who had really fucked me over, and how sad that must be for me. And I hated that they must look at me and think—or, rather, know—that I was faking half of how okay I was. I hated that, no matter what I'd done, they'd think about how responsible they were for it, while not doing anything to stop it.

I also hated that they probably nodded to each other and agreed that, yes, they had something much bigger to worry about. They probably figured that "Brooke will understand someday."

Whatever. I had one summer left in this shitty little town, and then this would all be a memory. An awful story that I would one day discuss and make light of over drinks on a back deck with my new—and real—best friend.

But that was in the future. Right now, I was pulling up at Black Hills for the graduation party I didn't want to go to, but had to. Everyone else was going. Everyone. I wouldn't care if it meant only that I would run into Aiden and Natalie. But I did care that the party was funded entirely by their senior class project. Every last potato chip was paid for by Natalie's creative thinking and Aiden's good work ethic.

Yeah. That stupid fucking wall. Everyone was all obsessed with how awesome it was, and people were constantly taking pictures in front of it. Another thing they'd taken from me. I couldn't even enjoy that with everyone else.

Fuck. What a great pair they made. What a superawesome team.

At least I looked fucking great. I grabbed the bottle of Jack Daniel's I'd talked an older friend into buying, and the lemonade I intended to mix it with. I tossed them in my sequined backpack from Victoria's Secret and started up to the party from the lot. I was in a red bikini, sheer white tank top, light jean shorts and feeling very *Baywatch* with my blond hair tumbling down over my shoulders. I had gotten a fresh set of highlights and was feeling pretty awesome.

The backyard was littered with people. The people I had spent the past four years with. Guys were making the tanning girls laugh. It was all string bikinis, belly button rings and the smell of grilling hamburgers. On the lawn in the shade a group of people had put their chairs in a circle and were tossing around Ping-Pong balls. I threw my bag on the grass and went up to Alexa, who squealed when a ball went in her cup. She chugged it, and then I tapped her on the shoulder.

"Hey, betch!" I said. God, I was good at faking it.

"Oh, my God, hi! We fucking graduated!" She jumped up and down and I squealed with her.

"I fucking know! Ahh!"

"Wanna play? Go get that chair."

I pulled it up and squeezed between her and her cousin Ryan. "How do I play?"

He leaned over to me and explained. "Basically, keep your cup in the same place, you can't move it. There are a bunch of balls being tossed around, you're aiming to get one in someone else's cup. If you get it, they have to drink it, and they have to finish it before someone else's cup gets sunk. If you break a rule, or if you don't finish it in time, you have to do three laps around the pitcher in the middle while chugging your drink.

"Is there—" I looked around, there were parents and teachers there "—any alcohol at all?"

"Obviously," he said with a wink. "In the punch."

Alexa handed me a cup.

Everyone erupted in a shout as Ryan's girlfriend Hilary's cup was sunk. She chugged it and then tossed the ball elsewhere.

"It's pretty easy to get fucked up," she said, stepping toward the pitcher to refill her cup.

I laughed. "What's this game called?"

"Hungry hungry hippos."

"Hah! I get it. That's awesome."

Someone sank my cup. I downed it.

It was hard not to laugh and have a good time playing. After about an hour at the party, I finally felt good again for the first time in weeks. In longer, maybe. This was my school. These were my people. I was okay. I did have friends. I could have a good summer with them, and not think too much about all the awful things that had gone on. These were my memories, and I refused to let two assholes ruin them. Even though I kept finding myself looking around for them. I knew they were there. They had to be.

Eventually, I did see them. They weren't together at first, but then they seemed to find each other. Why had they bothered keeping the distance to begin with? He'd probably even driven her here.

I looked over to where the parents were. Oh. Maybe he hadn't driven her. Her dad was there. With…oh, my God, was that Marcy? They were finally officially together? I'd have to ask—

No one. Nothing. Not Natalie.

After the game, Alexa and I sat together, chatting.

"I wish they didn't have to be here," she said. "I mean, like out of respect for you, you know?"

I knew it was stupid. But she meant it to make me feel better. To show she was on my side. "Yeah. Well. I expected them to be, so, whatever. Thanks, though, you are really a great friend." I gave her a smile and shoved her with my shoulder.

She did a pouty face. "I hate that you're not going to be in New York next year. We could have roomed together and everything."

"I know. Fucking blows."

She was going to be at NYU on an acting track. I had a feeling things would work out for her there. She was pretty, thin and a good actress. She was the only nonweirdo who did the plays at our school.

I didn't interact with either Natalie or Aiden until later that night. I was refilling my drink at the refreshments table, and they were nearby. Fueled by anger, feigned indifference and now a bunch of illicit alcohol, I decided it was time to speak to them. Bethany had joined Alexa and me, so the three of us marched over.

"Well, hey there, guys, so glad to see you."

They were both silent at first, but then Aiden nodded. "Yeah, you, too. Glad to have graduated?"

"Yeah, I'm so thrilled." My voice was so fake it hurt. "Wow, Natalie, not even drinking at the grad party?"

She bit her lip, and I could tell she wanted to cry. *Fucking good. Do it.*

"No, I don't feel like it."

"Sure you don't want some, Nat?"

Bethany and Alexa didn't know that I was being rude about her pregnancy. I hadn't told them. It was a line that I wouldn't cross, even though I knew it would become obvious soon enough. Something stopped me.

"Yeah, I'm sure."

"How about some ice chips?" I took a handful of ice and chucked them at her bare legs.

Aiden stepped forward. "Hey, Brooke—"

"I really think you should shut your fucking mouth, Aiden."

But I saw that his gaze went behind me. I followed it, and saw Natalie's dad.

God. Dammit.

I loved that man. He was like a father to me. And he had seen me, like, bully his real daughter.

"Hi, John…" I said. I almost literally hung my head.

I could tell from looking at him that he knew the whole situation. He knew why I was mad. Why I had just done what I did. But that didn't mean I wasn't filled with a horrible, horrible shame. This was worse humiliation than puking in my own hand at senior prom.

"Congratulations, Brooke. I'm so proud of you for graduating." He reached for me and gave a real hug. I couldn't even stop the tears. I could hide them, but not stop them. He and Natalie were family to me. "Your mom told me about Pennsylvania, and your plans for New York. I know you're going to do great."

It almost felt like a goodbye. Would that be it? Was I that worthless and disposable? So useless and unimportant that Natalie and Aiden could do this and not even worry about me? That after the fact, they could stay together, and live without me? And that Natalie's dad was okay with letting this be essentially goodbye?

"I gotta go."

I ran across the lawn, found Reed and made him take me back to Alexa's, where people would be going later.

AT ALEXA'S HOUSE, we went inside to the vacant kitchen and I got my Jack Daniel's from my backpack.

I poured two shots, and we each picked one up. "What shall we cheers to?"

He was in high spirits. He didn't know I wasn't.

"Fuck it," I said, clanging my shot glass on the counter.

"I'll drink to that."

I took a step toward him, pushed on his abdomen and then kissed him hard.

He pulled me to him roughly, his hand flat on my back.

Still kissing me, he turned us, picked me up by my thighs and put me on the counter.

He grabbed my hair by the base of my neck and pulled just hard enough. I wrapped my legs around his inked hip bones and my arms around his neck. I kissed him. The thrill shot through me, the same as it had all those months ago, and as it did every time he touched me. Something about the electricity of his lips and tongue and the hardness of his body turned me on like no one else's. In that moment, I didn't care about Aiden and Natalie. They were a thought long gone.

"Take me to a bedroom." I spoke into his ear.

He pulled me off the counter effortlessly, grabbed the bottle and took me into a dark room. The only light was coming through the blinds from the pool outside. He let the bottle slam on the glass nightstand, and lay down, allowing me to be on top of him.

I kissed him everywhere, unable to stop touching his muscles, which were tight and taut and everywhere without exception. I kissed and bit his hip bones before pulling down his shorts.

It also helped that he was huge, making me feel immediately like he was more of a man than Aiden. Messed up? Maybe. But it made me feel better.

He let me go for a few minutes before wrenching me back up by the waist, flipping me on my back and peeling off my bikini. He did so in about two point five seconds. I couldn't even be quiet. I wasn't sure if people had followed us yet or not, but I didn't care.

He kissed me with an intoxicating force, his hand in my hair, his mouth buried in my neck. I grabbed his back and scratched, maybe a little too hard, but he didn't cringe.

It was the hottest thing I'd ever done. I didn't even hesitate before letting him go all the way. He paused only to put on a condom—it hardly slowed him down. He was clearly a pro.

He groaned, his teeth on my collarbone and one hand on the middle of my back pulling me slightly off the bed.

It was as much passion as I had ever seen in movies, and never really had in my own experience. I was light-headed as he did whatever it was he was doing to make me feel that way.

But then, for the first time since we had begun, he kissed me on the mouth. The spinning in my head got far worse, and I kissed him back. He slowed to a stop and flipped me back on top. My hair was long and tangled, and in the way, but it didn't matter.

I kissed him again, my heart light as air, my body on fire, sticky and tingling.

WHEN WE FINISHED, I put on my bikini, prepared to act like it had been nothing. But as soon as he put his shorts back on, he pulled me close into his tight body. He looked down at me, his mouth slightly open and his hair all over the place.

Whatever I felt for him, I hated it. I knew he could never be anything real to me, or for me. I was just a different kind of fuck. I knew that. Or hell, maybe I wasn't even different. I hated that he was making me feel special right now.

All I could do was act like I didn't care.

So I bit my lip and smiled, kissed him under the jawbone and tossed my hair to one shoulder before leaving the room. Right before we went back into the living room, he smacked me hard on the ass. I giggled and then regained my composure in front of the people who'd started to gather. As if what we'd been doing wasn't superobvious, anyway.

CHAPTER TWENTY-SEVEN

MY LIFE BECAME this hot, summery haze of sex and drinking. It was only a few short months, and then I would be somewhere new. Somewhere lame, somewhere that I would be studying a subject I didn't want to study, with no one I knew. Not that I would have anything to miss here anymore. It was all gone. High school. Proms. Assemblies. Games. Being the football star's girlfriend. Sleepovers with my childhood best friend. All gone. I couldn't do anything to get it back.

So now I felt fake. Like an illusion that didn't have a body. Nothing I did felt like it mattered.

I slept as long as I could sleep, as often as I could. I woke up in the middle of the afternoon, often at Reed's house. I spent almost all my time with him.

It was a Saturday—or maybe a Sunday—and it was almost eight at night. We'd woken up and had sex, fallen back asleep for a while, both of us hungover, and now we were awake again for the night. I couldn't remember the last meal I'd eaten. I was living off midnight runs to McDonald's, pizza ordered

by other people, Excedrin Migraine, and the occasional bottle
of Gatorade to recover in the morning. But only if someone
else brought it to me.

On this particular night, we rallied by having a 5-hour
Energy shot each.

I was lying on the side of the bed closest to the wall in only
a bra and a thong. He was in a pair of black Volcom shorts he'd
tossed on to go outside and get the energy shots.

"You are so fucking hot," he said as he kissed my inner
thigh, holding my ankle on his shoulder.

"Yeah, yeah, yeah. You didn't even want to hook up with
me back in the day."

"When?"

"My birthday. You fucking dropped me at home."

He gave me a look and then shook his head before kissing me again.

"What is that look?" I asked.

"Nothing." He bit me.

"Ow!" I laughed and grabbed him by his tousled hair.
"What was that look?"

He shrugged. "It seemed fucked up to hook up with you.
I don't know. I liked you, I guess."

I raised my eyebrows. "That went away, then? Now that
you don't like me, you can hook up with me?"

He gave me a mild glare. "Brooke..."

"No, stop." I sat up. "Do you not even like me?"

"It doesn't matter."

"Doesn't matter. Why's that?"

"You're going away. We're not going to have a...relation-
ship or whatever. So what does it matter how either of us
feels? Let's not even bother with the subject. You want me. I
want you. We've got days and nights to fill. Let's not worry
about all the bullshit."

I squinted at him, my heart splitting a little.

But why? Wasn't he right? Did I even like him? Or was he one more example of someone I wanted to want me?

"Come on, Brookes." He gave me a smack on the ass. "You're just as cold as I am. Stop trying to fight it."

"You think I'm cold?" I said it with a sly smile, so I would still come off as playful. But I really wanted to hear the answer.

"I think you're a fucking ice queen." He grinned at me and adjusted me with my legs on his shoulders. He kissed my stomach.

"Why do you think that?"

He shrugged. "Everything. You just are. You're not one of those girls who wants to be loved. Well...you are, but you want everyone to love you. It's not about one person for you. You want what you want. And no one tells you who you are. I love it."

"Yeah." I smiled and sank into the pillows. "Yeah."

Was he right?

ON SOME WEDNESDAY or Thursday, Reed came out into the backyard where I was tanning and drinking a vodka and ginger ale—it doesn't go, but it was the only mixer I could find.

"Brookes."

"What?"

"You've got a visitor."

"Who?" I sat up. "Who, Reed?"

Natalie pushed past him. He shut the door, leaving us quite suddenly alone.

"Brooke, I have to talk to you. You and I have been best friends our whole lives, and I am telling you that I need you right now. You owe it to me to listen."

"I owe you? I don't think I owe you anything at all." But I took my stuff off the chair next to me. She came and sat down.

"I know that this is the worst possible thing I ever could have done to you. I know that. But you also know I would never try to hurt you on purpose."

"I don't care if it was on purpose or not. You might not have been trying to hurt me, but you weren't trying *not* to hurt me."

I immediately regretted saying it. That was an Aiden-ism.

"I did try. But...I failed. I didn't want it to happen. But you know you didn't want to be with him anymore. And I'm sorry that I did. But I couldn't help it. I'm weak, Brooke. I'm not like you, I can't just turn it off or you know that I would. I've never had to try, you know I'm completely inexperienced here."

"I might not have wanted to be with him—" I groaned in frustration. "It doesn't matter, Natalie, you can't just decide that I'm not good enough for him, or that you're better."

She looked at me like she was trying desperately to find the words to express what was in her head. "You and I have watched romance movies and read romance novels our whole lives. You know he isn't your It. And I know that, no matter how much you act like you don't care, you want that one guy who is perfect for you. You want the one guy who makes you want to be your best, and who you would rather flirt with one hundred percent of the time than get attention from other guys. I know that's what you want. Aiden isn't that for you. You know that. But there's a chance he could be that for me. And this situation I'm in...it's so real. It's really happening. It's not about boyfriends and rules...it's so real...." She shook her head. I could see that she was scared shitless.

She was saying exactly what I'd known she'd say. And I knew it was kind of true. But that didn't mean I was okay with it. Maybe I wasn't mature enough to be that noble. Whatever.

"And I know it sucks," she went on. "I know it. I don't expect you to forgive me for this. But I miss..."

She bent forward over her knees and wept. The kind of tears you can only cry in front of someone you love and know loves you.

I had to literally stop my arms from reaching for her.

"I miss my best friend so much, and I—I—" She gasped for breath. "I need you for what I'm...for all the—"

"You're keeping the baby, aren't you?" I clarified.

She breathed deeply, her eyes fixed intently on a spot in the yard somewhere. "Yes."

I knew it.

Fuck.

I was supposed to be there for her. This was one of the deals about having a best friend. That when you get knocked up at eighteen, your best friend helps you with whatever your choice is.

"And what does—" saying his name would be difficult here "—*he* have to say about this?"

"He's being really mature about it...he's being really nice and everything."

No surprise there. "I see."

"Brooke...Brooke, am I doing the right thing? Keeping it?"

One of Natalie's most defining traits, the thing that defined her psychologically more than anything, was her mom.

I had hated her mother for her.

And I knew that now, being faced with the opportunity to be a mother herself—how was this happening right now?—she was afraid of being the same way, or of messing up the kid in a totally different way.

Separately, I knew that Aiden would be great to a kid. Even at eighteen. I knew he was the kind of person—maybe the only kind of person—who could handle something like this and end up having the greatest kid ever.

A reluctant and frustrated part of my brain told me that

they might—cringe—be good together. And that maybe this was all for the best. Not ideal. In any way. But not the end of the world.

It definitely was if the other option was me being faced with these decisions.

Natalie would be okay. She would be good at this. She might even be great at this. I wanted to tell her that. I wanted to tell her that, yes, she was making the right choice.

I started to answer honestly, and then my throat closed up like I was allergic to the words. My bitter tongue responded before my opening heart could. "I think you should go."

She looked hurt. I wanted to take it back, but I was paralyzed.

She nodded, got up…and left.

As soon as she was gone, tears rose up from somewhere deep in me, and made my eyes burn. I couldn't sit out here and cry. Reed was not the type to help, or to even know how to. I kept them in, which was painful and nearly impossible.

I sat there in the sun, Natalie gone, not coming back, and focused on breathing.

I didn't want to be in my head. I went inside, found Reed and told him to take me to his room. He was always down for it.

ONCE WE FINISHED, I snapped my bra back on and pointed at the bottle on the dresser.

"Give me that."

"Isn't there a nicer way of asking?" he said, grabbing it, his cigarette hanging out of his mouth.

"I think I already gave you all of my magic words."

He laughed. "Yeah, that's true." He leaned down and kissed me. "I like your dirty words a lot better than your magic ones."

I gave him a challenging nose-crinkle and then snatched the bottle from him.

"I'll be out there when you're ready to go, Brookes."

"'Kay. Close the door please."

"You got it."

He shut the door and went into the living room, where he got a round of cheers from the other guys.

I unscrewed the bottle top and swigged. More than I wanted to. More than I should. More than I could without starting to cough.

I put the lid back on and dropped the bottle on the ground. I was almost shocked it didn't break. If it had, I wouldn't have cared, though.

I wrapped my arms around my naked knees and let my head fall onto them.

"Fuck," I muttered.

The tears came suddenly and intensely.

Why? Why was I even crying?

Natalie's face drifted into my mind. An annoying sense of forgiveness had been creeping up on me in the past few weeks, a frustrating, sickening desire to tell her to forget it. And now more than ever I wanted to go to her and start being there for her.

I thought of Aiden. When I thought of Aiden, I felt nothing. No anger. Why wasn't I madder at him?

But this wasn't only about forgiving my ex-boyfriend and my best friend. This was about the fact that I was so entirely not worth their respect that they hadn't even given it to me. This wasn't just about the act, or the fact that they had allowed themselves to exchange looks in front of me and made it obvious enough for Reed to notice.

This was about the fact that I hadn't mattered enough for them to control themselves.

And there was no way to fix that.

I shouldn't have, but I reached for the bottle once more and took another big sip.

I stood up, tossed on my tiny dark denim Hollister shorts and pulled on my black tank top. I pulled my slightly knotted hair from the inside of my straps and looked at myself in the warped and tarnished mirror that leaned against the wall on Reed's dresser.

"Jesus Christ," I said to myself, licking my fingertips and wiping the mascara from under my eyes.

I grabbed my makeup bag and loaded up on concealer, then put on a new coat of mascara. I tossed on some dark liner to cover up the red rings around my eyes, and called it a day. I tried to brush my hair, but it was too much of a challenge right now.

I grabbed my clutch and headed out the door.

I WAS GRATEFUL when the alcohol started to take me. I was able to let go. Reed's friend drove. I sang along to all the random punk songs I knew. The other guys thought I was sexy for knowing the words to songs by bands like the Sex Pistols. In the state I was in right now, having the approval of the scrawny drugheads I was in the car with was enough. I sat on Reed's lap, even reaching between his legs on the way there and making out with him unselfconsciously.

In another life, I would have seen myself and thought I was trashy. I would have texted Natalie, and said something like, *Oh, my God, this nasty blonde hobag can't keep her fucking chapstick lips off her stupid boyfriend for a car ride. Like, don't get a room, get a fucking STD test.*

In that world I also had a phone. In that world, I hadn't chucked it out the window.

I chose not to think about it and instead just let his mouth be on mine.

The party was at some cheerleader's house on the opposite side of town. Judging by the toasts they were taking, they were all juniors going on senior year in the fall.

All the girls were dressed to the nines. I recognized a lot of their outfits and shoes. They all shopped at Nordstrom, my favorite store. One stupid bitch was wearing the Valentino pumps I had been ogling for months.

And here I was in ratty Rainbow sandals, Daisy Dukes and a black tank top.

I ran my hands through my hair, trying to untangle more of the knots.

I stood back, leaning against the counter, debating the benefits of finding Reed and sneaking into a bedroom.

"Seniors!" said a girl who reminded me a lot of Bethany.

"To a fucking awesome year—I know it's going to be hard to top this past one, but we can absolutely do this shit." The girl now speaking was thin and pretty, with bright blue eyes, dark black lashes and shocking red hair. Her skin was perfect porcelain, and she had a spattering of freckles on the tops of her cheeks. When she smiled, I saw a set of perfect, white, attractively big teeth. She was the kind of girl who you could tell could wear any color lipstick.

She tossed her hair and held up her shot. Everyone else followed suit, and I watched how the boys watched her. Then I looked at the expression on her face right before she took her shot.

This girl knew exactly what she was doing.

She wanted all the boys to like her. They did.

She wanted the girls to like her. They did.

She was loud, and people listened.

She was me.

Fuck. I hated her suddenly. I crossed my arms and kept watching.

"Brookes!" I heard Reed call my name from across the room.

I tore my eyes away from the girl, who was now dancing in an annoyingly sexy way with her Bethany-type friend.

I followed Reed into a bedroom where a tall skinny guy handed something over.

"Cool, cool. Thanks, dude."

The guy left, and Reed closed the door after him.

"What?" I asked, looking at the excited grin on Reed's face.

"I got a present for you."

I narrowed my eyes at him, knowing it was not going to be Tiffany's. "What kind of present?"

He held up a little bag. It had two pills in it.

I raised my eyebrows, and responded a little breathlessly. "Oh…it's…"

"Ecstasy, baby."

The child in me wanted to shake my head and go home. No. This was too real.

Somehow that child found a small voice. "I don't think… I don't want…"

"Okay, okay. No pressure. I wasn't sure what you would say."

He took out one of the pills and popped it into his mouth.

"You're still—" I stopped myself.

He tilted his head at me. "What?"

"Nothing." This frustrating part of me feared who else he'd give that pill to. "Okay, thanks, anyway, I'm going to go take a shot."

I opened the door and went back to the kitchen. I poured a shot of the awful-quality whiskey they had.

"Want someone to take a shot with?"

It was the redhead.

I smiled at her. "Yeah, definitely. I, uh, I missed the toast, so…figured I'd catch up."

"Betch, I'll always take another round." She smiled and gave me a little wink.

God. She really was me.

"Awesome."

"But hey, let's not do that shit whiskey. That is dis-gus-ting. Have you ever shotgunned a Red Bull vodka?"

She held up a sugar-free can. No, I hadn't. I'd never even thought of it.

"Yeah, let's do it."

"Cool!"

She popped open two cans and handed one to me. She swigged, so I did, too.

She pulled it away from her lips. "Okay, now the vodka."

She poured in Pearl vodka, until it almost overflowed. She filled mine, too.

"All right, now…" She handed me a steak knife, took one herself and then stabbed a hole in the bottom of her can. I did the same, and then we chugged.

Once finished, I wiped whatever had gotten on my chin.

"What was your name again?" I asked.

"Oh, I didn't tell you." Her response was the hint of a power struggle with me. "It's Lana."

Stupid bitch had a cooler name than me. An undeniably hot-girl name.

"Lana, okay."

"And you're…"

"Oh, I'm Brooke."

"Brooke…" She narrowed her eyes. "Brooke from Churchill? I knew you looked familiar!"

I smiled more genuinely at the thought of being known of. "Right, yeah."

"Oh, gosh." She gave me a slight up-and-down. For once in my life, I was embarrassed at what she was seeing. "I have heard of you. You were with Aiden Macmillan, right?"

"Yeah. For a long time."

"Right."

Apparently the news of him cheating on me with my best friend had traveled school districts.

And here I was, looking like a mess of all messes.

"So you're a senior this year, huh?"

"Yes! I'm so fucking pumped." She rolled her eyes in excitement. "It's going to be the best year."

I nodded at her and felt like one of those old, jaded people looking at a wide-eyed child. I felt an urge to tell her Santa wasn't real, that Peter Pan was really about dead children stuck in purgatory and that too much ice cream would one day make her fat.

"I'm sure it is. Well, enjoy it! I have to go talk to my…" I pointed toward Reed. "I'll see you later."

"More shots in, like…fifteen." She looked at her watchless wrist and then gave me a big smile.

I nodded. "Totes."

As I turned my back, I knew she was going over to her Bethany-friend, and that they were going to talk about how I wasn't like how they had thought I would be. How they didn't get what all the fuss was about. They'd say how shitty I looked.

I found Reed, dancing on the dark porch in a mass of bodies, with another girl. I shoved her aside and grabbed him.

He only laughed, not caring about whoever she was.

"Still have that pill?" I shouted in his ear to be heard over the deafening music.

He nodded and gave me a questioning look.

I want it, I mouthed.

He hesitated, but then reached in his pocket and pulled out the little bag. He licked his finger and reached into the bag, pulling the pill out on his fingertip.

He held it out for me, and I looked him in the eyes, which were caught by a red light from somewhere behind me. I took a deep breath and then put his whole finger in my mouth. I slid the pill onto my tongue and then swallowed it. It was done. No going back.

I pulled my mouth off his finger, giving the tip a quick bite before turning around and dancing on him.

The songs blended together in my drunkenness, but not too long after, I started to feel different.

My heart began palpitating a little. Just nerves. I was scared of this drug. I had never done anything like this before.

Overabuse of Excedrin, and a little pot every now and then, yes. But not real drugs.

It wasn't long before my body started to give in. I grinded against Reed, and then turned around, burying my face in his neck. He was sweating, but I didn't care. I touched him as much as I could. His cold skin, the sweat on top of it, it felt good on my face. I felt aware of the tiny space between his skin and mine when it touched. I grabbed his hair and pulled it, and took his face and pulled his mouth onto mine.

I was so hot. Some time passed. My hair was kind of wet, and sticking to my cheekbones and collarbones. There was no air-conditioning, and more people pouring in every minute.

I let my body grind into his, never letting go of him.

A song picked up the tempo. There were heavy drums. Fast double bass drums. My forearms started to feel like they had fire shooting through them. My neck muscles tensed and started to cramp. I looked up to see Reed's eyes, like something of a horizon, but he wasn't there. I was alone. When did

I let go of him? I realized my hand was still holding someone's arm. I didn't know him. I let go.

Fuck. Where was I?

It was dark. There was a TV on. The redhead was in my sight, laughing at something someone said. My chest hurt. My head was splitting. My legs felt like I'd been overworking the muscles. They shook, and I thought maybe I'd collapse.

I suddenly felt like I was falling down a deep, dark hole.

Part V

NATALIE

CHAPTER TWENTY-EIGHT

I'D NEVER GRIPPED anything harder than the handle on the car door that night. My fingernails bent against the leather, and I didn't even notice until I saw the cracks later.

No one spoke on the ride to the hospital. My dad drove us up to the door to the E.R., then said he would meet us inside. My dad had talked with Brooke's mom to put us on some list so we could go right in.

Aiden got out of the backseat. He didn't try to touch me or talk to me.

My hands trembled as I went to the reception desk and said her name.

I signed in. Aiden did, too. Then we followed the directions through the doors they let us in, and down the hallway. It was freezing cold. Bright lights. I couldn't help but look in each of the little rooms as we passed. Old people, on their last legs. Little kids with doting, terrified parents. But no Brooke. Finally we arrived at her curtained–off area. I felt the awful plunge in my heart and stomach before I even stepped in.

"Brooke…"

Her name tumbled from my mouth as I saw her. Pale. The same color as her hair. Tubes in her nose and down her throat. IV in her hand. Pulse monitor on her finger.

I stared at her, and shook my head. "I can't…she's got to be okay."

I felt Aiden rub his face next to me. "She's got to be."

I don't know how long we stood there. I stared at the creepily identical breaths that made her chest rise and fall. I reacted to nothing around me until I heard the squeak of sneakers on the tile behind me. I turned, expecting to see my dad, but instead saw Reed.

I felt my mouth curl into a snarl, and I felt this urge to hit him. Before I could even tell myself not to, however, Aiden had done it for me.

The hit went straight through Reed, knocking him to the floor.

A nurse came over and started to yell at them. Reed held up his hand at her.

"It's fine, it's fine, I deserved it. Just…back off." He said the last part more quietly as he stood. She went away, clearly feeling out of her element. I got the feeling she was new.

"Fuck you, man." Aiden glared at him.

"Fuck me? I'm the one that fucking called you."

"I don't care, this is your fault and you know—"

He gave an awful, humorless smile. "Yeah, I gave her the drugs. It's my fault. But I'm not why she's here, am I?" He looked between both of us, holding his cheekbone.

That stung.

He pulled away his hand, exposing some blood from where his skin had split.

"I don't think it's really any of your fucking business. Don't imply that it's because of us—" Aiden started.

"You're both kidding yourselves if you think she doesn't care about what you did. She's not even mad, man, she's fucking hurt. I can't believe that I have to be the one to recognize that she's sadder than she is mad. You're her best fucking friend, you can't tell the difference? You can't see that you made her feel worthless and like she didn't matter to either of you, and that that's the problem? Because that *is* the problem. This isn't about popularity or her being pissed because you broke a secret 'BFF' rule." He used finger quotes, and his cheek bled freely. "This is because you're the only people she really gives a shit about. Not the people who are up her ass at school, not fuckin' Bethany or whatever, not me. You two. And you fucked her. I get it, man, I get that you're in love and that shit, but you have to realize that you sacrificed her happiness for yours. You have to fuckin' recognize that, the both of you."

Aiden and I were stunned into silence. He was completely right. *Reed*. Was completely right.

"I just wish you hadn't let her get to this point," said Aiden, his voice rough.

I thought Reed might argue some more, but he didn't. "I know, me, too. She's not the kind of girl that should be in this shit. It was my turn to watch her." He gave a small smile, and then it faded when the truth of what he said seemed to hit him. "Anyway, I'm going to go. I think it's best I don't hang around her anymore." He looked toward her body in the other room. "Plus, it's fuckin' hell looking at her like this."

I nodded.

He put up his hand in goodbye and took off down the hall.

"Reed," I called after him. He turned. "Thanks for getting her here."

He tightened his lips and kept walking.

I looked at Aiden. He couldn't make me feel better about what Reed had said. Because he knew, as I did, that it was true.

It was us. We were why she was there.

I opened my mouth to say something, but I didn't even know what. Things were all way too complicated for me to even begin to know how to fix it.

I stepped out of the room and leaned against the wall across the way. I looked down the hall and saw Brooke's parents.

They looked simultaneously angry and scared out of their minds.

A few minutes later they came over. We made awful small talk for a while and waited for the doctor.

Finally he came over. His voice was loud, too calm and brash. He was so matter-of-fact. He told us what had happened. Reed had given them the information they needed to know, and they had deduced that it was a combination of alcohol, poor nutrition, caffeine and MDMA.

"Ecstasy?" Aiden muttered to me. "Since when...?"

"I don't know." I shook my head, my eyes shut tight to keep from crying.

The doctor told us she was only unconscious because she was on a sedative. It made it easier for her to have the tube down her throat.

After getting all the information, Brooke's parents talked to my dad. He shook his head and discussed whatever parents discuss in these situations with them. Aiden and I sat quietly like children in time-out.

My dad came over to us after they finished talking, and said we needed to go. I didn't want to, but he insisted nothing would change, and that I would only get upset sitting here.

I made her mom promise to call me the second she woke up, day or night.

THE CALL FROM Brooke's mom didn't come until late the next night.

The second it did, I bounded out of bed and took my dad's car. I booked it inside the hospital and to the room they'd relocated her to.

Once there, I hesitated before moving into sight. She was awake. She'd almost died. Last we had spoken, she didn't want to see me. And now I was here.

I gathered my strength and knocked.

"Come in."

I stepped in.

She gave a small flicker of her eyebrow before biting her bottom lip and saying, "Hey."

Her eyes went elsewhere, and I didn't know what to do.

I walked over and sat in one of the awful chairs they had next to the bed.

"How are you feeling?"

She nodded her head. "You know. Like a fucking idiot." She gave a weak laugh. "I'm okay. Little nauseous. Headache. You know. The usual hangover shit."

I watched her. She still wasn't looking at me. But her eyes shifted from the wall straight ahead of her and then down to her hands. She was trying to keep her face passive.

I exhaled deeply, and put my head in my arms on the bed next to her.

She didn't reach for me. I didn't expect her to. I sat back up a few minutes later.

"I have never been more terrified, Brooke."

She didn't answer.

"I can't do this. I can't not know you. I can't not be talking to you every day. I can't pretend you're not my best friend."

"Yeah, well. You really showed me how much you care, Natalie."

The words stung, and my eyes filled with tears. "I know…
God…I…it all feels like a nightmare…."

"I just don't understand." She tightened her shoulders, and
the heart monitor next to her beeped a little faster. "How did
this happen? You and Aiden, how did it happen?"

"I…"

"I mean, seriously, Natalie."

"You wanted me to come out. I wish I never had. I told
you I couldn't. I told you I didn't want to."

"Yeah, I thought that was because you were scared. Of
what people would think of you. Of not fitting in. Of…fuck,
I don't know. Whatever else. I didn't think it was because you
were going to do *this*."

"I always liked him. You knew I did, back when he first
started here. I'm…I hate myself for it."

"Yeah, well…" We were silent for a moment. "It feels to
me like you decided you loved him more than you love me.
I mean, certainly he feels…whatever for you more than for
me, but…"

She looked determinedly at the ceiling and then groaned
loudly.

"What?"

"I guess there is no more than that. He loves you more than
he loves…loved me."

"Oh—"

"And," she interrupted, "you love him more than I did."

I had nothing to say. She was right. But I didn't know that
agreeing with her was the right move.

Finally she looked at me for real. "This is so fucked up. And
so not okay. But…I know you both too well to act like…I
mean, neither of you would have done it if it wasn't…impos-
sible not to. I guess."

Again, I didn't know what to say. So I extended my hand to her.

After a moment, she took it.

"You can't fall apart like this, Brooke. You're way too smart for this. Way too smart for Reed. Way too smart for fucking Ecstasy and a solid alcohol diet."

She took a deep breath. "I know that. It's...I've had enough of this now. I know that. I don't want to be a mess."

"I don't want you to, either. I can't ever be scared like that again."

"I know. Me, neither." She breathed deeply. "You know it can't be okay right away, right? I can't...be okay with this. I can't sit across from a table with you guys, or...give you any kind of blessing. I hate it still. For right now. Or maybe I always will."

"Of course. I know."

"But I guess...I kind of have to get my shit together if I'm going to be Auntie Brooke."

The words immediately sent me into unexpected tears.

"Oh, great, you're going to be all hormonal now," she said. "This is going to be a fucking nightmare. A guilty and hormonal best friend." She rolled her eyes, and smiled.

"It's going to be worse for me," I said, laughing. "I'm getting fat!"

"Let me see it."

I moaned. "No..."

"Lift up your sweatshirt, fatso. Do it. Let me see it. Seeing you fat might be the only thing to help right now."

I sighed and stood, lifting up my shirt to show her my stomach. Which had started to seriously show.

"Eee...yuck..." she said, staring.

"Hey!"

"I mean, oh! How...beautiful! There's life inside you."

"Okay, yeah, yuck."

Now teasing me, she sat up. "Just think, in only a few months, it'll be you in the hospital bed, and me sitting there. Feeling smug."

I was still crying, but laughing, too. Suddenly we were both in stitches, unable to breathe or speak.

When it came down to it, I knew that she was the most important person to me. And that because I had made the choices I had, it didn't mean I wouldn't do anything to keep her as my best friend.

Epilogue

Brooke

Two and a half years later

I SAT IN the middle of my tiny apartment, surrounded by boxes. Alexa had the living room furnished, but I had to find a place to put all my crap.

It was everything from my room at home and my off-campus housing apartment in Pennsylvania that I had chosen not to sell at yard sales.

I was newly twenty-one. And really on my own for the first time. I had spent two years at the school my parents wanted me to go to, done the program they wanted me to do. And I recognized that I'd learned skills that would only ever benefit me. But in the end, I knew I still needed more. I saved money working my butt off as a waitress during the summers and saved almost enough money to come to New York. I hadn't wanted to, but I'd accepted the financial help my parents gave me. After how hard I'd worked, they were all right with my relocation.

Alexa and I had stayed in touch, and when I'd realized it was a real possibility I would be going, I'd started talking to her more. When I'd gotten accepted to the Fashion Institute again, I'd told her I was coming. She'd been thrilled, and we'd started making plans to move in together.

I had recently visited home to get my things and fill a small U-Haul with the furniture my parents were donating to me. My parents respected me for trying the program they'd wanted me to and for boldly making my own independent decisions.

For most of high school, I had looked forward to the years of college where I would be free to go as long as I wanted without seeing them. But the truth was, now that I didn't live at home and didn't technically have to listen to them, we had a much better relationship. My mom and I had even, somehow, shockingly, developed something of an adult relationship. I called her when something happened in my life. This might sound like a simple thing, but it was something I couldn't have imagined for most of my life.

After my embarrassing hospitalization senior year, during the Reed era, I had realized, in a way I don't know if I could have otherwise, what I wanted and what I didn't. I took school seriously once I went, and amazingly enough, my being kind of "over it" about partying and getting fucked up all the time had only made me seem cooler. I also started to make friends that I actually had things in common with. Friends who didn't just like me because I was popular, but who liked me because I got their movie and book references—thanks, Natalie—or because we could laugh together on a Friday night in, eating Oreos and playing Apples to Apples.

I visited home often. After all my years spent with Aiden and Natalie, and even after the animosity, I missed them both all the time. And ever since meeting their daughter, Jem, named for the boy character in *To Kill a Mockingbird* (one of Natalie's favorite books), I couldn't help but miss her, too.

She was freaking cute. She had brown hair, pretty green eyes, and I swear she almost never cried or screamed. She was easygoing and sweet, like both of her parents. She didn't whine and throw Cheerios. She was pretty quiet, and when you looked in her eyes—which she had so totally gotten from Aiden—it seemed like she was having actual thoughts.

Aiden and Natalie were still together.

I guess in the end, it was a good thing they had done what they did.

Aiden was already almost finished with his program at College Park. Natalie was finishing up a program at a culinary institute.

This past time I'd gone home, Natalie and I had gone to lunch at Chin Chin, which the owners had finally remodeled. Jem sat quietly in my lap as we finished chicken fried rice and drank sodas.

"So did you leave behind a broken heart in Pennsylvania?" Natalie asked, taking a spoonful of egg drop soup. "I mean, I know you weren't dating anyone, but that doesn't mean someone wasn't in love with you." She smiled.

"Nah," I said. "I've had, like, no time. Seriously. That program was near impossible. But I got a lot of credits, and they're going to transfer, which is awesome. They might not have, and then I could have ended up a year or more behind. Which would have been god-awful."

"I think you're going to meet someone amazing in New York. I have this feeling about it."

I shrugged. "Maybe."

"You will. I'm like a mom, you know. I know things."

I shook my head. "A mom, ew, you're a mom!"

"Shut up, I love it! Bitch!"

I covered Jem's ears. "Excuse me, do not fuck up my god-daughter's language before I get a chance to."

Jem wrapped her fingers around mine and squeezed. She looked up at me, wide-eyed, and said my name. Actually, it sounded more like "Book!" But I knew what she meant.

I smiled at her.

"Do you really love it?" I asked.

"I really do. I've never been good at much, really. I have never loved doing something every single day. I was always afraid I would never find whatever it was that I would be re-ally good at that I'd enjoy forever. But—" she cocked her head at her daughter "—I really did. Even though it happened su-peryoung. And unexpectedly." She made a whoops face.

"At least it was you that got knocked up," I said. "I mean, let's face it, the odds were in my favor."

"Definitely true."

"Are you calling me a slut?" I narrowed my eyes at her and took a bite of my dumpling.

"Yeah. I am."

We both cracked up.

Later that night, we had gone out to dinner with Aiden, Natalie's dad and his new wife, Marcy, and I insisted on her not getting a sitter for Jem. I loved the little monster.

I loved my trips home. And I was so glad to feel like I had family when I went there. I had feared for so long that I would become an island, and that I would always be surrounded by people who kind of mattered, but who ultimately were noth-ing to me. But I had them, and I knew I always would.

My phone buzzed on the floor of my New York apartment. I reached over and picked it up. Alexa.

Superhot musician guy at the bar on 2nd ave. Come meet!
I'm with girls from work but they're cool.

I sighed and responded.

How hot?

She responded immediately.

Worth the makeup.

I laughed aloud.

Be there in 15.

I got up. Boxes could wait. I slithered into my skinny den-
ims, tossed on my favorite Aldo boots, disheveled my hair, put
on a little blush and a coat of my favorite mascara. I grabbed
my brown leather jacket, my purse and headed out the door.

I went up to the door, where I was not charged the typical five-dollar cover, and found Alexa. She said he had just
gone on break, but that he would be back in a few minutes.
I ordered a Corona—I didn't drink a ton anymore, but I was
twenty-one and I was hardly going to let that go to waste—
and took off my jacket.

I introduced myself to the girls. They commented on how
pretty my hair was. I smiled and thanked them, tossing it to
one side. I told them the name of the guy who did my highlights. Our conversation became drowned out as the musician came back to the stage. I talked to Alexa animatedly at
first, not paying attention, and then finally turned to see the
singer. I immediately loved his voice.

When I saw his face, I almost died.

I narrowed my eyes and started laughing to myself. *No freaking way.*

His songs were good. I couldn't even verbalize what was going on inside my brain as Alexa yelled into my ear that he worked at an elementary school that one of her friend's daughters attended. I listened but mainly gawked at him.

His gaze caught mine on a lyric about time going by. He did the slightest double take. It could have been because he thought I was good-looking. I didn't know yet. But I found out when he came off the stage and over to our table.

The girls watched in awe.

He held out his hand. "I'm Paul."

"Hi, Paul," I said, smiling. "I'm Brooke."

He gave me that look you give someone when you're not sure if it's weird if you remember meeting them. "I think…"

"Yeah, I've seen you play before."

"In Bethesda, Maryland, like…a million years ago?"

"Yep. I hope you put that twenty toward something really worth it."

He smiled. "I can't believe you remember seeing me."

"I can't believe you remember me passing by."

"Are you kidding? Definitely the hottest girl I had ever seen. Even in beautiful Bethesda."

I felt the girls watching our conversation like a tennis match. In fact, I felt the eyes of a lot of people in the bar on us.

"Hey…so for the sake of…fate and all that…" He gave a nervous laugh.

"And all that, yeah."

"Do you want to…go get some dinner?"

"Tonight?"

"Yeah, I'm done at midnight…is that weird?"

"No." I couldn't stop smiling. "Let's go get dinner. I know some all-night places."

"Okay, cool." He laughed again. "This is crazy. All right. Awesome. I'll, uh, I'll meet you here…yeah. I gotta…" He gestured at the stage.

"Cool."

He went back up, and every once in a while, he would sing a line in my direction and shake his head at the craziness that we remembered each other.

Sometimes things work out the way they're supposed to.

★ ★ ★ ★ ★